# I JUST WANT
# *you*

NEW YORK TIMES
BESTSELLING AUTHOR

# KAYLEE RYAN

Cover Design: Perfect Pear Creative Covers
Cover Photography: Sara Eirew
Cover Model: Alex Boivin & Karine Lefebvre
Editing: Hot Tree Editing
Formatting: Integrity Formatting

# PROLOGUE
## Crew
### One year ago

I'M JOLTED AWAKE by my ringing cell phone. Reaching over, I tap around on the nightstand until I feel it. Forcing my eyes to open, I see 'Mom' on the caller ID and I groan. It's too early, but I know if I don't answer she'll just keep calling.

"Hello," I mumble into the phone.

"Crew, were you still sleeping?" she asks the obvious.

"Mmhmm."

"Good grief, son. It's eleven o'clock. The day is half over."

"The guys and I went out last night. Didn't get in until late." I yawn.

"I see. Well, you have some mail here."

"I'll get it at some point."

"A certified letter came today. It looks important. You shouldn't let it wait."

"Just open it," I say, pulling myself up to sit against the headboard.

"That's illegal." I can hear the smile in her voice.

"Really, that's the angle you're going with?"

"Don't fault me. I'm your mother and I will use any means necessary to get you to come and visit."

"Mom, it's been, what? Two weeks?"

"Tomorrow, yes. I made homemade apple pie this morning. It will

1

be waiting on you when you get here."

She knows she has me. Not only can I not say no to my mother, but her apple pie is so fucking good. I miss her cooking and she knows it. "Fine, give me an hour."

"I'll make lunch too. See you soon."

The line goes dead. I drop my phone to the mattress and wipe the sleep from my eyes. If I sit here I know I'll just fall back asleep, so I drag my tired ass out of bed and into the shower. Forty-five minutes later I'm pulling into their driveway.

Mom feeds me while Dad and I talk about the '69 Mustang he's rebuilding. It's a sweet ride, and we make plans to make a trip to the junkyard a few towns over next weekend to look for parts. After calling around dad found out they have a radiator that he needs.

"Okay, woman, I'm stuffed. Where's this letter you were talking about?" I ask.

Mom just grins. She knows I'm on to her, and it doesn't faze her a bit. She hops up from her chair and returns with a yellow envelope addressed to me. It's from an attorney's office in New York.

Holding it in my hands, I look up at them. "Any idea what it could be?"

They both shake their heads. I can see worry etched on their faces.

Curiosity is killing me, so I tear open the envelope and scan the letter. When I'm finished, I have to read it again just to make sure my mind's not playing tricks on me.

"Well?" Mom asks.

I can't speak. Instead, I hand the letter over and they read it together.

"Son of a bitch," Dad says under his breath.

"Dad?" I ask, needing to understand what this means.

His face is pale. I watch as he swallows hard. "She's your grandmother. My mother, Linda Ledger."

"I don't understand." Growing up, they told me she was gone. I assumed that meant she had passed away.

"You got plans for the rest of the day?" Mom asks.

"No," I say, never taking my eyes off my father.

"Good. This story is long overdue."

# ONE
## Berklee

HAVE YOU EVER had one of those days where you question everything? You know, the ones where you dig deep and ask yourself the questions that you so often try to avoid. That's me. That's my day. I arrived to work at six this morning for the early shift, prepared for a morning rush just like every other day, but today it never came. It's raining so hard it seems as through Mother Nature is standing over the city and pouring piss out of a boot. Okay, maybe not the best metaphor, but I'm bored out of my mind. Boredom leads to thinking, and that's where those heavy questions come into play. This is not where I saw myself at the ripe old age of twenty-two. I wanted to be a college graduate, starting my career. Moving forward with life, you know? Maybe not married with kids on the way, but a steady male companion, my other half making me whole. Yeah, corny as hell, I know, but that was the naive sixteen-year-old girl, dreaming about the unknown.

I never wanted for anything growing up. We weren't rich by any means, but we made ends meet with extra left over. My parents spoiled me rotten. I'm an only child—by choice, mind you. My parents said that kids were expensive and they wanted to be able to provide me with the best of everything. Truth is, I was an oops. My parents started dating in college and just a short six months later, the stick turned pink. Luckily for me they were committed to each other even though it was such a short amount of time. Apparently my grandparents on both sides were not thrilled, but my parents were both just weeks from graduating college, so there wasn't much they could say to their adult children for doing the deed. Dad proposed, Mom said yes, and we lived happily ever

3

after.

Literally.

Sure, my parents fought, but they never went to bed angry. That was a hard and fast rule in our household, one they both lived by. Never did either of them sleep on the couch or in the spare room. Never did I lie awake listening to them argue and wondering if they were splitting up. I can remember my best friend Maggie always coming to school and saying how she was worried that this time it was going to happen. Her parents fought all the time, and just mere weeks after our high school graduation they called it quits. They stayed together for her, but looking back I'm not so sure that was the best solution. They were all miserable.

So you see, I don't have much to complain about. However, on this dreary Monday morning, I sit here on my stool behind the counter of the coffee shop where I work watching the rain pour from the sky. I'm pondering what I'm doing with my life. I have a Bachelor in Business Administration and I work at a coffee shop. It's hard for new graduates to find jobs. Everyone wants experience, but how in the hell am I supposed to get experience if no one gives me a chance? See my dilemma? So, instead of putting my education to good use, I work the early shift at the local coffee shop.

Before I can let myself get lost in my own pity party, the bell over the door sounds and the noise from the thunderous rain fills the small shop. I quickly stand to greet my first customer of the day, but when my eyes land on him, I freeze.

Sweet mother of all that is good in life, he's gorgeous. Dark hair, cut short on the sides and a little longer on top, but not so much that it hangs in his eyes. His strong jaw is covered in a light beard. It's sexy, more than a five o'clock shadow, but not as prominent as a full-on *Duck Dynasty* beard. His eyes, like milk chocolate, study me like I have two heads. It's not until he smirks that I realize this super sexy man has just busted me checking him out. I want to feel embarrassed and I do, kind of, but not really. Trust me, if you could see what I see, you would roll with it too.

"How can I help you?" I finally say.

"Coffee, black, biggest cup you have," he replies, reaching up and wiping the rain from his forehead.

"It's wet out there, huh?" My lame attempt at making conversation.

I blame Mr. Super Sexy Beard. He's distracting and has my brain scrambled.

That smirk again. "You could say that."

I can feel my face heat. Funny how when he blatantly caught me checking him out, I couldn't care less, but the minute I open my mouth and words fly out, I'm embarrassed. Lesson learned: ogle the sexy man, but do not engage in conversation.

I fumble with the cup, making an even bigger spectacle of myself. I focus on the task at hand and fill the extra-large to the brim with steaming hot brew. Carefully I add the lid and then turn to face him. "That'll be two dollars," I say, carefully sliding the cup across the counter.

He gracefully pulls a five out of his wallet and hands it to me. I don't make eye contact as I make his change from the register. When I lift my head to count back his change, he's already at the door. "Sir," I yell out, waving his three dollars in the air. "Your change."

"Keep it." He winks.

Then he's gone. Like a figment of my imagination, no one here to witness that he truly does exist. I should have snuck a picture. Damn! I always think of that after the fact. Not that I could have been covert about it anyway. I barely held on to the stupid cup.

The rain is still pouring outside and Mr. Super Sexy Beard has been my one and only customer all morning. With a heavy sigh, I perch on my stool and pull out my phone. I scroll through my social media accounts and get lost in what everyone I know had to eat in the last twenty-four hours. This is what my life has been reduced to.

# TWO
## Crew

IT'S AMAZING HOW money can change your life. A year ago I was working construction, busting my ass day in and day out, living paycheck to paycheck. I enjoyed the work, being able to build something from the ground up, seeing my progress. I started right out of high school, since college wasn't my thing—hell, *school* wasn't my thing—and I was good with the choice I made. I knew I would never be rich, but I was able to support myself.

Life was good.

Then it got better.

At least after the initial shock wore off. The condensed version is that my grandmother, my dad's mom whom I thought was dead, wasn't. Until she was. When she passed, she left me, the grandson she'd shunned, her fortune.

Ten million dollars.

At first I refused it, but after some thought and talks with my parents and my best friend Zane, I decided to accept. My first order of business was to pay off my parents' house. I tried to buy them a new one, but they threw a fit insisting that their home was all they needed for the two of them. Mom cried and said all of our memories are there, and her tears had me conceding. I also bought them both new cars and transferred a million to their bank account. They were pissed but soon got over it.

My next step was an investment banker. I wanted to use the money wisely. I kept my job at the construction company and pretty much just laid low. Six months after meeting with the investment banker, I had gained just under one million.

"Sleeping on the job, I see," Zane says, pulling up a bucket beside me.

I motion toward the laptop I'm holding. "Not hardly. Just thinking about how things have changed in the last year."

"True that." He holds his fist out for me and I don't leave him hanging.

"Why are you not at work?"

"Got rained out. How are things coming along?" He surveys the room.

"Good. I met with the contractor when I got here this morning and everything is on schedule."

"You settle on a name?" he asks.

"Yep." I click the file on my desktop and pull up the logo. "Club Titan," I say, spinning the screen so he can see it.

"Hell yeah!" He grabs my laptop to get a better look at the logo. "This is sick, man."

"The designer nailed it. Actually, I'm glad you stopped by. There's something that I've been meaning to talk to you about."

"Shoot," he says, handing me the laptop.

I close it and put it back in the case. "I want you to come work for me."

He opens his mouth, but I stop him by raising my hand. "Just hear me out. I've known you my entire life. I need people I can trust along for the ride in this adventure. No matter how hard I've tried to hide my inheritance, word gets around. You have your choice of capacity. Security, bar, overall management. I don't care."

"Do you even need all those positions?" he asks.

I shrug. "Honestly, I have not the first fucking clue what I need at this point."

Zane throws his head back and laughs. "Count me in, my man. You name it and I'm there."

"Yeah? Why don't you go ahead and put in your notice and you will be the first official employee of Club Titan. We can work out the specifics of your position as we go."

Zane doesn't hesitate; he pulls his phone out of his pocket, taps the screen a few times, and places it next to his ear. I hear a deep voice pick up on the other line, and Zane tells him he's giving his notice. The voice on the other end gets louder, but I can't make out what they're saying. Zane gets a huge grin on his face as he hangs up.

"Well?"

"Marty, the dick that he is, was pissed. Said not to bother with two weeks and that he would mail me my last check."

"Looks like you start today." Reaching into my laptop case, I pull out the legal notebook I was working on last night. I rip off a corner of the top sheet and write his new salary. "This is what I was thinking. Salary, of course. I'm working with an agency to get a full benefits package, so that will come later."

"Crew, this is . . . a lot of zeros."

I try not to laugh. "It's a six-figure salary. For you, my right-hand man. I'm really going to be relying on you, so I need you to be well compensated."

Zane studies me for a minute. He must realize that I'm not budging on this. "All right," he concedes. "Where do we start?"

"Staff, I think. Construction will be finished in two weeks, at least that's what they tell me. At that point we'll need to get the place furnished and staff trained."

"You have an opening date in mind?"

I've thought about this long and hard, and after talking to the contractor, I settled on a date. "Yeah, Halloween weekend. The thirtieth is on a Friday. My hope is to have an invite-only soft opening the weekend before."

"That's just under two months away."

"Right. All the more reason you starting today is a good thing. I'm thinking we run some ads in the local papers. Maybe put some fliers up at the college."

"Okay. I'll get something made up today and start getting the word out."

"I have an appointment today to meet with the city to finalize my liquor license. The designer is supposed to be here at three. You can sit in on that too."

"Done."

I nod. I wasn't kidding when I told Zane he was going to be my right hand in all of this. I have a ton of shit to get done in a small amount of time if I want to meet my opening night of Halloween weekend.

# THREE

*Berklee*

THE RAIN FINALLY stops, but it's still dreary outside. My shift ends in ten minutes, which I'm sure will feel like an eternity. This has been the longest day ever. It's been slow and boring—well, unless you count the visit from Mr. Super Sexy Beard. He's been on my mind all day. I've never seen him in here before, but I can only hope that he becomes a regular. That will most definitely be the highlight of each shift.

I stare at the clock on the register, waiting for it to flip over to three. Two more minutes. Pulling out my phone, I text my roommate and best friend, Maggie.

> **Me:** *You at home?*
>
> **Maggie:** *Yep.*
>
> **Me:** *Barry?*
>
> **Maggie:** *Yep.*
>
> **Me:** *Takeout?*
>
> **Maggie:** *YES!*

*So she does know how to spell something other than 'yep.'*

> **Me:** *Harold's?*
>
> **Maggie:** *Yum! The usual for me and B.*

I knew that's what she would say. I slide my phone back in my pocket and look up at the register just as the time ticks over. Three o'clock—

finally! Hopping off my stool, I untie my apron and quickly type in my code to clock out. Carrie, my boss, looks up from her book and gives me a nod. She's working on her master's in something or another, so her nose is always stuck in a book. Not that I mind; as far as bosses go, she's pretty cool.

Thankfully the rain has let up enough that I don't get drenched during the mad dash to my car. Harold's is just around the block, but no way am I walking in this weather. I pull up in front of the building just as it starts to pour once again. Hoping that if I wait it out it will slow down, I grab my phone from my purse and call them, placing our usual order. They tell me fifteen minutes, so I spend the time carelessly scrolling through my social media. Same old stuff, nothing new and exciting. Then I check my e-mail, hoping there might be some correspondence from the what seems like hundreds of résumés I've submitted. Nothing, not even a simple 'thank you for your submission.'

The rain is still pouring and my fifteen minutes are up. Time for another mad dash. It's maybe fifteen feet from my car to the door, but by the time I'm inside I'm drenched.

"Hey, Berklee. Still raining?" Harold asks.

Harold and his wife, Martha, have owned this place for years. I've been eating here my whole life and it's always been one or both of them behind the counter. I love the guy to pieces. Looking down at my soaked clothes and then back at Harold, I grin. "What gives you that idea?"

He chuckles, a deep belly laugh that only Harold can pull off. "I could have brought it out to you, girly," he says after he has his laughter under control.

"You're too good to me, Harold."

"Berklee, dear. My goodness, look at you. Let me get you a towel," Martha says.

"No, it's okay," I say quickly to stop her. "I have to go back out in this and I'm just ten minutes away from home. I'll be fine."

"You sure, dear?" she asks.

"Absolutely. Now, fill me in. How have you been?"

Harold gingerly places his arm around his wife's shoulders and holds her next to him. "I get to spend my days with this beauty, so life is good," he says proudly.

I watch as Martha blushes. Blushes! They've been married for over forty years and he still makes her blush. I want what they have. Is that too much to ask?

"Oh, you," Martha says, removing his hand from her shoulders. "How about you? Any news on the job hunt?"

Told you I was here a lot. "Nothing yet. One day I'll get a break and find someone willing to give me a shot."

"Really," Martha huffs. "You are a bright, beautiful young woman. How are you to get experience if they don't give you a chance?"

See why I love them? "The struggle is real," I say, defeated. "I'm just going to keep trying."

"I'll put you to work," Harold says for what must be at least the tenth time since graduation. I know he means well, but they don't need me. They have each other and this place is a well-oiled machine. A small mom-and-pop operation that has been able to withstand the test of time.

"You don't need me. You two make owning a business look effortless." I tell them the same thing every time.

"The offer stands," Harold says sternly. It's his way of letting me know that he's serious.

"Well, I better get going. Maggie and Barry are probably starving to death by now." I give them a big grin.

"How are they? We don't see them much anymore," Martha says.

"Good. Barry is still teaching at Garrison High. Maggie is actually subbing several days a week at Garrison Elementary. Of course, it helps that her dad is the superintendent and her mom is the principal."

Martha shakes her head. "The whole lot of them teachers. I sure do bet their parents are proud to see them follow in their footsteps."

They are. I remember I asked them both why education, and they said that teaching gave them a happy life. Their parents were able to be home with them during the summer and snow days, and they never went without. "Why mess with a good thing?" Barry had said. They both always liked school, something that formed from having parents as teachers, I'm sure.

"That they are," I say, reaching for our bag of dinner. "Thank you. I'll see you all soon." With that I turn and head back out into the rain. It's a little lighter now but still a pain in the ass.

Once I'm in the car, I look over and see Martha and Harold waving in the window. I wave back before pulling out. Those two are like my surrogate grandparents. They never had kids of their own, but not for lack of trying. Martha told me once that after you lose a few pregnancies your heart just can't take it again. I remember that day and the pain in her eyes. I could see how badly she wanted kids, but it didn't work out for them. Despite the struggles, they're still together and more in love than ever.

By the time I get home, which is a three-bedroom condo I share with Maggie and Barry, the rain has reached an all new level of downpour. I grab my purse, shove my phone in the side pocket, pull the keys from the ignition, and grab our bag of dinner. I survey my car, a Honda Accord that I've been driving since I turned sixteen, to make sure I have everything. I don't plan on trudging back out in the tears of Mother Nature to get whatever it is I might leave behind.

Suddenly my door is pulled open, scaring the shit out of me. I look up to see Barry grinning, holding a huge umbrella over his head. He sticks out his hand and I give him our dinner before he steps back to let me climb out of the car.

"Thank you." I raise my voice over the rain.

Barry just smiles and maneuvers the umbrella to the same hand as our bag of food. The other slides around my waist, holding me close so we're both under what little safety the umbrella gives us.

"Shit. It's really picked up out there," Barry says, wiping his feet on the rug once we're inside.

"I know. Thanks for that. You didn't have to come out and get wet just for me," I tell him. I see the sexy smirk cross his lips and quickly replay my words. Damn it. I always leave myself open like that. I can tell by the smirk that he's going for it.

"That's my line," he says over his shoulder as he carries our dinner to the kitchen.

Maggie and I have been best friends since kindergarten. We were seated beside each other first day of school. Being an only child, I was shy, but Maggie not so much. She asked me if I wanted to be her friend and I said yes. We became inseparable. So much so that our parents are now also close friends, as are her brother and me. Hence the reason that Barry, Maggie, and I all live together.

Barry is three years older than us at twenty-five. He's a confirmed bachelor so living with us is not a big deal to him. For all intents and purposes, he is my big brother. He's always watched out for me and protected me just as he did Maggie.

He's gorgeous. About six-two, with light brown hair and light brown eyes. He's defined, complements of his daily trips to the gym. If it weren't for the fact that I see him as nothing but a brotherly figure, I could see what all the fuss is about.

"I can smell that all the way in my room. I'm starving," Maggie says, walking into the kitchen at the same time I do. "How was your day, dear?" She giggles.

"Fine." I try to fight my grin and can't. "Boring as hell. We were dead most of the day." I get napkins and the ketchup while Maggie grabs us each a bottle of water. Barry is already at the table and has started eating. I swear I don't know where he puts it.

"That makes for a long day. You didn't even get to people watch," she says, taking her seat next to me.

That's when I remember Mr. Super Sexy Beard. "Oh, but there was this guy. Holy shit, Mags, he was gorgeous."

"I'm listening," she says, shoving a fry into her mouth.

I go on to tell them about how I got caught checking him out, and how I blushed like a school girl when I fumbled over my words.

"I'm sure he enjoyed it. I know I would have," Barry says, crumpling one cheeseburger wrapper and grabbing the second.

"Doubtful." I reach for the ketchup.

"What's up with you?" Maggie asks.

"I'm just . . . I don't know. I didn't expect to be here, you know? I thought I would be at my first real job out of college—you know, one where I can actually utilize my education. I feel like I'm at a standstill."

"It's only been, what, four months?" Barry asks. "Rome wasn't built in a day."

"I know. It's just been an off day. This rain is depressing."

"Tell me about it. I spent the day in bed." Maggie laughs.

"Must be nice," Barry says.

"Oh, like you have it rough. You were home by two-thirty today. I thought you had practice after school?"

"Nah, we canceled. No point in trying to practice football in this kind of rain. No way they could hold on to the ball."

"I'm surprised Coach Brown let that happen," Maggie says.

"He said he wasn't feeling all that well and he didn't want a team of sick players. We have our first game Friday night."

"I can't wait. I love football season," I say.

"Me too. Do you work Friday, Berklee?" Maggie asks.

"Yeah, I get off at five."

"I sub that day, but I'll be home by three at the latest. I'll make a quick dinner so we can eat before we go."

"Sounds like a plan."

Barry finishes eating almost before we get started and retreats to his room. Maggie and I sit and talk while we eat and then do the same. What is it about the rain that just makes curling up in bed and napping so appealing?

# FOUR
## Crew

I OFFICIALLY BROUGHT Zane on board on Monday and he's already taking a load of stress off me. Today is Friday and he's just informed me that he has interviews set up next week for servers and bouncers.

"So, what else do we need?" he asks.

"Bartenders. At least two to start, although three would be better. I know we're cutting it close."

"Okay, anyone else?"

"I have some names of a few cleaning crews that I'll need to interview."

"I can do that." He holds out his hand. "Give me the list."

Without hesitation, I hand it over.

"So, what exactly is going to be my official role? I mean, I know you said right-hand man, but I don't know the first thing about running a nightclub," Zane confesses.

"Join the crowd. What are you thinking? What appeals most to you?"

"Security," he says immediately.

"Done. Zane Davis, head of security of Club Titan," I say with authority.

He laughs. "Okay, so what about you? You plan on orchestrating all this yourself?"

I pull my hat from my head and run my fingers over my hair. "Nah, man, I'm in over my head. I guess we need someone to keep up with the books, ordering and that type of thing. I really just want to be the owner. If we can find someone who we really feel is trustworthy, I would love nothing more than to pass that shit off."

"What's that? Mr. Always In Control is passing the torch?" Zane chides.

So I might be a little bit of a control freak. I like routine and order. I like to say it keeps life tidy, but my mother says it's 'only child syndrome.' Whatever it may be, it's who I am.

"I want this place to be a success, so yeah, I'm going to need someone to help with payroll, scheduling staff, ordering, those types of things. They can report to me. Besides, that stuff doesn't interest me in the slightest."

"Bartenders and one administrative person of sorts. Got it. I'll call the cleaning crews and get them in here too. You want to meet with them?"

I knew this was going to be a huge undertaking, but damn, there is a hell of a lot more involved than just hiring builders and picking out a name and logo. "Yeah, I guess so." I pull out my phone and look at my calendar. "I'll be here every day next week, so whenever is fine."

"Done. Now I'm headed out for the day."

Looking at my phone, I see that it's a little past four. "Where you going in such a rush? You got a hot date or something?" I know better, but I ask anyway. No way could he have not mentioned it before now.

"Nah, Barry's first game is tonight as assistant coach. I'm going to watch. You want to go?"

His cousin, right. I forgot he said he was coach at the high school now. I think about his offer and my mind drifts to the second stack of paperwork I was given this week in regards to the liquor license. "Not tonight. I have a ton of paperwork to get through so I can submit it Monday. I don't want to take the chance of the club not opening on time."

"All right, man. If you change your mind, hit me up." He stands. "See you later, boss man." His laughter carries him out the door.

Reaching for my laptop bag, I pull out the stack of papers. *I'm going to need some caffeine for this.* Grabbing my keys, I head a few doors down to the coffee shop for my afternoon dose.

It's a warm sunny day in September, the rain from earlier in the week long forgotten. Inside the coffee shop there is no line. Perfect. I'll get my tall black and head back to the club. I have a feeling that packet is going to take me a while to get through.

Walking up to the counter, my eyes immediately spot what appears to be a very fine ass high in the air. The owner is bent over grabbing more supplies. I should alert her to my presence, but I don't want to. I'd rather enjoy the show. She shimmies a little and I have to bite down on my lip to keep my laughter from bubbling over. When she finally pops up, she turns toward the counter and drops the box of spoons when she sees me.

"Nice moves," I can't help but say.

Her face pales and she pulls the single earbud out of her ear. I watch as it drops over her shoulder. *That explains where the shimmy came from.*

"You're back," she says her face turning red.

I think back to Monday and how she was blatantly checking me out. I guess I returned the favor today, but I just didn't get busted. Not that she seemed to mind. "That I am," I say, taking her in. She has long red hair like the color of autumn leaves, soft curls falling down her back. Her apron hides her figure, but when she was bent over I got an eyeful. She's rocking a tight little body.

"What can I get you?"

You. "Coffee, black, biggest cup you have."

"Your usual," she says, grabbing a cup and turning to fill it.

So she remembers my order. Interesting.

I take her in, head to toe. Those tight black pants that make her ass look fucking edible. I can't seem to pull my eyes from her—don't want to, really—which is why it's me who is now busted. Like her, I'm not the least bit embarrassed to have been caught. I give her what I'm told is my panty-melting grin and hold out a twenty. She slides my coffee carefully across the counter and reaches for the money. I make her work for it, not easily letting go. Her fingers brush mine and my cock twitches. The huge packet of paperwork waiting on me has me groaning internally. Once the club is up and running I can think with my cock; right now, it's the head on my shoulders that needs to remain in charge.

I scan her chest for a nametag and come up empty. However, I do get a feel from the outline or her apron that she is more than a handful.

Damn paperwork!

She reaches out to hand me the change and my eyes lock with hers. "Keep the change . . ." I let my words hang in the air, waiting for her to take the bait and give me her name.

"Berklee," she says, never breaking eye contact.

Berklee. I let her name roll around in my head. It's hot as fuck. "Berklee." I caress her name with my tongue, I had to see how it sounded. "Keep the change." Reaching out, I fold her fingers around the money if for no other reason than to touch her. I'm just torturing myself, but her skin is so damn soft. It's worth it. "See you around, Berklee." I grab my cup and turn to leave. If I don't go right now, I won't. She's too damn tempting, that one.

I make my way back to the club and settle in for the long haul. I have to keep my eye on the goal: opening before Halloween. Then maybe, just maybe, if the sexy little Berklee is still there we can get to know each other better, or at least intimately.

The grin never leaves my face as I bury my nose in paperwork for the night.

# FIVE
## Berklee

O F COURSE HE would have to stop in at the end of the day. He could not have been there earlier and given me the day to fantasize and get it out of my system. Now I'm going to be distracted tonight.

I need to snap out of it. I had given up hope that he would ever step foot through those doors again. I had myself convinced that he was just in the area, and that was that.

As I drive home, I'm caught up in him and those dark chocolate eyes, and the ink. I want to strip him of his shirt and see just how far up his arm those tattoos go. Nothing wrong with a little fantasy to keep a girl . . . motivated. Yes, we'll go with motivated. It's not far off since his face is what's single-handedly had me reaching for my vibrator every night this week.

The condo is quiet when I arrive home. I can hear the shower running in between Maggie's and my room. We share, with connecting doors. Barry has his own, and we have a half bath for guests. Quietly, I shut and lock my door. I make sure the bathroom door is locked from my side and tap the screen of my phone to pull up some music. Carefully, as if someone might be watching, I slide open the nightstand drawer and reach for B.O.B. Settling on the bed with the lowest setting, I let myself get lost in the image of Mr. Super Sexy Beard. I didn't have enough wits about me to ask his name in return today. No, instead I just stared, memorized his features, which brings me to now. It doesn't take long, like I knew it wouldn't.

As soon as I drop B.O.B back in the nightstand, Maggie knocks on my bedroom door.

"Berklee, shower's free," she says.

"Thanks," I call back, trying like hell not to sound like I just got off. Then I would have to explain what got me in this mess at five thirty in the evening. Maggie and I tell each other everything, but our families will be with us tonight, and well, she and I don't really have much of a filter. I want this fantasy—because let's face it, that's what it is—to be all mine.

Needing a shower, I rush through, soaping up all the important parts and then quickly washing my hair. I'm lucky to have natural waves so some mousse and a diffuser for about ten to fifteen minutes and I'm good to go. I'm pretty low maintenance. Besides, it's a high school football game; who there do I need to impress?

"Ready," I say, walking into the kitchen. Maggie is sitting at the small island eating.

"Made you a plate." She points beside her to a plate of spaghetti and garlic bread.

I take a seat and dive in, suddenly famished. I grin, thinking of how I worked up an appetite.

"What's got you grinning like the cat that ate the damn canary?" she asks.

"Nothing really. Just had a good day, I guess."

"Did he come back?" she asks, abandoning her fork for her bottle of water, all ears.

I hesitate at first. I can keep the part where he was checking me out and basically what felt like eye-fucking me to myself. I won't tell her about what the touch of his hand on mine did to me. That's a story for another time. "Yeah, he was back. Right before my shift ended."

"Did you get his name?"

"No, I didn't really think about it. He was in and out, just his usual order and then he was gone."

"Usual, huh?" She leans in.

"You know what I mean." I laugh. "So far he's ordered the same thing both times. Black coffee, extra-large."

"Damn! Next time you need to sneak a picture, or at least get his name so we can google his ass and maybe do some social media investigating."

"Right, because taking a picture of him while making his coffee is not going to throw up red flags. Come on, Mags."

"Okay, so you might have a point. At least work your feminine charm to get a name."

"He got mine," I let slip. *Damn.*

"Oh, did he? And how did that happen?"

*Shit.* I decide to give her a fraction of the interaction. "He told me to keep the change, but left it open so I filled in the blank for him."

"Did he say it? How hot was that to have sex on legs say your name?"

I laugh. "Eat, we don't want to be late."

"No, you are not leaving me hanging, B," she scolds.

"It's just like you're imagining it would be. His deep voice is just as sexy as he is. It was over before it even began. Now eat."

She gives me that look, the one that says 'I've know you almost my entire life and I know when you are not telling me everything.' The one that only a lifelong best friend can master.

I ignore her and dive into the rest of my dinner.

"I'll drive," she says, standing to put her plate in the sink.

I'm right behind her, as I basically inhaled my food. It beat the alternative of talking about . . . him. All the talk about his name has me irritated that I didn't ask for it. I want—no, need—to put a name to this gorgeous man.

"Our parents are riding over together, and I think Aunt Jenny and Uncle Jeff are coming too," Maggie says as we circle the packed parking lot looking for a spot.

"Is Zane coming?"

"I think so. I didn't ask, but you know he and Barry are tight. I'm sure he wants to be here for this. That's all he talked about was going to college to be a teacher and coaching football."

"I still think he was good enough to go pro," I say.

"Maybe, but that's just not the life he wanted."

"He's such a great guy. Too bad he's on this 'bachelor for life' kick."

"Right?" She laughs.

Finally we find a spot, grab our hoodies from the back seat, and head toward the entrance. After paying, we walk in front of the bleachers looking for our people. I spot my mom and then Maggie's as they stand and wave their arms in the air at us. "Girls," they call out.

We make our way into the bleachers and take the seats that are saved for us. Mom and Dad are there along with Sue and Tom, Maggie and Barry's parents. We wave hello and I lean down and give Dad a quick hug before taking my seat.

"Are Aunt Jenny and Uncle Jeff coming?" Maggie asks.

"They're here. They just went down to grab a drink. I'm surprised you didn't pass them," Sue tells her.

"There's trouble," Jeff calls out.

This causes us all to turn our heads and see who he's talking about. That's when I see Zane striding up the bleachers, his long legs eating up the steps. He could easily be Barry's brother. Same height and build, although Zane's hair is darker. I've always sort of crushed on Zane. Well, when I was younger, that is. Sure, he looks like Barry, but it was always different when he was around. Of course, that ship sailed long ago.

Zane squeezes Maggie's shoulder as he steps past her, winking at me and then taking his seat next to Tom. His parents are right behind him, so we have the entire row occupied.

The game starts and we all focus in. I watch Barry as he paces on the sidelines. He's always been passionate about football and teaching. My heart smiles for him knowing that he's doing what he's always dreamed of.

I was never that focused, really. I knew I wanted to do something business related, but I didn't have it planned out like Barry and Maggie. I'm just floating by, waiting for my opportunity. Shaking myself out of my mental woes, I focus on the game and supporting Barry.

"Hell yeah!" Zane exclaims as the clock hits zero, ending the game.

Garrison brings home the win 28–3. We're all on our feet, clapping and cheering. Barry looks up and his face is lit up like a Christmas tree. He's stoked, as he should be. This is his first year as assistant coach; his first two years he wasn't officially a coach, but volunteered his time. He's earned his spot, and I couldn't be happier for him.

"Where we going to celebrate?" Tom asks.

"You name the place and we'll follow you," Jeff says.

"Right behind you," Dad agrees.

"I'd say they'll all be at the pizza place across the street. Let's go on over and

get a table before it gets busy," Maggie says, looking left and right at our entire row. "We're going to need a big table."

"I'll text Barry," Sue states, standing. We all follow suit and make our way down the bleachers.

"We'll see you there," Maggie yells over her shoulder as we walk to her car.

The drive is literally right across the street. Thankfully we beat the crowd and are able to get a table for ten. The waitress didn't bat an eyelash. We come here a lot and she knows we're good for a decent tip.

I take a seat at the far end of the table, Maggie grabbing the one beside me. The others file in and we get ourselves sorted while we wait for Barry. As soon as drinks are delivered, he comes strolling in with what looks like most of the team. The place erupts in cheers as we all celebrate a win for the home team.

"Hey hey," Barry says when he reaches our table. He takes a seat between Maggie and me at the head of the table. "Where's Zane? Did he not stay?"

I turn to scan the room. I thought for sure he was with us. The table jerks, causing me to look back at Barry. Zane's standing behind Barry with his arm around his neck, rubbing the top of his head.

"I thought we stopped giving noogies in grade school." Maggie laughs.

"You're next, cuz." Zane winks at her.

Maggie holds up her hands in surrender. "Don't even think about it, Zane."

He laughs, releasing his hold on Barry and taking the only remaining seat next to Maggie.

"Good game," I say to Barry.

"Thanks, Berklee. The guys played hard."

That starts the conversation, everyone reminiscing about the game. A few of the players stop by the table to give Barry a fist bump, and he's all smiles. Once the waitress takes our order, the parents are already on to their own conversations, so Barry changes ours.

"So, what's up, man?" he asks Zane. "Feels like forever since I've seen you."

"Don't I know it. Was working construction for a while. You know how it is: long days when you can get them in, trying to beat the weather. I actually just quit though," he says, taking a drink of his beer.

"New job?" Maggie asks.

"Yeah, you remember me talking about my friend Crew?" Barry smirks and Zane laughs. "Well, he came into some inheritance about a year ago. He's been working on getting his own club up and running, and he brought me on to help get staff hired. I'll be the head of security."

"That seems like a big change for you," Maggie says.

"Yeah, but a good one. I have no doubt that Crew will make this place a success. He's determined, that one."

"You'll have to let us know when it opens. We'll stop by," Maggie says.

"Sounds like fun," I add.

"You got it. I'll make sure to hook you up with VIP."

"Nice." Barry holds his fist out and they bump.

Our food comes and we spend the rest of the night listening to Zane and Barry talk about their antics with this guy Crew. Maggie assures me that I've met him, but I don't recall.

"He's gorgeous, Berklee. You would remember, trust me."

I laugh at her. "We pretty much stopped following this guy around like a puppy once high school hit." I point to Barry. "Sounds like I missed out."

"Oh you did, B. You so did." Maggie laughs.

# SIX
## *Crew*

LOOKING AT THE clock on the microwave, I see I have thirty minutes until I have to meet Zane at the club. I gulp back the rest of my coffee, place the cup in the sink and gather my stuff. It took me all damn weekend, but I finally finished the packet for the liquor license. I'm sure someone with a business background could have done it faster, but I found myself consulting Google more often than not. I've been putting in countless hours of research but it's worth it. I want Club Titan to be a success.

First order of business for Zane today is for us to find a manager or administrator or whatever we decide to call it. As owner, I want to do just that—own the club. See it thrive. I'll do whatever it takes to make that happen.

I'm almost to the club when Coffee House comes into view. Before I even realize what I'm doing, I'm parked in front of the building and climbing out of my car. The bell jingles when I open the door, announcing my presence. My eyes lock on the counter and there she is, the blue-eyed, autumn-haired girl from last week. I flash her a smile and make my way to the counter.

"Good morning," she says.

"Morning," I reply, never taking my eyes off hers. Their color reminds me of the sky on a clear summer day.

"Coffee, black, biggest we have." She smiles.

That smile. She's fucking gorgeous. I remind myself that I have to focus on the club. I can't let myself get distracted. Keep my eye on the

27

prize and all that. As far as mental pep talks go, it's a good one, but it doesn't change the fact that I've already had three cups of coffee at home today and yet here I am.

Looking for her.

"You memorize all your customer's orders?" I ask.

"It's been a slow week," she says, turning to grab a cup.

It's a hit to my ego, but the sting is long forgotten as I stare at her ass in those tight little pants as she pours my coffee. All too soon she's turning around, and I curse the fact that I don't add all that other shit to my drink. Surely that would take her longer than to just pour my cup of black.

When she slides the cup my way, I reach out and place my hand next to hers, feeling her skin. "Thanks." I bring the cup to my lips for a drink. Her eyes follow my every move. Setting the cup on the counter, I pull a twenty out of my wallet and hold it out for her. She doesn't notice at first, her gaze locked on mine. I motion toward my hand and she blushes.

Damn.

"Keep the change, Berklee." My voice is husky even to my own ears.

"I can't. I don't even know your name."

"You can." I lean in and rest my forearms on the counter. "If you know my name there's no more mystery. You'll forget my order with all the others," I say with a smirk. "See you around." I stand, grab my coffee and turn to leave. Once I make it back to my car, I make a conscious effort to not look back at Coffee House. Her pull is too strong. She has no idea what she does to me. It's unlike me to feel this kind of attraction with just casual conversation. It has to be the fact that I've put myself on a hiatus from dating, from women in general. I'm not exactly much of a dater. I need to stay focused and a girl like Berklee, she can make a man lose more than just his focus with a simple look.

Pulling into the lot of the club, I see Zane sitting on the bench outside the front door, talking to the contractor. Beckett Construction came highly recommended, and Ridge has proven that he and his team know their stuff. I almost hired Zane's company, but I knew I wanted him to work for me, and that would have been all kinds of uncomfortable. Besides, Beckett Construction has one hell of a reputation. I wanted the best.

"Write it down." Zane grins. "I never beat you. You feeling all right, my man?" he chides.

I hold up my cup. "Had to stop for coffee."

He laughs. "I see how you are. Didn't bother to bring me one."

Honestly, I should have, but Berklee kept me from thinking of anything but her. "Sorry, man." I almost volunteer to go get him one. It's just around the corner and I could see her again; that would certainly throw her for a loop. *No. Focus, Crew.* "Next time," I say instead.

"I've already had three cups, I was just giving you shit."

*Me too.* "So, I finished the liquor license packet, the second one. I really need to get someone with a business background in here. I know enough to get by and most of it is common sense, but I need someone I can depend on for this kind of stuff."

"Okay. So what are you thinking?"

"A business manager or administrator, Google suggested both." I laugh.

Zane joins in. "All right, I'll call a couple of agencies and maybe check in with the local college. You okay with a new grad?"

"Yeah, as long as they know their shit. Actually, I might prefer it. I can train them the way I want. I don't want some know-it-all coming in here telling me how to run things. I just need someone with the business savvy to monitor the books, payroll, staffing, and this fucking paperwork," I say.

"Got it. Our interviews start in an hour. I'll make some phone calls."

Taking a seat at the makeshift desk, I take out my laptop and pull up my e-mail. I've got an hour to put a dent in some of them.

"Crew." I look up to see Zane standing there with a brunette in a short dress and mile-high heels behind him. "Interviews are here."

I know from just looking at her that she's not what I want. Not for the club. Sure, she's easy on the eyes, but provocative is not the way to dress for a job interview, regardless of the position. Unless maybe you're trying to be a stripper. Instead of voicing my opinion, I follow Zane and the brunette to a small table we set up for the interview process.

Zane motions for her to sit and she makes a production out of it. Tossing her hair over her shoulder and crossing her legs, causing her already too-short dress to ride up further on her thigh. As a man, I appreciate the effort, and she's a knockout, but as an employer I'm not impressed. Sure, I want her to be friendly and even a little flirty with the patrons, but this is a respectable business, or it's my hope that it will be. This girl has drama written all over her, and I don't want or need that in my club.

"So . . ." I look down at the pink résumé she handed over that coincidently smells like flowers. "Mandy, what are you looking for in a job?"

Mandy grabs a lock of her hair and begins to twirl it around her finger, then giggles. "I'm looking for a job where I can . . . use my assets," she says, her voice low.

"And what might those assets be?" I ask, even though the answer is written all over the way she presents herself.

Mandy looks down at her cleavage that is spilling out of her dress, then back up at me as she licks her lips.

"Thanks for stopping by, but we're looking for something . . . more," I tell her.

Her mouth drops open and she narrows her eyes at me. "That's it?"

"That's it," I confirm before standing, hoping that she gets the hint. It's time for her to go.

She stands as well, only instead of moving toward the door, she steps closer to me. I catch Zane's eye and he's biting his lip to keep from laughing at this girl.

Mandy goes up on her tiptoes and leans in close, attempting a whisper that is anything but by the look on Zane's face when she says, "I bet I can change your mind."

I raise my eyebrows at Zane in silent question. *Are you hearing this shit?*

"That's all we have time for today, Mandy," Zane comes to my rescue. "Thanks for stopping by."

Mandy stomps her foot with a huff and turns toward the door.

"I'm just going to make sure she leaves," Zane says, following her out.

*Damn. This is going to be a long and grueling process if all of our candidates are like this.*

Zane comes back to the table with a guy about our height and built like a damn tank. "This is Tank. Tank, meet Crew, the owner of this club."

I hold out my hand. "Nice to meet you."

He shakes my hand, his grip strong. "You too."

"So, Tank, what position are you applying for?" I ask. I have a feeling it's bouncer, but after our last interview, I'll let him tell me.

"I've been a bartender for the last four years. I've also done some work bouncing. I just moved back to Tennessee from LA. My mom is sick and it was just time to come home."

I nod in understanding. "Tell me about your previous employer."

Tank goes on to tell us how he started out in the kitchen, and the day he turned twenty-one he begged his manager to make him a bartender. With no family close by, when he wasn't at work he was at the gym. One night things got rowdy, and he jumped from behind the bar and took care of it. From that day on he worked both roles.

I look over at Zane and give him a subtle nod. He does the same. I fight my grin at finding our first employee. "Tank, I'd like to offer you the same type of position here. I can't say which you will be working more of as we've just started interviews, but I feel you would be an asset to Club Titan."

Tank nods. "Thank you. I look forward to working with you."

"We hope to be through the hiring process this week, and then we'll start training in the next week or two. Construction will be done this week and then tables and supplies can be ordered."

"I'd be happy to help out with all of that as well," Tank says.

"We might just take you up on that." I stand and offer him my hand. "Welcome to Club Titan."

Zane tells him that he'll be in touch early next week and then Tank's gone.

"Let's hope the rest of them are that easy."

"From the looks of the line, it won't be many." He laughs. "There are always a few diamonds in the rough. We'll figure it out."

I nod and take a sip of my now cold coffee while he goes to get the next candidate.

# SEVEN
## Berklee

I COVER MY yawn with the back of my hand. I stayed up way too late last night drafting cover letters and sending out résumés. I dropped off another ten in the mail this morning on my way to work, something I do every week. I've got the process down. I write the cover letter, really just changing it to match the company, add my résumé and seal the envelope. I also have a spreadsheet on my laptop of every job that I've applied for and the date. I make follow-up calls a week later. Still nothing, but I'm hopeful.

I'm setting out a fresh batch of muffins from the back when the bell jingles on the door alerting me to a customer. I check my watch and it's the same time Mr. Super Sexy Beard was here yesterday. I'm still kicking myself in the ass for not asking for his name yet again. I apparently lose the ability to think clearly when he's around. He's just that gorgeous.

Taking a deep breath, I turn to face the counter and am greeted with Zane's smiling face. "Berklee!" he exclaims. "I didn't know you worked here."

I try not to let my embarrassment show. He knows I graduated college with Maggie. "Yeah, just filling time, paying bills until I find a job in my field."

"What's your major? Education?" he asks.

I laugh. "No, much to my roommate's dismay, I was a business major. My bachelor's is in business administration."

"Really? And still no luck on the job front?"

I lean against the counter, as does he. "Not yet. They all want experience, but how am I supposed to get that if no one gives me a shot? Anyway, what can I get you?"

"Large coffee, cream and sugar. That sucks about your job search. What area of business are you interested in?"

I pour his coffee and add his cream and sugar before answering. "Anything, really. I don't want to work here at Coffee House the rest of my life. Don't get me wrong, I'm not knocking it and it pays my bills, but I worked hard for that degree and I'd like to use it." I place the lid on his cup and slide it across the counter to him.

"How much do I owe you?" he asks.

I wave him away. "It's on me. You off to work?"

"Yeah, the club I was telling you about is just around the corner."

He stops and studies me. I try not to squirm under his scrutiny.

"You know, we're looking for a manager/administrator for the club. I can't guarantee you the position, but I can get you an interview for sure. You interested?"

I stand there staring at him like a crazy person.

"Berklee."

"Yes, sorry, yes. I would love to interview. I can't thank you enough." I step out from behind the counter and launch myself at him, giving him a huge hug. He laughs and catches me.

"Like I said, I can't guarantee you the job, but I have some pull with the boss." He winks as I step back and release him.

"Just the opportunity is more than what I've gotten in weeks. Even if I don't get the job, the interview experience will help me too. Thank you so much, Zane!"

"Anytime." He pulls out his phone. "What time do you get off today? We're actually interviewing this week."

"At three." I look down at my leggings and sweater. "I need time to run home and change."

He lifts his head and takes me in. His eyes roam up and down my body, making me squirm. "You look fine to me," he says once his eyes reach mine once more.

My cheeks heat. "You might think so, but I refuse to attend a job interview looking like this, even if you will be the interviewer."

He grins. "It will be Crew and me both, and I can assure you he will have no issues with what you have on."

"Four o'clock," I counter.

He laughs. "Sounds good, Berklee." He reaches over and grabs a pen and a business card for the shop, then starts writing on the back. "Here's the address. You have my number?"

"I think so." I pull my phone out of my pocket and scroll through my contacts. Once I reach his name, I tap on the screen and then turn it to face him.

"That's me. Call me if something comes up."

"I'll be there," I promise. "Thank you again, Zane."

"You're welcome. See you later." He waves over his shoulder and walks out the door.

As soon as the door shuts behind him, I tap on Maggie's number and place my phone to my ear.

"Aren't you supposed to be working?" she asks in greeting.

"I am, but you'll never guess what happened?"

"You got his name?" she asks excitedly.

"No, not yet. He didn't come in today. Zane did though."

"Okay . . ."

"His friend, the club owner, is looking for a manager, and Zane got me an interview!" I shriek a little too loud. Thankfully the shop is empty.

"Berklee, That's awesome!" Maggie squeals.

"It's today at four. He said I could come right after work, but I need to change first. No way am I going to a job interview in leggings and a Coffee House T-shirt."

"Agree. I'll look through our closets and throw something together. That will save you time when you get home."

"Thanks, Mags. I'm trying not to get my hopes up, but even just the chance to interview will be good for me."

"You got this. I feel good about this one, B," she says.

The bell jingles over the door. "Customer just walked in. I gotta go. See you later." I quickly end the call, slip my phone into my back pocket and turn to face the counter.

It's him.

"Hi," I say cheerily.

"Berklee," his deep, sexy voice replies.

"Your usual?"

"Please."

I turn and make quick work of pouring his cup of joe. Not even Mr. Super Sexy Beard can distract me from thinking about the job interview this afternoon.

"You seem like you're having a good day," he comments with a grin.

"I am." I slide his coffee across the counter. "This one's on the house." He shakes his head and tries to hand me money. "Not today," I say, still grinning like a fool.

"Thank you, Berklee." He drops the five-dollar bill in the tip jar and turns to leave. I watch him go; it's not something you want to miss, trust me. "Berklee," he says, turning to face me once he reaches the door.

"Yeah?"

"That smile looks good on you." He flashes those damn dimples and walks out the door.

*Can this day get any better?*

The rest of the day drags on as I watch the clock slowly move its way toward three o'clock. Luckily we've been steady, so that helps pass the time. When the clock strikes three, I'm clocked out and in my car in less than a minute. When I get home, Maggie is there waiting on me. She has my black pencil skirt, my favorite blue silk blouse and my black pumps sitting on my bed.

"Gah! You're a lifesaver! Thank you so much," I yell out my bedroom door before I rush into the bathroom to take a quick shower.

"You're welcome," she yells back.

I take the fastest shower ever, hitting all the important parts, then quickly dry off and apply lotion. Thankfully I shaved this morning; I hate wearing hose, and time does not allow for that today. I apply some mousse to my hair, then pull out the hair dryer and diffuser. That's going to take the longest. I almost didn't wash it, but there is no way I'm going into an interview with my hair smelling like Coffee House.

Fifteen minutes later, my curls are hanging freely down my back. I apply some mascara and lip gloss and call it good. Slipping into the outfit that Maggie laid out for me, I look over at the clock. It's three thirty. Grabbing my purse, I head to the living room. "Well?" I ask Maggie and Barry who are sitting on the couch.

Barry gives me a thumbs-up, then turns his attention back to the television.

"You look great. Very professional, yet still sexy," Maggie comments.

"Not going for sexy, Mags. Just professional. Maybe I should go change?"

"No, it's understated sexy. I promise you look great, respectable for a job interview. Now go. Call me when it's over."

Leaning down, I give her a hug. Barry pats me on the shoulder while I'm doing so and mumbles, "Good luck," never taking his eyes off the screen.

With a final wave, I'm out the door and headed to what I hope is the job that starts the next chapter of my life.

Finding the club was no issue at all; it's literally just around the corner from Coffee House. There's a banner hanging over the door, "Coming Soon—Club Titan" sprawled across it in bold black letters.

"Showtime," I mutter before climbing out of the car. Once I reach the door, I'm not sure if I should knock or just go on in. I decide to try the door and find it's unlocked, so I take two steps that place me inside the door. "Hello," I call out.

"In here," I hear a deep voice call back. It sounds like Zane, but I can't be sure. I've barely taken two more steps when he comes around the corner. "Berklee, hi. Sorry, I lost track of time. This way." He turns and I follow him down the hallway. "Have a seat." He points to one of the four folding chairs nestled around a small table.

I do as told and let my eyes wander the room. High ceilings overlook the bar and dance floor, and there's a set of stairs that leads up to what appears to be a loft. I assume that will be for VIP or private parties. This place is really amazing.

"It's actually just going to be us today. Crew's been working to get our liquor license. He submitted his second stack of paperwork yesterday and they called today with questions. He just decided to go down there to see what the issues are. All the more reason we need someone with a business mind to help. He's out of his element and, frankly, so am I."

"Licenses and permits are tricky. Each section of the application needs to be completed correctly. Something as simple as not having a box checked can void the application," I comment.

Zane grins. "See, we need you," he states matter-of-factly. "So, tell me about your job search so far."

I explain to him that the company I did my internship with closed their doors after the owner passed away. His children wanted nothing to do with the small printing business, so they sold out. "I was hopeful to get on full time but that didn't work out," I tell him. "And no matter how many phone interviews or face-to-face interviews I go on, when they hear that, it's as if I caused them to sell and they shoot me down. It's always the same excuse. 'You have the education but we're looking for someone with more experience.'" I stop there before I go on a rant about my job search. Yes, I know Zane, but I need to keep this interaction as professional as possible.

"Well, we're looking for someone to run the behind-the-scenes stuff. Payroll, human resources, deposits, paying bills, those sorts of things. Crew is the owner, but he doesn't want to be that hands-on. He's going to be here, so if there was ever an issue he would be available to you as a resource. So will I, although we really have no clue how to even begin with all of that stuff."

"With this being a club, what would the hours be?" I ask.

"You wouldn't be expected to be here until closing every night. The ideal situation would be that you're here at least when the staff arrives in case they have payroll or HR issues that need to be addressed. We plan on opening at five Wednesday through Sunday. When Crew and I talked earlier, we were thinking you could work eight to five with the understanding that some days you would have to alter your schedule or stay late. The staff are all going to report an hour before opening, so that gives them an hour to see you for anything they might need."

"I don't mind working into the evening. I have no other responsibilities that would keep me from being devoted to the position."

"Between now and a few weeks after opening, it will be long hours. It would be nice to have you here for all the training and even later into the shifts once we first open in case any issue were to arise."

"That won't be a problem."

Zane and I spend the next hour talking about the club and what I could do for them. We talk salary, which puts mine at Coffee House to shame, plus benefits.

"So, what is the title, exactly?" I ask.

Zane laughs. "We actually just decided on that before Crew left today. We settled on club administrator. You will be over the staff, just as Crew and I will be. The three of us will hopefully keep this a well-oiled machine. At least that's the goal. What do you think?"

"Off the record, I think I'm trying really hard not to get my hopes up." I laugh. "On the record, I feel as though my education and experience, although limited, would be a great asset to Club Titan."

Zane grins. "I could not have said it better myself. How much notice do you need to give Coffee House?"

*Wait, what?* "You mean?"

"Yes. Berklee, welcome to Club Titan."

It takes every single ounce of control that I have not to jump out of my seat and hug him. "Don't I need to meet Crew first?"

"No. He left this up to me. He trusts me and I trust you. I've known you forever, and I honestly think you're exactly what we were hoping to find."

I hold my hand out for him to shake. "Thank you, Zane. I promise I won't let you down."

He takes my hand and grins. "Now, how much time do you need to give them?"

"I want to give them two weeks. It's the right thing to do, but I don't know that they'll need me to stay that long. We have several people who want more hours. I've worked there all through college so I have seniority. Besides, most days I'm off at three, so I can come here after work. It would only be for two weeks, so I can start as soon as you need me to."

"Tomorrow, then. Be here at four?"

I nod.

"I'll introduce you to Crew and we can get started on all the employee paperwork. We've hired a few in the last two days but we're starting from scratch. You're going to have your work cut out for you."

"I got it," I tell him confidently. I do. This is what I went to school for.

"All right, be here tomorrow at four with all of those ideas you just rattled off."

"Thank you, Zane. I won't let you down."

With that I turn and make my way back down the hall and out onto the street. I focus on not walking too fast and not screaming and fist pumping into the air in celebration. It's not until I'm in the car and a block away that I let out a scream of excitement and do a little shimmy in my seat.

Things are looking up.

# E I G H T
## Crew

THREE HOURS LATER, I have my liquor license in hand. Apparently, I forgot to check a few boxes and they were going to deny me. Lucky for me I was able to lay on the charm and the lady was willing to sit down with me to help. We need an administrator yesterday.

> **Me:** *Any luck with the admin interview?*

> **Zane:** *Yeah, I hired her. I think she'll be perfect for what we're looking for.*

> **Me:** *Hell yes! When does she start?*

> **Zane:** *Tomorrow at four.*

> **Me:** *Even better. Thanks for taking care of that.*

> **Zane:** *I got you.*

I slip my phone back in my pocket and release a sigh of relief. Maybe now that we have an administrator, this feeling that I'm drowning, that I've taken on more than I bargained for, will go away.

My original plan was to head back to the club, but instead I'm going to go home and just relax for the night. Tomorrow starts a new day. Placing my truck in Drive, I try to put it all out of my mind and not worry about anything club related.

When I get home, I throw a frozen pizza in the oven, change into some sweats, grab a beer and turn on ESPN. Nothing like a little preseason football replay to clear the mind. The timer on the oven reminds me that dinner is ready. I don't bother with a plate, just cut the pizza into quarters and stand at the island to eat it. I have a clear view of the TV and it's less to clean up. That's the life of a bachelor.

Dinner done, I grab another beer and head to the couch to watch the game, but my mind drifts. Suddenly autumn-colored hair and sky blue eyes are all I see. With my focus on the club, I've had . . . a dry spell. Self-imposed, of course, but my body feels it. I try to block out the image of those tight black pants and focus on the game.

Fifteen minutes later I find myself staring blankly at the screen as I imagine what it would feel like to have that ass in my hands. Needing some relief, I slip my hand under the waistband of my sweats and palm my cock. I've gotten used to taking matters into my own hands since I made the decision to make the club my focus. No distractions.

But this . . . this is different.

I ache.

For her.

I slide my sweats down my hips and waste no time fisting my cock in quick, even strokes. Closing my eyes, the first thing I see is her. Berklee with her auburn hair flowing down her back in soft curls and that ass. In those pants.

I grow harder.

Pump faster.

I let myself get lost in the fantasy of her. My cock nestled between those tight cheeks, my hands in her hair. Grunting, I squeeze tighter as my release spills onto my stomach.

My phone rings and I jump. Surveying my current situation, I decide to let it go to voice mail. Standing from the couch, my sweats slide to my ankles and I kick them off. Picking them up, I wipe off my stomach and head to the shower, stopping on the way to throw my sweats and a few other items into the washer.

After a quick shower, I slide into another pair of sweats and resume my spot on the couch. I look at my beer that sits untouched and undoubtedly warm on the coffee table. Grabbing it, I take it to the kitchen and pour it down the sink, then grab another. My phone dings, reminding me I missed a call.

Grabbing it from the table, I see it was Zane. Swiping the screen, my phone dials him automatically.

"What's going on?" he says in greeting.

Thoughts of my little jack-off session along with the image of Berklee filter through my mind. "Just having a beer, watching last night's game." It's not a complete lie. "What you got going on tonight?"

"Nada. Barry called and wanted to know if I wanted to get a beer, thought I'd see if you wanted to go. You've been nothing but the club these last few months."

"Nah, I'm thinking it's a night-in kind of night."

"All right, man. Let me know if you change your mind."

"Later," I say, ending the call. Taking a big swig of my beer, I attempt to leave thoughts of the sexy Berklee alone and focus on the game once more.

Kicking back on the couch, I can feel exhaustion setting in. Closing my eyes, I fall asleep to visions of her.

A loud thud and pain in my side wake me up. Opening my eyes, I blink to focus and realize I'm on the floor of my living room. Reaching under me, I pull out the remote that is jammed into my side. I must have rolled over and fallen off the couch.

Stretching up to the table, I grab my phone and check the time. Two minutes until six. Time to get the day started. Pulling my tired ass off the floor, I pad to the kitchen to make coffee. Just as I'm about to hit Start on the coffee maker, I change my mind. With my sudden obsession with Coffee House, and the lovely Berklee, I've been consuming way more caffeine than what I need. I forgo drinking any here with plans to stop and pick up my usual. I'm asking for trouble and I know it, but that doesn't stop me.

I rush through getting ready and am out the door in forty minutes.

Parking outside the shop, I peek through the windows and see she's working today. I've been lucky that she's always here when I need my caffeine fix.

Climbing out of the truck, I casually make my way inside. Berklee looks up at the sound of the door and gives me a warm smile.

"We have to stop meeting like this," I say. It's lame as hell, but this girl . . . last night . . . yeah, I'm not exactly on top of my game this morning. I think I should probably feel bad or embarrassed that I stroked my cock to images of her, but I can't find it in me to care. She's gorgeous, and all guys have stock in their spank banks, right?

She laughs. "Well, you've only got two more weeks of run-ins, and then you never have to see me again," she jokes.

I feel a tightness in my chest. "New job?" I manage to find my words.

"Yep." She grins. "It's been a long time coming. I'm excited to finally be using my degree."

She's happy, and that makes me happy for her, but sad for me. Shit! I don't even really know this girl. I've seen her a handful of times, talked to her just as many. My self-imposed dry spell is affecting more than just my orgasms.

"Congratulations," I say halfheartedly.

"Thanks." Her face lights up. "Your usual?"

"Yeah, thanks," I mumble. She turns to pour my coffee and I give myself a mental kick in the ass. It's not like I planned on asking her out. She's just a girl in the Coffee Shop who happens to be sexy as hell and gorgeous. Nothing to lose sleep over.

"Here you go." She hands me the cup and I quickly reach for it, letting our fingers graze. Her skin is so damn soft, same as before, but this time there's a current that races through me. It has to be a result of last night's extracurricular activities.

"Thank you," I say, handing her a five-dollar bill, and turn to leave. I need to get my head on straight.

"Bye," she calls out. I don't turn around, just wave and walk straight out the door. It's a dick move, but that's the reason I do it—my dick. I need to subtract him from the equation.

I climb back in the truck and drive around the block, parking in front of the club. 'Club Titan' is now written in large letters hanging above the door. This is what I've sacrificed myself for all these months. This is what my focus should be on. I need to get this club up and running. Everything else needs to fade into the background until that happens.

As I reach for the door handle, my phone alerts me to a text.

> **Zane:** *Have a meeting with a temp agency today. Hoping they will be able to help with the rest of the staff.*
>
> **Me:** *What about the new Administrator?*
>
> **Zane:** *She'll help too, but we'll need time to bring her up*

*to speed on your vision.*

**Zane:** *BTW, she'll be there today at four.*

**Me:** *Got it.*

I shove my phone into my pocket, grab my laptop bag and head inside. Ridge and his staff are wrapping things up.

"Hey, man." Ridge holds his hand out and I shake it. "We just finished all the items on the punch list. I thought you and I could do another walk-through while the guys finish cleaning up."

"Sounds good." I follow him through the club and nod as he points out items on the list that have been fixed.

"That wraps it up," he says, handing me a copy of the list with all the items checked off.

"Thanks," I say. "Looks like you get an early day."

"Yeah." He grins. "I plan to use it wisely. My wife and kids are home today."

"All good, Ridge," one of the guys says. I think his name is Tyler.

"Great. We're going to head out. Call me if something comes up."

"Will do," I say, handing him the check from my wallet. "You and the guys should come to the opening. Bring your wife for a night out."

"You know we might do that. She would love it. I love my kids, but sometimes I just want her to myself." He grins.

I walk him to the door and say goodbye to the rest of his team. Turning, I look around me and take in my vision. When I inherited the money, I wanted something that would continue to make me money. Once the club idea got in my head, it just wouldn't leave. After weeks of thinking of not much else, I started putting my plans to paper, looking for a location. Now here I am, just under two months from opening night. It's surreal to see it all come together.

Grabbing my iPad, I begin walking through and making notes in regards to furniture we're going to need. Beckett Construction built a custom bar, but we need bar stools, as well as tables, chairs, and booths for the upstairs VIP. There are also three offices and a conference room that looks down over the entire club. It has a mirrored effect; people can't see in, but I'll be able to see out. So will Zane and our new administrator. All three offices are now spoken for. I quickly get lost in taking it all in and planning.

"Hello," I hear a female voice call. I'm in the back storage room measuring for shelves.

Looking at the time, I see that it's four o'clock, which tells me that this must be our new administrator. "Sorry, I lost track of time. Zane should be . . ." My voice trails off when I come face-to-face with Berklee. "Hey," I say hesitantly.

"Uh, hi. I'm, um, looking for Zane."

*No fucking way is he dating her.* "He's supposed to be here any minute. Can I help you with something?" *Like telling Zane to fuck off?*

"I don't know exactly. I'm supposed to start working here today." She gives a shy smile. "This is the job I was telling you about. I'm the new administrator for Club Titan."

*Holy. Fucking. Shit.*

My words are stuck as I process what she just said.

Berklee, the girl I stroked my cock to not even twenty-four hours ago, is my new administrator.

## NINE
# Berklee

"**H**EY, YOU MADE it," Zane says, rushing into the club. "Sorry, I was hoping to beat you here." He stops in front of me and pulls me into a hug.

"What the fuck?" Mr. Super Sexy Beard says. I'm still trying to figure out what he's doing here. Surely, he's not . . .

"Crew, I see you've met, Berklee. Berklee, this is Crew Ledger, owner of Club Titan."

Shit. Shit. Shit. Mr. Super Sexy Beard is my new boss. I mentally replay all of our interactions, making sure I didn't make a fool of myself. The flirting, that first day when I checked him out . . . Oh no. This isn't good. I'm going to be fired before I even get to start.

His name fits him. It's sexy like him.

*Oh no.* I fight the blush that I know is rising to my cheeks. *I used my boss to fuel my fantasy. This is not good. So not good at all.*

"Yes," Crew says, bringing my attention back to them. "Would you care to tell me why you're hugging our new employee? That has sexual harassment written all over it." He's looking at Zane like he wants to rip his head off.

This guy is always calm, cool and collected when he comes into Coffee House. I guess first impressions can be wrong.

"Relax, Crew. She's Barry's roommate."

"Barry and Maggie," I speak up. "Maggie and I have been best friends for . . ."

"Your entire life," Zane finishes for me.

I shrug. "Anyway, Barry's a confirmed bachelor and when Maggie and I graduated college, he offered for us to move in with him and split the bills. It works for us," I say.

"When you're here it needs to remain professional. Is that going to be a problem?" he asks.

"No, sir," I say quickly.

Crew, who is staring Zane down, breaks his gaze to look at me. I think I see his face soften just a fraction when he says, "I was talking to Zane." Still not the friendly guy I've come to know, but this is his business after all. His livelihood.

"Calm down, Ledger. Berklee and I go way back. There is nothing sexual between us. Well . . . not yet." Zane winks at me.

"Enough!" Crew thunders, causing me to jump. "It's my name and reputation on the line. This can't and won't happen, do you understand me?"

"I got it. Now, Crab Ass, can we get started?"

I hold my breath, waiting for Crew to tell me that Zane made a mistake and that I no longer have the job. I'm sure Coffee House will let me stay. I've been there for years now.

"Show her around. Keep your damn hands to yourself," Crew grumbles before marching back upstairs.

"That was pleasant." Zane chuckles.

I slap his shoulder. "Zane! What if he fires me before I even get started?"

"Relax, Berklee. He's not going to fire you. He's just under a lot of stress with getting this place up and running. Neither one of us really know what it takes to run a business. Crew has been researching and doing a lot of reading, but we need you. He knows that. He also knows that since I know you, you can be trusted. He doesn't trust new people easily. They find out he has money and that's what drives them."

"People suck," I say.

"That they do. All right, let's take the tour."

I nod and follow him as he points out the bar, stage, storage closets and security room. He explains that state-of-the-art cameras will be installed, so there will be eyes in the sky, and the team will be in the room next to the door. That way they can get to any potential issues faster than if their office was housed upstairs with the rest.

"Level two." He motions for me to go first.

As I reach the landing, Crew is standing there, his arms folded over his chest and a stern look on his face.

"No touching, and none of that eye shit you got going on either," he says with authority.

"Eye shit?" Zane chuckles.

"Berklee, we need a minute. You can go into the first door on the right. That's going to be the administrator's office."

I don't miss how he doesn't say "your office," but I do as I'm asked anyway.

"Stop fucking her with your eyes," I hear Crew demand.

Zane laughs.

My knees begin to shake as adrenaline rushes through me. I'm afraid to get busted eavesdropping and losing my job all at the same time. Emotional roller coaster.

"Damn it, Davis!"

"Okay, geez. Listen, Berklee has been at practically all of my family functions growing up. She's like a little cousin. Relax. I'm not going to do anything to screw this up for you. I'm invested too, you know. I quit my job to be here."

I hear a heavy sigh, then Crew says, "Okay, I got it, but can you tone that shit down? Please?"

The way he says "please" sounds as though it was painful for him to get the word out.

"Done. Now, can we please show her the rest of the club before we scare her off and we're screwed? We need her and you know it."

Hearing that, I quickly move to the opposite side of the room and look down over the club through the glass.

"It's one-way," Crew says from behind me. "You can see out, but they can't see in."

"Great idea," I reply, keeping my back to him.

"This will be your office. I'm going to be ordering furniture in the next couple of days. You can decorate however you want."

I relax at his words. He's not firing me.

Taking a deep breath, I turn to face him. "Zane and I are friends. I can promise you that we will be completely professional. Nothing other than two friends working together. You have my word." I stare into those dark brown eyes, willing him to believe me.

"Good." He walks to the glass to stand beside me and looks below. "It's a far cry from Coffee House. You up for this?"

"Without a doubt," I say confidently.

He nods.

"Ready to see the rest?" Zane asks from the door.

Funny, I didn't even notice he wasn't in the room with us until now. Crew Ledger is my sexy new distracting boss, and I need to learn to be around him every day and not lose my head.

"Yes, lead the way," I say, walking toward him. I follow him as he shows me his office and Zane's. They are the same size as mine, and all three look down over the club.

"I ordered you both laptops. They'll be here Monday." Crew looks down at his wrist. "It's just after five. You have time to stay?" He looks at me, then Zane. "I'd like to get furniture ordered."

"I'm good with anything, but yes, I can stay."

"I'm thinking deep cherry wood, tall bookcase and a chair made for a king," Zane says, puffing out his chest.

I can't help the small laugh that escapes my lips. Crew whips his head around to look at me before moving his glare to Zane. "The books are downstairs." That's all he says before leaving us to follow him.

"Is he always like this?" I whisper to Zane.

"Nah, he's got a stick up his ass today for some reason. It's going to be fine, Berklee, you'll see."

Although I'm skeptical, I nod and follow him down the stairs.

# TEN
## Crew

I STOMP DOWN the stairs in a pissy mood. I have to get a grip on this situation, keep my head in the game. I've been around beautiful women before, so this should be a piece of cake. Although, I don't ever remember their skin being as soft as hers, and those eyes . . . I want to get lost in them.

*Shit.*

*Focus, Ledger!*

On the makeshift desk, I grab the furniture book and slide it across the table where Zane and Berklee are now sitting. Next to each other. Zane grabs the book and starts flipping to the pages I've flagged. Berklee leans in and I clench my teeth as her full breast brushes against his arm. In Zane's defense, he doesn't even seem to notice. *How is that possible?* I shove my hands in the pockets of my jeans to keep from pulling her away from him.

*What the fuck is wrong with me today?*

"I really don't have a preference," Zane says.

"Pick your favorite, Berklee," I tell her, my tone clipped. Those blue eyes stare up at me. I know I'm being a dick, but I just don't know how to stop.

"Well, I think they should all match. It will give a more professional feel to the club. The rooms are all the same dimension, or they seem to be. I think a simple L-shape with matching credenza and bookcase is sufficient." Her voice is confident despite the fact that she can tell I'm not impressed. I just don't know why.

"Cre-what?" Zane asks.

I'm glad he did because I have no idea what a fucking credenza is either.

Berklee laughs. She covers her mouth trying to keep it in. It's a magical sound I can see myself getting addicted to. "It's a filing cabinet, just fancier. Lateral and wood to match the other office furniture," she explains.

"Okay. Pick what you think will work and I'll get it ordered," I tell her.

She nods, grabs the book and flips through the flagged pages. I watch as she removes flags one by one. Within a few turns she's narrowed it down to two. "Do you have the room measurements? I want to make sure they'll fit."

*Smart girl.* "I did that before I started looking. All the sets I flagged will fit."

"Okay." She bites her bottom lip, and I have to shift in my seat at my body's reaction to that simple move. "Then I say this one. Black is sleek and will go well with the ash-colored carpeting."

I nod and take the book when she hands it to me. "Thank you."

"You're welcome. How about chairs? You all should go to the local office supply store and sit in a few. You're both tall and you'll want to make sure it fits your height."

I look down at my watch. Almost six. "What time do they close?"

"My guess is at least nine," she says.

Standing, I pull my keys out of my pocket. "I'll drive." I start toward the door. I hear them talking and the scraping of chairs. It's not until I hear her high heels clicking against the laminate flooring that I know they're following me. This is not something that has to be done today, but I've already opened my big-ass mouth so we need to follow through.

When I get in the truck, I start to rethink that. The back seat is full of boxes of flyers for opening night that I picked up today and never got around to unpacking.

"Thank God for bench seats." Zane laughs.

*Damn it!*

Zane steps back and motions for Berklee to slide in. I watch as he offers her his hand and helps her step up. Immediately she tugs at her skirt and slowly slides to sit beside me. She smells like fresh strawberries and I hide my smile; it fits her. Zane climbs in, and with his big body and broad shoulders, Berklee scoots just a little closer to me. Her leg, which is bare a few inches from her knee down, is leaning against my thigh.

"Sorry," she whispers when I move over toward the door.

"No worries," I croak out. I sound like a fucking frog. She's throwing me off my game today; that's not something I'm used to. The ride to the office supply store is thankfully only ten minutes. I don't know that I would have survived longer. She kept her hands on her lap, and I wanted to reach over and lace her fingers with mine. Lightly brushing my hand against her thigh, I feel the softness of her skin and fuck if I don't want to feel more of her.

Yeah, any longer and I don't know that I could've held out.

As soon as the truck is in Park, I hop out and reach out and offer her my hand without thinking. I don't want to see him helping her, touching her. I've had about all of that I can take for one day.

"Thank you," she says, holding her skirt with one hand and placing the other in mine. It takes Herculean efforts to not run my thumb across her soft skin.

I nod. Once she has two feet safely on the ground in those heels, I close the door. We meet Zane at the back of the truck and his face is lit up with a grin. I roll my eyes, which causes him to throw his head back in laughter. I give in to temptation and place my hand on the small of her back.

"What did I miss?" Berklee asks.

"Oh, nothing," Zane says, wiping tears from his eyes.

Berklee shrugs like this is normal Zane behavior and leads us into the store.

"Eyes," I grumble, and he laughs harder. He opens his mouth and I throw my hand up, stopping him. "Not a word," I say, then quicken my stride to catch up to Berklee. I keep step beside her, placing my hand on the small of her back once again, not moving it until we're in the store. I've crossed the line of unprofessional and I shouldn't risk it any further, but when I see the sales guy eating her up with his eyes, I want to knock his ass to the ground and take her away.

"Looking for tall office chairs," I hear her tell him. I watch as he takes her in from head to toe, lingering on her legs.

"For me," I say, stopping next to her. I'm not standing so close that we're touching but close enough that this jackhole gets the drift. *Don't look.*

His head pops up and he has to tilt it back to look up at me. I'm six-one, so not a giant, but this guy, he's not much taller than Berklee, whom I'm guessing is about five-five, five-six. "Right this way," he says, turning and walking away.

"Damn, Crew, did you have to scare the guy?" Zane says from beside me.

"I didn't scare him," I grumble, then follow Berklee who is behind the sales guy.

"This is our tall chair section," he says.

Berklee turns to me. "Start sitting." She grins.

I can't help it; I grin back at her. I try out the "tall" chairs, as does Zane.

"How do they feel? Lean back, slouch, all that. Make sure you're going to be comfortable."

We do as she says, moving around in each chair. It doesn't take us long to find what we want, both choosing the same one. "What about you?" I ask her.

"I'm sure mine will be in the next row over."

"I can show you," the sales guy pipes up.

"Oh, no, thank you. We would like two of these if you could get them ready. I'll find mine in the meantime."

She effectively dismissed him. She was polite and professional, but I can read through the lines; she was either pissed from how he was looking at her earlier or trying to diffuse my anger. First day on the job and she has me pegged. If she only knew where that anger was coming from. She probably thinks I'm pissed that he's objectifying her, and I am, but even more so that he's looking at her at all. I don't want anyone looking at her. Not like that.

Zane's laughter captures my attention. Shaking out of my thoughts, I look over and see what's so funny. Berklee is sitting in a black leather chair and spinning in circles. She looks like a little girl, and that smile on her face.

*Beautiful.*

"You like that one?" I ask her. I have this irrational twisting in my gut. I want to be a part of her joy, her laughter.

She plants her feet on the ground to stop spinning. Looking up at me, her face flushed, she smiles sheepishly. "Yeah, this one will work." I can tell she's trying to bring herself back from the high she just spun herself into and be professional.

Little does she know, professionalism walked out the door the minute I found out Zane hired her.

"Nice choice," the sales guy says to Berklee.

*Does he have a death wish?*

"We'll take it," she says, her tone all business once again. She stands and smooths out her skirt. "Do we need anything else? Printers? Office supplies?" she asks me.

"Printers, no. I ordered those when I ordered the computers. Office supplies, yeah," I say, placing my hand on the back of my neck. What the fuck do I know about ordering office supplies.

"For the three of us?" she asks.

"Yeah, and maybe for behind the bar too, just in case," I suggest.

"I'm on it." I watch as she grabs a cart that seems to have been abandoned at the end of the aisle and walks off.

"I did good, huh?" Zane says, knocking his shoulder into mine.

"Too early to tell," I say, lying through my teeth. This is . . . more than I bargained for. However, if I'm being honest with at least myself, I can admit that Zane did good. Real good.

Zane chuckles and I walk off to follow Berklee. I catch up to her in the Post-it aisle, watching as she checks each pack carefully. "What are you doing?" I ask.

She quickly raises her head, apparently unaware that I was watching her. "Getting the best bang for our buck. Checking the number of Post-its versus the price." She says it like I should've known.

"Berklee, I can afford whichever ones you want."

"Doesn't matter. It's about getting the best deal. That's great that you have money, and it's my job to make sure you keep it that way."

She settles on what I assume is the best—what did she say, bang for my buck?—and throws two packs in the cart. I step behind the cart and motion with my head for her to move down the aisle. "I got this," I tell her.

"We need pads of paper, and printer paper. I assume the printers will come with at least starter ink. I can order more once I know what kind we're going to need. Oh, and we'll need pens. I think that's it for now."

I follow her as she stops and studies the pens. Looking down to the cart, I see three staplers and three tape dispensers, along with a sleeve each of staples and tape.

"Now the paper," she says, placing some pens and highlighters in the cart.

I don't say anything, just follow her down the aisle and into the next. Cases of paper are lined up and she immediately goes to the lower price. She bends as if she's going to pick it up. "Stop!" I say, probably louder than I needed to. "Sorry," I mumble. "Let me get it." I rush to her side and easily lift the case, placing it in the bottom of the cart.

"Thank you." She looks around. "Where's Zane?"

Why is she looking for him? "Left him at the chairs," I say, trying to keep my voice calm. This causes her to laugh.

"What's so funny?"

"You don't know how many times all of us would get together to go out and Zane would end up getting lost in the crowd. I swear that guy doesn't know a stranger."

Relief and more annoyance that he knows her. That he's spent time with her. It pisses me off because I can't have her. She works for me and I have to focus on the club. A guy could lose himself to a girl like Berklee. I would lose myself to her. All the more reason to keep this professional.

She works for me. That's the extent of our relationship.

I hear a woman laugh and I would bet my life Zane is with her.

"I think we found him." She smiles up at me.

"You know him well."

"Not really. I mean, we've hung out, and he's at all the family functions that I go to with Maggie and Barry, but I wouldn't say that I know him. I do know that he likes the ladies, and with his looks and personality I can only assume that he's behind that throaty, 'I want you' laugh."

I choke back a laugh of my own. "What exactly is an 'I want you' laugh?" I have to ask.

She waves her hand. "Oh, you know, the one that makes women seem desperate. The laugh that you know is fake, and so does the offender, but she doesn't care. She wants the guy's attention and she knows stroking his ego will get it."

Sure enough, we get to the end of the aisle and find Zane standing too close to one of the store employees. She's looking at him like he's her next meal and laughing at almost everything he says. She reaches out and touches him, and he moves closer.

"See what I mean?" Berklee whispers.

"You nailed it," I whisper back.

"It's sad, really. She's a pretty girl. She should hold out for someone who really makes her laugh."

It's with those words that she walks toward the couple. Zane spots her and introduces them. I follow behind and watch her as she says hello and then tells Zane that it's time to go, almost like a mother hen. I watch as the girl grabs a business card off the counter and scribbles something on it—her number, I assume—then hands it to him. Zane winks at her and then turns his attention to Berklee, looking over her shoulder to find me.

"Got everything?"

"Yeah," I mumble as I roll the cart to the checkout line.

# ELEVEN
## Berklee

WE PULL UP outside the club and I'm ready to get out of this damn truck. I'm sexually attracted to my very hot, very close boss, and the ten-minute drive felt like a lifetime. I need some space to separate us, to move away from his musky scent, the one that has me rubbing my thighs together.

"Berklee, we can get this stuff. You've worked all day. Go ahead and head home," Crew says, opening his door.

I nod and start to turn toward Zane's door when Crew's deep yet soft voice rumbles next to my ear, "I got you." He offers me his hand. My body instantly reacts to his voice, to the feel of his hot breath against my ear. *Get a grip, Berklee. You can't go there.*

Taking a deep breath, I place a smile on my face and take the hand he's offering. I hold my skirt with the other and, as graceful as possible, hop out of his truck. I stumble on my heels and his other hand—his rather large hand, I might add—wraps around my waist and pulls me close to him, saving me from falling to the pavement but heating my body even more. "Thank you," I say, resting my hands in his chest. I take a little longer than necessary to get my bearings because he's so close. I eventually push back, stepping out of his hold. I keep my eyes on his chest; I don't want to see those dark eyes, the intensity in them.

"You good?" he asks, holding his hand close to my hip as if I might fall again. Part of me wants to stumble just to feel his arms around me one more time, but I know it's a bad idea. I need to get my attraction to him and lock it down tight.

*I need this job. I want it.*

"Yeah," I say, taking another step back so I'm out of his reach. "Same time tomorrow?" I ask him—well, his chest.

"That works, as long as it's not too much for you."

"It's fine. I'll be here around four."

"Hope to have some interviews set up," Zane says, walking to where Crew and I are still standing by the driver's door.

"Great. I'm excited to get started." I take another step away from them. "Well, gentlemen, I'll see you both tomorrow afternoon." I wave awkwardly and turn toward my car. I don't look back. I don't make eye contact. Instead I make sure my Bluetooth is connected and call Maggie.

"How did it go?" she asks.

"Mags!" My voice comes off as a whine.

"What?"

"It's him. Crew, it's him."

"Crew? What are you talking about?"

"Mr. Super Sexy Beard is Crew Ledger, aka my new boss."

"Oh shit." She laughs.

*Really?* "It's not funny," I scold.

"Yeah, it really kind of is, B." She laughs harder.

Ugh! I hit End on my cell phone.

I just hung up on my best friend. I don't think in all the years that we've known each other have I ever done that. She immediately calls back, but I don't answer. I'll be home soon, and then she can laugh at me face-to-face all she wants.

When I pull into the driveway she's standing on the porch. I take my time getting out of the car and slowly make my way to where she's standing.

"I'm sorry," she says immediately.

I feel the stress of the day weighing me down. "What am I going to do, Maggie?"

"What do you mean?"

"I'm attracted to him. He's my boss."

"Let's go inside."

I follow her in the house and look around. Thankfully, Barry isn't home. "Let's hear your wisdom, oh wise one," I say, flopping down on the couch.

Maggie laughs. "Okay, so Crew, the guy you've been flirting with the last, what, week or so?"

I nod.

"Right, so he's your new boss and you're crazy attracted to him."

"I think we've covered that."

"Just doing a quick replay. Honestly, I say try to fight it."

"Great advice," I deadpan.

"I wasn't finished, smartass. Once you spend some time with him, you'll know if it's just his looks or the man himself who attracts you."

"Okay, I'll bite. What happens if I try to fight it and I find out that it's him, the whole package, that has me panting after him? Then what?"

Her reply is immediate. "Then act on it." She shrugs as if it's not a big deal.

"Hello." I wave my hands in front of her face. "Did you forget the part where I told you that he was my boss? As in my livelihood depends on me working for him?"

"I didn't forget, but honestly, Berklee, life is too damn short. If you're that attracted to him and he returns that sentiment, you're both mature adults. I say go for it. If it doesn't work out, you'll have the experience from the club under your belt and can cut your losses and move on."

"I don't want to move on. I'm excited about this job," I whine.

"How do you know you'll have to?"

"You have your dream job," I tell her. "I want mine."

She laughs. "Right, I'm just a sub right now, B. No matter how badly I want to work at Garrison full time, it's not yet my reality."

She's right and now I feel like a bitch. "I know. I'm sorry, I just don't know how to handle this."

"How is he treating you?"

I tell her about how he warned Zane of interoffice relationships and then the way he treated the guy at the office supply store.

"He wants you." She grins. "He's fighting it too. When this"—she swirls her finger in a circular motion around me—"finally comes to a head, it's going to be combustible."

"Not helping," I tell her. I hear the front door open and groan.

"Let's get a man's perspective," Maggie says, motioning for Barry to join us in the living room.

"What's going on?" he asks, eyeing me. He knows me just as well as Maggie does.

"Have a seat, big brother. I want to run something past you." Maggie pats the couch beside her.

I stay silent as I listen to her catch Barry up to speed.

"So wait, Crew Ledger is the guy you've been all swoony over from Coffee House?" he asks.

I nod.

"Crew's a good guy. Although, I don't ever remember him being serious with anyone. He and I aren't close, but we've hung out a few times with Zane."

"Yay, he's a great guy. What the hell am I going to do, guys?"

"Why do you have to do anything?" Barry asks.

"I told her to see how it goes. See if this attraction still goes both ways once they get to know each other," Maggie chimes in.

"I have to agree with Mags on this one. Maybe in a week you'll wonder what you ever saw in the guy."

I release a heavy sigh. I wanted them to fix this situation for me, but they can't. I have to be the one to decide that I can or cannot work for him. If I decide to stay, which is the decision I'm leaning toward, I just need to be the mature adult I am and fight it. I can't be the first person in history attracted to her boss. I can do this.

"I'm going to bed."

"Don't stress over it. Whatever happens will happen," Maggie says.

I give them both a hug and head to my room, stopping by the kitchen on my way to make myself a bowl of cereal. I don't plan to come out until morning.

# T W E L V E
## Crew

WHEN I PULL into a spot in front of Coffee House, I tell myself it's because I slept later today and didn't have a chance to make coffee after tossing and turning most of the night before exhaustion finally took over. Taking a deep breath, I climb out of the truck and head inside. Berklee looks up when she hears the bell over the door. Her eyes light up when she sees me, but otherwise nothing changes. She plants a polite smile and greets me.

"Good morning, Mr. Ledger. Your usual?" she asks.

*Mr. Ledger?* "Crew," I correct her. "Yeah, the usual, thanks, Berklee."

She nods once and turns to pour my coffee. Today she's wearing tight jeans that hold her ass just as well as the blank pants she usually wears, paired with a black sweater and boots that come up to her knees. "That will be two dollars," she says, sliding the cup toward me.

Just like all the mornings before this one, before she was my employee, I reach out before she can pull away just to get a small feel of her soft skin. That's partly the reason I couldn't sleep last night; I kept feeling her pressed against me, her bare knee begging for me to rest my hand there.

"You're welcome." Her voice is soft.

"I'll see you later?" It's a stupid question, but it keeps me here, just the two of us, a little longer. The bell over the door tells me we are no longer alone. I curse it and bless it at the same time.

"Yeah, I'll be there around four," she agrees.

"Damn, good help's hard to find," a male voice says from behind me.

I instantly whip my head around, ready to pound the fucker for his comment.

When I turn, fists clenched, I see Barry and . . .

"Barry, Maggie, what are you two doing here?" Berklee asks from behind the counter.

"I was called in last minute to sub so we decided to stop in and say hello on our way to work," Maggie explains.

"Hey, man, how've you been?" Barry asks me.

I force myself to relax and unclench my fists. Something they both take note of. *Fuck me.* "Good, just staying busy getting the club up and running."

"You got a good one there." Barry points over my shoulder toward Berklee.

"That's what I'm told." I'm being a dick, but what else do I say? That I know that she's a good one from the feel of her soft hands, or that her scent of strawberries is still in my truck? Maybe I should tell him that I fisted my cock to the image of her burned into my brain. I don't say any of that. Instead, I watch her as she talks and smiles at her friend.

"Hi, Crew, I'm Maggie. I don't know if you remember me." She holds her hand out for me to shake.

"Yeah, I think you were there when we stopped by to pick Barry up a time or two," I say, pulling my eyes off of Berklee.

"Yeah. It's odd that the two of you have never met, considering Berklee was always at our place growing up."

"Uh-huh," I agree.

"It's a small world." Maggie grins.

"Right, so what can I get for you two?" Berklee takes control of the conversation.

"The usual," they both say in unison.

This has me turning to face Berklee. "You remember all your customers' orders?" I ask her.

"Just the ones I care about." She immediately slaps her hands over her mouth and a beautiful blush coats her cheeks. "I mean, they're family," she tries to backpedal.

Leaning over the counter, I motion for her to lean forward. When she does, I place my lips next to her ear. "What am I?" Moving back, I reach out and tuck her hair behind her ear, my eyes never leaving hers. I watch as she swallows hard and takes a deep breath. I don't wait for her reply; her body spoke for her. "Keep the change. I'll see you later." With that, I pick up my coffee, wave goodbye to Barry and Maggie, and head back to my truck.

When I pull up to the club, I sit in my truck and stare at the coffee in my cup holder. That's how this started, me needing a dose of caffeine. That's when Berklee was just a gorgeous girl at Coffee House who I busted checking me out. Now that same girl works for me and I don't know how to turn it off. I don't know how to not see her as the girl with autumn-colored hair, sky blue eyes and the tightest ass I've ever seen. How do I see her as just an employee?

I'm startled out of my thoughts when Zane bangs on my window. "Got ya." He laughs.

Grabbing my coffee, I climb out of the truck.

"What were you doing just sitting there?" he asks.

"Just running through a mental checklist of all the shit that still needs to be done."

He spies the cup in my hand. "You see Berklee this morning?"

"Yeah, she was there. So were Barry and Maggie."

"Sounds like a family affair. Should I feel bad that I wasn't invited?"

"Not my family," I remind him. "Maybe you should ask them."

"So, I have some more interviews set up for today—servers, bartenders and a few more guys for security. I thought we could let Berklee lead them, see how our new administrator conducts business."

"Probably not a bad idea, considering neither one of us really knows the legality of interviewing."

"I'm sure there's shit we're asking that we're not allowed to," he agrees. "I have them all starting at five. I thought that would give Berklee an hour or so to look over the applications." He hands me a stack of papers. "These are your copies."

I don't bother looking at them, just shove them in my bag and head inside. "You know what we're looking for," I tell him.

"So, what's on the agenda for today other than the interviews later?"

"I ordered the office furniture last night. I have a meeting with a supplier for the liquor and beer at eleven, and an appointment on Friday with a security company. That's the soonest they could be here."

Zane claps his hands. "Now we're talking."

"Other than that, just waiting on the bar mirrors to come in and some additional lighting. Ridge said he or one of the guys would come back and hang it once it comes in."

"What do you need from me?"

I toss him a book from the liquor vendor. "They have the best prices around. I need to compile a list of what we want to stock."

"This I can handle." He grins. Walking over to the bar, he grabs one of the new pads of paper and a pen and starts working on his list.

I open my laptop and pretend to be engrossed in e-mails, but all I can think about is getting my fucking head straight. I look at the clock; I have seven more hours until she shows up. Time to get my shit together.

"List is done," Zane says, laying the paper on the table in front of me.

Glancing at the clock, I see that's its almost noon. "I'm going to go hang some flyers and grab a bite to eat while I'm out." He rubs his stomach. "You need anything?"

"Nah, I'm going to run out too. I have to get Mom a card. It's her birthday next week."

"All she gets is a card?" he asks.

I laugh. "You know better. I like to mail her a card, but I have a gift for her too. It's actually for both of them. I got them a cruise to the Caribbean."

Zane whistles. "She's gonna love that."

"I know. Dad already knows. I had to swear him to secrecy, but I needed him on board to make sure their schedules were cleared."

"All right, man. I'll see you in a few hours."

I grab my keys and follow him out. It takes me no time at all to pick out a card for Mom, and then I hit the drive-through and grab a burger and fries. By the time I make it back to the club, it's gone. Seeing it's now almost two o'clock, I decide to answer some e-mails while I wait for Zane and Berklee.

A few minutes before four, I'm pacing. Zane's not back, and I need him to be a buffer. The sound of the door opening and her heels against the floor tell me that's not going to happen. I stop pacing like a crazy person and turn to face her.

"Hey." She waves.

My cock comes to life, not sure if it's the sweet sound of her voice or just her, just Berklee. What I do know is that it's wrong of me to imagine picking her up and pushing her against the wall, her long legs wrapped around my waist. I know that it's wrong to think about kissing her neck while feeling her body tighten around me. I shift my stance, trying to hide my reaction to my little daydream and greet her. "Hi. We have some interviews set up around five." I look down at my watch. "Zane should've been back by now." All business. I need to remember that. Keep things professional, no fucking hard against the wall.

"No worries if he's not. Do you happen to have résumés or applications so I can get an idea about the candidates before they get here?"

I walk over to where my laptop bag is sitting on the bar and pull out the stack of papers that Zane gave me earlier today. "Here you go," I say, holding them out for her. This time I make sure we don't touch.

"Thanks. What are we interviewing for?"

"Let's sit." I motion for the small table that's still set up in the middle of the room. "Bartenders, servers, and security are still on the list."

"Cleaning crew?" she asks.

"I have that lined up already."

"Good." She begins to flip through the applications. "This girl, Carly, she's got bartending and server experience. That's good."

"Mmhmm. I'm going to go make a call. I'll be right back," I say, standing abruptly. I need to distance myself. She nods but never takes her attention from the applications in her hand.

Stepping outside, I pull out my phone and call Zane.

"Yeah," he answers.

"Where the hell are you? We have interviews soon."

"Flat tire. The spare is shit, so I had to call Dad to pick me up. We're going to get a new one."

*Shit.*

"You and Berklee are going to be flying solo on this one."

"All right, later." Taking a deep breath, I head back inside so Berklee and I can make a game plan.

"Crew, there are some good applicants here," she says when I join her back at the table.

"Yeah, Zane's been spending a lot of time finding them. Speaking of Zane, he's not coming. Flat tire."

"Oh, no worries." She waves her hand in the air. "We got this."

"I was thinking I'll let you take the lead on this. The only experience I have are the interviews we held last week, and I wouldn't exactly call them professional."

"Got it." She grins. "So, how many of each are we looking for?"

She and I spend the next half hour discussing hours of the club and staff needed. She's very smart and thinks about the big picture.

She's definitely an asset to Club Titan—as long as I can keep it professional.

# THIRTEEN
## Berklee

"SORRY ABOUT THAT," I tell Crew.

"For?" he asks.

"I kind of took over during the interviews. I'm just excited to be using my degree. This is what I enjoy and I got caught up."

He laughs. "Berklee, that's your job. You don't need to apologize to me for doing your job."

"I know, I just . . . Oh never mind. It's just me being silly. I'm not a control freak, I promise."

Again, he laughs. "Good to know. Now, what do you think about the candidates?"

"I really liked Carly, Janet and Casey for servers. Carly is also trained as a bartender so she could float. Heath for security, for sure, and Sam for the bar," I rattle off.

"Zane and I already hired one for security. His name is Tank."

"Does the name fit?"

He studies me. "He's a big guy, why?"

"No reason, just his name alone screams 'security.'"

Looking at my watch, I see that it's after eight. Just as I'm about to ask if he needs me for anything else tonight, my stomach growls loudly.

"Shit," Crew mumbles. "We're done for the night. Let's go grab some dinner."

"I'm so embarrassed," I tell him. I know my face is red, so I might as well own it.

"Don't be. I knew you were coming here straight from your other job. I should've made sure you'd eaten." He stands and holds his hand out for me. "Come on, my treat."

I don't argue, although I know I should. I should stand on my own and not take his hand, should drive my ass straight home. Instead, I place my hand in his and allow him to help me from the chair.

"I know a great pizza place. How's that sound?"

My stomach growls again. "Great, actually. I love pizza."

He looks down at me with a boyish grin. "Me too."

I watch as he walks around turning off lights. Suddenly we're in complete darkness except for the glow of the exit signs.

"Berklee." His deep voice echoes in the darkness.

Before I can answer I feel his hand on the small of my back. The heat from his palm seeps through my thin shirt.

"Careful," he whispers next to my ear. My body shivers and I know he feels it. I don't say anything; I can't without my voice betraying me. Instead I walk slowly with him leading me to the door. Once we're outside under the gentle glow of the streetlights, I step away from him. From his heat.

*Distance. I need distance.*

"Let me get that," he says, reaching around me and opening the truck door.

"Thank you," I whisper, afraid my voice will betray me. I take a big breath as Crew climbs behind the wheel. I slowly exhale and try to relax against the seat. Looking over, I see his fingers gripped tight on the wheel.

He catches me looking. "Pizza." He winks and puts the truck in Drive.

"So, why a club?" I ask, trying to break the silence and distract myself from my racing heart. Surely he can hear it.

"I wanted to invest in something, something I could be proud of. I inherited . . . some money from my grandmother, and I wanted to put it to good use."

"I admire that. So many would blow through it, or gamble it away."

"I didn't go to college. School was never my thing. I was working a job living paycheck to paycheck, and when I found out about the money, I just . . . wanted something for me, you know?"

"I do, actually," I tell him. "I graduated four months ago and I've been hitting road block after road block while job hunting. Everyone wants experience, more than just internships, and well, as you know, I have none."

"How did they expect you to get it?"

I laugh. "Right? That's my complaint. I appreciate you and Zane giving me this chance. I won't let you down."

He nods. "So, you and Zane know each other?"

*Haven't we been through this?* "Yeah, causally. Like I said, it won't be an issue. There has never been anything between us."

"Right, your boyfriend would kick his ass," he remarks.

"Yeah, you kind of need one of those for that to happen," I say. He mumbles something under his breath that sounds like "idiots." I can tell just from the sound of his voice that he's being nosey. *Two can play that game.* "What does your girlfriend think about you opening a club?" I ask.

He chuckles. "You kind of need one of those for that to happen." He pulls up to the pizza place. "Best in town," he says with a boyish grin, then climbs out of the truck, me following quickly behind.

The smell of warm melted cheese and sauce greets us at the door. My stomach again growls.

"Let's get you fed," Crew says from behind me, his lips next to my ear.

Damn! Does he not realize what that does to me? What him being that close does to me? Of course he does—he's one of those. You know, the type that knows he's damn sexy and isn't afraid to show it.

Crew leads us to a booth in the back.

"Hi, I'm Alice, and I'll be your server. Can I start you off with drinks, maybe some breadsticks?"

"Sweet tea," Crew says, then points at me.

"I'll have sweet tea as well."

"Breadsticks?" he asks.

I grin. "Only if you add cheese."

"Breadsticks with cheese and an extra side of sauce."

"Man after my own heart. The more sauce you dip them in the better." I chuckle as Alice walks away.

"So, why business?" he asks.

"I guess since I already have the job, I don't have to worry about being fired if I answer this question the wrong way?"

"Berklee." His deep voice is scolding. "The job is yours, and the only answer is the honest one."

The waitress delivers our drinks and I take a sip. "I'm one of those weird people. I love organizing and problem solving. I also enjoy paperwork."

He raises his eyebrow in question.

"Really. I never minded writing papers in college. Homework in general didn't bother me. I think it's my organizational trait. My mom has it too."

Before he can ask another question, a basketful of cheesy carb heaven is delivered to our table. "Are you ready to order?" the waitress asks.

"I like it all," I tell Crew.

"Meat lover's?" he asks me.

"Sure."

"Large," he says, handing over his menu. I do the same.

Grabbing a plate, I add a breadstick with some sauce. I take a bite and close my eyes, savoring it.

"So good," I murmur. Crew clears his throat and my eyes pop open. His are trained on me. "So, uh, the interviews went well today."

He nods, takes a sip of tea, and then places a breadstick on his plate. "They did."

I take another bite. He watches me. I grab my napkin, wipe my face, and then take a peek. Nothing. "What?" I ask, paranoid.

"You're sexy as fuck when you eat."

"I don't even know how to respond to that. You're my boss." I'm not sure who I'm reminding at this point, him or me.

"Doesn't matter."

"Crew."

"Doesn't change the fact that you're sexy as fuck."

I don't miss that he left off "when you eat" that time. I look down, trying to hide the blush that covers my cheeks.

"That." I look up from under my lashes at him and he's waving his fork at me. "Sexy," he says. "The way your skin pinks . . ."

*Oh my God!*

"Here you go. Careful, it's hot." The waitress sets the pizza in the middle of our table. "I'll be right back with some refills. Y'all need anything else?"

"No," Crew replies, his eyes still locked on mine.

"Looks good." I serve myself a piece and then hand the spatula to him. "Here you go," I say, as chipper and unaffected as I possibly can.

He takes it, his fingers brushing over mine. I swear from the smirk he's wearing that he did it on purpose. I let go and resume eating.

"When's your last day at Coffee House?" he asks.

I swallow my bite of pizza. "I actually meant to tell you. One of the girls wanted the hours, so this is my last week." I don't know if he can sense my unease, but the rest of the meal the conversation is focused on the club and what's to come. I'm grateful that the topic remains neutral. Work I can discuss.

"Can I get you all any dessert?" the waitress asks.

Crew looks to me. "No, thank you." I push my plate away. I've already eaten too much.

"Just the check," he tells her.

"All right, you all have a great night." She lays the check on the table.

I reach into my purse and pull out my wallet.

"What the hell are you doing?" he asks.

"Getting some money."

"Put it away." He shakes his head.

"You don't have to buy me dinner, Crew."

"No way you're paying when you're with me, for anything. Put it away." He stands, grabs the check and stalks off toward the register.

I do as he says and put my wallet away. I know there's no amount of arguing that's going to change his mind. I reach the register just as Crew finishes up. He places his hand on the small of my back and leads me to his truck.

"Thank you for dinner," I say once we're on the road. If I weren't looking at him I would have missed his nod, acknowledging me. We make idle chitchat about nothing of importance. I even bring up the weather. Lame, I know, but the silence gives me too much time to think. Time to analyze and replay his words from dinner. Talking about the weather is a much better option at this point.

"You don't have to come in tomorrow. There's not a lot going on right now. Next week the furniture is supposed to be delivered, and I have a supplier coming in so we can pick the mugs and all that for the bar area. I'll also need you to start files on the staff we've hired so far, process background checks, and I'm sure a bunch of other shit I have no clue about."

I smile at him. "I've got you covered. That's what you hired me for. If you change your mind about tomorrow, let me know."

"I won't. Enjoy your weekend. I'll see you Monday at nine."

"You got it, boss," I say, climbing out of the truck.

"Crew," I hear him correct me before I shut the door.

I wave and turn to head toward my car. "Wait!" Crew quickly catches up with me with his long stride. "I'll walk you."

"It's like twenty feet," I tell him.

"I'll walk you," he repeats.

Again, I don't bother to argue, letting him have his way. I hit the remote to unlock my car and he pulls open the door. "Have a good weekend."

"You too, Berklee." He waits until I'm buckled in before shutting my door and tapping on the roof three times.

I drive away without looking back to see if he's watching me. My mind is already coming up with ideas. Ideas that I need to shut down.

# FOURTEEN
## Crew

ROLLING OVER, I look at the clock. Just after six and I'm wide awake. I told my parents I would be at their place around nine. Dad wants some help finishing up the deck he's building, and Mom, of course, insisted that she make breakfast.

It's been a couple of weeks since I've seen them. I've let the club consume me. Like Berklee, I told Zane to take yesterday off as well. I tracked some deliveries, returned some e-mails and spent the rest of the day and night looking through the new website and sending off changes to the designer. We messaged back and forth until close to one this morning.

Deciding I'm not getting back to sleep, I climb out of bed and head to the shower. Mom will be thrilled that I'm early.

When I pull up, Mom's already at the door. "Crew." She rushes out onto the porch and wraps her arms around me. Pulling away, she swats my arm. "It's been too long," she scolds me.

"Hi, Mom." I throw my arm over her shoulder as we walk in the house. "I'll do better I promise."

"You better," she says, stepping out from underneath my arm. "I'll get breakfast started."

"How you been, son?" Dad asks from his spot at the kitchen table. He's reading the paper and drinking his morning coffee. That's his routine, has been for years.

"Good, just getting everything up and running with the club. Got some staff hired." My mind immediately goes to Berklee.

"That's good to hear. Things are coming along good, then?" he asks.

"Yeah, I hired an administrator. Zane is taking lead on security, and we've hired a few bouncers, bartenders, and servers. We still need to add a few more to the roster. I hope to have Berklee do more interviews next week."

"Berklee? What a unique name."

I don't comment. "How are things? How's the deck coming?" I ask Dad instead.

"Good. I just need to finish the railing."

I look at him and he must see the question in my eyes. If he's already at the railing he didn't need my help, obviously. Dad tilts his head toward where Mom is standing at the stove and winks. Figures. She must have been saying how it had been two weeks since I've been by, and Dad took it upon himself to make that happen for her. He's always been one to give her whatever it is she wants. I just shake my head and he grins.

"You need any help down at the club?" Dad asks. He's trying to change the subject.

"Thanks, but we've got it. Berklee, Zane, and I are getting it done."

"You let us know if we can do anything."

Mom sets a big plate of pancakes in front of each of us and one for herself. "How is Zane?" she asks.

"You know Zane, still breaking hearts." I laugh.

"Well, he needs to settle down. You both do. Hey, what about the new girl, Berklee? Maybe with them working together—"

"No!" I state, louder and more intense than what I intended. I feel like a dick for snapping at her. "What I mean is they're coworkers. I don't need office romance to run my staff off. He needs to look elsewhere." What I don't say is that if anyone gets close to Berklee, it's going to be me.

"Oh poo." Mom waves her hands in the air, dismissing me. "There is nothing wrong with dating someone you work with."

"You can't be serious." I'm surprised at her statement.

"Of course I am. Tell me, if they both do their jobs and it doesn't interfere with the club, how is that wrong?"

*It's wrong because she's my employee. I'm the boss, as she likes to remind me. It's wrong because I can't stop thinking about how it would feel to be inside of her. It's wrong that I want her.*

"I mean, that kind of thing happens all the time. Did you put a rule in your employee handbook that states that coworkers can't date?"

I make a mental note to get Berklee on an employee handbook. Just another item I wouldn't have thought of.

"What happens when they split? Then you have jealousy and animosity, and I don't need that in my club. Not to mention if one of them can't handle it and quits. That leaves me in a bind."

"Not all splits are terrible, Crew. Have a little faith, my dear." Mom reaches across the table and pats my hand.

"You ready to tackle this deck?" I ask Dad, changing the subject once more. Talking relationships with my mother is the last thing I want to do.

Dad chuckles as he pushes back from the table. "Let's get started."

He doesn't have to tell me twice. I pick up my plate and carry it to the sink.

"I got those. Go on now," Mom says.

I drop a kiss on her cheek and follow Dad outside. We spend the rest of the day taking our time putting up the railing on the new deck. Neither of us is in a hurry to get the job done.

"I think that's got it." Dad stands back, hands on his hips, admiring our work.

"Not too shabby," I agree. Quickly we pack up the tools and head in the house.

"Just in time," Mom says over her shoulder. She grabs the casserole dish from the stove and sets it on the island. "Dig in." She turns back to get the garlic bread.

One thing I miss about no longer living at home is Mom's cooking. If I didn't know better, I would swear that's why Dad married her. The woman is a genius in the kitchen. Dad and I grab plates and pile them high with Mom's baked spaghetti. She adds a huge piece of garlic bread to each and we take a seat at the table.

"Don't wait on me." She nods toward us. "Eat."

Not needing to be told twice, we dig in.

"So, I was thinking, it's been a while since your dad and I have been to the club. When is a good time to stop in and see the progress?"

"Mom, you don't need an invite. You know that."

"We just know that you have a lot going on, and we didn't want to get in the way or delay you in any way."

"Any time next week is fine. I'm there most days all day." Mom smiles at my comment and my work here is done. I finish up and take my plate to the sink. "Thanks for feeding me, twice." I pull Mom into a hug when she stands to take her plate to the sink as well. "I need to get going. I'll see you two one day this week?" I ask, looking at Dad.

"You can count on it," he says, standing from the table as well. They walk me to the door and we say a quick goodbye.

As soon as I get home, I take a shower and wash off the day, dressing in lounge pants and a T-shirt. My plan is to get caught up on e-mails and go over the ever-growing list of items that need to happen before Club Titan opens its doors.

Three hours later, e-mails have been knocked off the list. Now to look at everything that still has to get done. As I'm making notes, I remember Mom mentioning an employee manual. I add that to the list. Maybe I should tell Berklee, give her a heads-up to start thinking about it. Not giving myself time to change my mind, I grab my phone and send her a quick text.

> **Me:** *I know it's the weekend, so don't reply. Just wanted to have you put an employee manual on your radar for the club.*

I hit Send and set my phone on the arm of the couch. A message alert sounds not a minute later and although I doubt it's her, I reach for it, almost dropping my laptop in the process. *Fuck, this girl has me acting like a horny-ass teenager.* Tapping the screen, her name appears.

> **Berklee:** *Got it, boss. That was already on my list.*

> **Me:** *Good to know you're all over it. And it's Crew.*

> **Berklee:** *Got it, Crew.*

> **Me:** *Better.*

Just as I'm about to put the phone down, it alerts me to another message.

**Berklee:** *Do you ever stop working?*

I think about her question. I used to. I used to live for the weekend, grabbing a beer, hooking up with a beautiful woman. Then I got the letter, the inheritance, and everything changed. Suddenly I was leery that those women were out to trap me, tap into the funds. More than that, I wanted to do something with it. Build an empire, so to speak. Sure, I inherited the money, but I wanted to make something of myself with it. The club is that for me. Failing is not an option, so yeah, I'm at home working on a Saturday night.

**Me:** *If you knew me a year ago, you would not have asked that question.*

**Berklee:** *So, what changed?*

**Me:** *Life.*

Yeah, the answer is vague, but I'm not much of a spill-my-guts kind of guy. She must sense that with my reply because she ends the conversation when her next text comes through.

**Berklee:** *See you Monday, Crew.*

I lock the screen on my phone and toss it beside me on the couch, focusing on the to-do list. At least I try. Texting Berklee completely broke my concentration. It happens any time she's around. Hell, even when she's not, I let my mind drift to her. Texting her is not good for my productivity.

# FIFTEEN
## Berklee

I'M WIDE AWAKE when the alarm goes off at seven. I didn't sleep well last night, thinking about today—my first official first day at Club Titan. Well, not really, but it's now my only job, my only source of income, so it feels like the first.

I took full advantage of my three-day weekend. Friday, Maggie was off too, so we hit the mall. I needed more professional clothes, not just skinny jeans and leggings that I wore at Coffee House. Saturday night, Maggie, Barry, Zane, and I along with a few other mutual friends hung out at our place to watch the UFC fight.

At first I was reluctant and was planning to go to my parents'; Crew didn't seem too impressed that Zane and I knew each other outside of work, and the last thing I need is to get fired before I even really get my feet wet. Barry assured me it was fine. He even went so far as to call Zane and made me talk to him. He assured me Crew was just cranky with the stress of the club and all was fine. Maggie also made a good point that Zane and I are just friends, nothing romantic, and there's no law against that. Although, pissing off my new boss is not on my to-do list at the moment.

Sunday, I just caught up on laundry and lounged around with Maggie. We had a Lifetime movie marathon.

I stare at the alarm clock as the time rolls over to seven fifteen. Groaning, I climb out of bed and head to the shower. I'm going to need a huge dose of caffeine to get me through the day. Good thing Coffee House is just around the corner. I wasn't super close with my coworkers, but it'll be nice to see them when I stop in. With the close proximity,

I'm sure I'll be a frequent flyer.

Once I've showered and dressed, I make my way to the kitchen. The condo is quiet, Barry and Maggie both long gone. She got the call yesterday afternoon to sub all this week. Popping a bagel in the toaster, I head back to my room, grab my shoes and slip on a couple bangle bracelets and my earrings. I look at myself in the full-length mirror and grin. I'm wearing a gray pencil skirt, a coral silk shirt, and my natural wavy hair is hanging down my back. I grab my black strappy heels and call it good.

Quickly scarfing down my bagel, I grab my purse, lock up and head to work. I feel like . . . an adult. It sounds crazy, but this is my first "big girl" job after college. The first job I get to use my degree. I feel like today starts a whole new chapter in my life. I can't keep the grin off my face as I make the short drive.

Checking the clock, I see that I have plenty of time, so I stop at Coffee House. A new guy is behind the counter. "Hi, what can I get you?"

He's easy on the eyes, and of course I'm still on my "big girl job" high, so I give him a cheesy grin. "Good morning, Noah," I say, reading his name tag.

He grins back and his dimples show. "I'll have two extra-large black and one extra-large pumpkin spice."

"Berklee!" Carrie, my boss—scratch that, former boss—comes out of the back and greets me. "You just can't stay away." She laughs.

"What can I say?" I shrug. "The club is just around the corner, and this is the best coffee in town."

"Noah," Carrie says, "Berklee gets the employee discount always."

"Carrie, you don't have to do that."

She waves me off. "You worked here for years, and I want to. You will always be a part of the Coffee House family."

"Thank you."

She nods, pats Noah's shoulder and walks back to her office.

"Here you go, Berklee," he says with a flirty wink.

"Thank you." I hand him my card and he swipes it. Reaching into my purse, I pull out a couple of ones and drop them in the tip jar.

"Have a good one," he says, handing me my card and receipt.

I grab the drink carrier and leave Noah and his flirty winks behind. When I arrive at the club, Zane and Crew are both parked out front. "Good morning," I say, pushing open the door with my hip, careful not to spill the coffee.

"Let me help you." Zane comes rushing toward me.

He takes the carrier and I pull mine out. "Those two are the same, tall and black." I grin.

"Thanks. You're taking all kinds of care of me." Zane chuckles. "I finished off that dip you made yesterday." He rubs his stomach.

I laugh. "It's so easy even you can make it. I'll write it down for you."

"Or you could just make it for me again," he says as we reach the table where Crew is sitting with his laptop in front of him.

"Fine, I'll make it for you, lazy man. Just tell me when you want it."

"Make me a list. I'll buy whatever you need. It just tastes better when you make it." He bats his eyelashes at me.

"Really? You might want to make it yourself first before you make that assumption."

He places his hand over his heart. "I can feel it." He winks and I roll my eyes.

"What the hell are you going on about?" Crew asks. Zane hands him his coffee and he looks up at me, those dark eyes so intense, taking me in. "Thank you." He holds up his cup before taking a sip.

"You're welcome." I'm proud that I'm able to tamp down the lust enough to even reply. When I graduated college, I never dreamed that my biggest hurdle after actually landing a job would be my sexy-as-hell boss.

"Berklee made this dip, dude." Zane closes his eyes and groans. "So fucking good."

"Dip?" Crew questions. I can see the confusion in his eyes.

"Yeah, I went over there Saturday and we watched the fight. Berklee here made this dip, and I'm telling you man, it's like crack," Zane boasts.

"You were at her place?" Crew asks. His voice is low and gravelly, his eyes flashing between the two of us.

"Well, yeah. I mean, it's my cousins' place. They all live together," Zane confirms. "Anyway, Maggie and Berklee made the food and this dip? So good. I was just convincing her to make it again." He turns to me. "Really, make a list. I'll buy whatever you need."

I laugh. "Okay. It's just a few ingredients. It's easy to make, so you really could handle it on your own."

"Nah, it's always better when someone else makes it." He winks.

"You didn't mention you had company," Crew says, his dark eyes piercing me.

I shrug. "Don't see how it matters."

"Wait a minute. Is he"—Zane points to Crew—"who you were texting when you missed the KO?"

I bring my cup to my lips and take a slow sip, buying some time.

Zane takes that as confirmation. "Damn, man, you made her miss the KO. Don't you know not everyone works 24/7?"

"I told you not to reply," Crew says, his voice softer. Almost apologetic.

"It wasn't a big deal. I know some of the fighters from living with Barry." Crew's jaw ticks at this. "But I'm not a hard-core, 'have to watch every minute' fan or anything." I point to Zane. "He's the one who insisted we rewind it so I could see."

"It was an epic KO, B, and you missed it!" Zane exclaims.

"We've got work to do," Crew snaps.

I immediately clamp my mouth shut. It's obvious he's pissed off, and I don't want to poke an angry bear.

Zane, on the other hand . . .

"Chill out, man. Did you wake up on the wrong side of the bed?" He smirks.

I can tell from the look on Zane's face that he's baiting his friend. Out of the corner of my eye, I see that Crew's not impressed.

Crew ignores him and turns his attention toward me. I hold my breath, waiting for the wrath and possibly the words "You're fired." They never come.

"Berklee, I have a list of things that need to be taken care of, much like the manual we talked about."

Releasing the breath I was holding, I reply, "Great. I brought my laptop, just let me run out to the car to get it."

"No need, I bought you both one." He points to the two white Apple boxes sitting on the bar. "The furniture is also being delivered for the offices today." He looks down at his watch. "Should be here any minute."

"Great." I don't really know what else to say. He's clearly pissed, yet trying to contain it by getting down to business.

The sound of the door opening has the three of us turning to look. "Delivery for Crew Ledger," the guy says.

"This way." Crew points up the stairs. "Berklee, why don't you set up your laptop. Zane and I are going to make sure they don't need any help."

I nod my agreement and watch as they walk upstairs to check that the furniture is placed correctly. I make my way to the bar and grab one of the boxes. There are no chairs yet, so I look around, making sure I'm not about to flash anyone, then hike up my skirt and lift myself onto the bar. I wiggle to get my skirt to a decent length before grabbing the box and getting to work on setting up my new laptop.

# SIXTEEN
## Crew

I STOMP UP the stairs, Zane on my heels. I'm pissed the fuck off. I know I have no right, but that doesn't matter. Once we clear the landing in the small lounge area, I turn to face my best friend. One look at me and he's throwing his head back in laughter.

"What the fuck?" I ask angrily. His laughter isn't helping my mood.

"How long have we known each other?"

"You know the answer to that question."

He nods. "It's safe to say we know each other better than we know ourselves, right?"

"What the fuck are you spouting on about?"

"You're jealous." He smirks.

"Jealous? What the hell are you talking about?" Shit. He's on to me. And hell fucking yes, I'm jealous.

"Berklee. You want her."

"She's my employee."

"You want her," he says again.

"You're delusional." I can't admit it to him. I have to tamp this down, this . . . want that I have for my new employee. My only saving grace is that I never told Zane about the sexy girl at Coffee House. I kept her just for me.

"Keep telling yourself that, buddy." He laughs and pats me on the shoulder.

Before I can try to convince him that he's wrong, the movers appear with the first of many pieces of furniture. It's probably better; one who protests too much looks guilty, right? Better to let the subject drop and work on my poker face.

Finally, the lead guy seeks me out. "There are only a few more pieces. You want to come down and sign the invoice?"

"Zane, you got this?" I ask.

"Yeah." He's already directing which office gets the next piece.

I follow the lead guy downstairs and review the packing slip he hands me. "Thanks," I say, signing and handing it back to him. He nods and heads back out to his truck.

Realizing we've been at it for over an hour, I decide to check on Berklee. That's what a good boss would do, right?

What I find has me biting back a curse. Berklee is perched up on the bar, her feet bare, those sexy heels thrown haphazardly on the floor. Her skirt's hiked up, showing the creamy skin of her thighs, and her curls hang over her shoulder. I walk toward her hesitantly when all I really want is to rush her and pull her into my arms.

She hears me and looks up from her laptop. "Hey." She smiles. "All set?"

I walk closer. "Yeah, just a few more pieces." I don't stop until I'm standing next to her. So close I'm sure it's deemed inappropriate. I look down at her laptop, sitting atop those creamy thighs. My dick twitches. "You?" I ask, nodding to her lap.

"Yes. I actually started making a list of things we'll need staffing-wise. Do you know if you want to do checks or direct deposit?" she asks, all business, while all I'm thinking about is stepping between her legs and kissing the fuck out of her.

I move closer. It's wrong and I know it, but being this close to her, it's my undoing.

Sensing that I'm now closer than professionalism allows, she looks up from her lap. An errant curl hangs over her eyes and without thinking, I reach up and tuck it behind her ear. It's so fucking soft, like silk, just as I imagined. Her breathing accelerates, causing me to inch a little closer. She's nervous, her expressive blue eyes giving her away. I can see this is a struggle for her too.

"Crew." She breathes my name and I have to fist my hands at my sides to keep from taking her into my arms.

"Hey, guys!" Zane yells from the top of the steps.

Fuck! I forgot about the two-way mirrors. I can only hope he was too busy to be watching me, us.

"Come on up and take a look," he calls out.

Berklee sets the laptop on the bar beside her and starts to move.

"Wait," I say, placing my hand on her bare knee. Fuck, her skin is soft and warm. Bending down, I grab her shoes and place them back on her feet. Rising to my full height, I stand directly in front of her. Reaching out, I place my hands on her hips and move in close. "Ready?" I whisper. That one word has so many meanings.

A blush coats her cheeks. "Yeah," she says, her voice low and sexy as fuck.

Gripping her hips, I fight the urge to wrap her legs around my waist. Instead I lift her from the bar and place her on her feet.

Looking up at me, she gives me a shy smile. "Thank you."

Now that she's on her feet, I tower over her. I'm still standing close, my hands on her hips. Looking down, her shirt is unbuttoned just enough that I can see the swell of her breast in her white lace bra. I swallow hard and force myself to release her.

"After you," I say, my voice gruff. She doesn't say anything, just turns on visibly shaky legs and heads for the stairs. It's not until I stare at her as she walks up in front of me that I realize being a gentleman in this case scored me a major view of that incredible ass.

Berklee stops in the doorway of the first office. "Wow, this looks great."

"Which one do you want?" I ask.

She turns to look at me over her shoulder, and her beauty takes my fucking breath away. "I don't have a preference."

"I think this one should be mine," Zane says from behind us.

I close my eyes and school my features before turning to look at him. "Once Berklee chooses, you can have your pick of what's left."

"You can have this one. Like I said, I really don't care either way. They're all the same size and have the same furniture."

"Yeah, I was just thinking that, even though it's not by much, this is a shorter distance to get downstairs should something security related happen."

"Makes sense," Berklee agrees. "Crew, maybe you should take the one at the end of the hall? Being the owner, you'll be bothered less being there. The employees should come to Zane or me, then you by last resort," she suggests.

"It's settled, then," I say.

"I'm going to get my computer and try it out." She grins at me.

"I'll get it," I offer, already turning to leave the room. I don't need her falling down the steps in those heels.

I grab her laptop and the box, plus Zane's as well. "Here you go," I say, giving Zane his. "I'll put yours on your desk," I tell Berklee.

She smiles and follows me into her office, watching as I set everything on her desk. "Let me know if there's anything else you need. We can make a trip to the office supply store and pick it up." Ordering online is just as easy, and from what I've read they have next-day local delivery, but I'll keep that tidbit to myself. It's an excuse to get her back in my truck. I have to take my doses of the sexy Berklee where I can get them.

"I started a list for that too." She blushes. "We're going to need employee files and things like that."

"Whatever you need, we'll get it." I watch as she bites her bottom lip and nods. *Fuck me. I need to leave her alone.* "Here's yours," I say, handing her the laptop box. Her hand brushes mine when she reaches for it and I feel that same zing of attraction. It's something that I've come to expect when it comes to her. "Right, so I'm just going to get my stuff and put it in my office." Reluctantly I release my grip on the box and slowly back out of the room.

Stopping at Zane's door, I see him with his computer out and sitting on his desk.

"What else you got on the agenda today?" he asks.

"We need to set up some more interviews. Berklee nailed the last ones, so I'm just going to let her handle it. You can do the security staff if you want or leave it up to her. It doesn't matter either way." I don't wait for a reply before jogging down the stairs to gather my stuff from the makeshift desk I've been using in the main part of the club.

When I head to my office, I don't look into either of theirs, just walk right past and settle in behind my new desk. Taking a deep breath, I take a minute to let it all sink in. This is mine, all mine. This club was my vision and slowly, day by day, I see it come to life. A sense of accomplishment washes over me, and every sacrifice I've made in the last year is worth this feeling hands-down.

Leaning back in the chair, I close my eyes and try not to think about the auburn-haired beauty just on the other side of the wall. Never have I felt this kind of burning attraction. Hell, I'm not even sure "attraction" is the right word; it's more like a deep-seated need that I have for her. It's fucking crazy since I barely know her, but there's just something about her that turns me inside out. From the first day at Coffee House until now, it's only grown stronger.

"Knock knock," her sexy-as-fuck voice says from the doorway. "I have some résumés for you to look at."

I don't need to look at them; I've seen her in action and I trust her already. However, I do want to be around her. All the damn time I want to be around her. "Come on in," I say, moving to take a seat in one of the two chairs in front of my desk.

"Servers, bartenders, and security. I talked to Zane and he said for me to move forward with the security applicants as long as you were okay with it."

"Sit," I say, motioning toward the chair beside me. She does as she's told and crosses her legs. Her skirt rides up, causing my cock to stand up and take notice. I shift a little to hide my growing problem. "Let's see." I hold my hand out for her to give me the résumés. When she does, I place mine over hers and rub my thumb across the back of her hand. Electric scorching heat races through me. From her intake of breath, she feels it too.

"I, uh . . . I just wanted to make sure you were on board."

I'm on board, and so is my cock. I leaf through the stack of résumés and then hand them back to her. This time she's careful not to touch me. "Go with your gut."

"Okay."

She stands to leave and I want to demand that she stay. I'm losing my damn mind. Instead I stand with her and walk behind her to the door. She stops and turns around, and suddenly her chest is bumping into mine. I fight back the grin that wants to break free when she braces her hands against my chest so she doesn't fall and I grab her hips to steady her. I couldn't have planned this if I tried. "Careful," I say, staring down at her.

"So-sorry." She pushes back from my chest but doesn't get far as I tighten my grip on her hips. I like her here, next to me. "I need to, um . . . " She looks down at the papers that now cover my office floor. I couldn't give a fuck where they ended up with her this close to me. She steps back, pushing against my chest once more, and this time I let her go.

I place my hands on the back of my head and try to keep from grabbing her and pulling her back into me. I watch as she gets down on all fours in that tight-ass skirt and starts picking up the papers. Before I can pull my head out of my ass and help her, she's trying to stand in heels and the skirt that fits her like a second skin.

Reaching down, I offer her my hand. She stares at if for what feels like a fucking eternity before she places her hand in mine and allows me to help her to her feet.

"Thank you." She gives me a shy smile.

*Fuck, I want to know what those lips taste like.*

She turns toward the door and I follow, placing my hand on the small of her back. I can't seem to help myself—not that I'm actually trying at this point. I'm too far gone with this burning need for her.

Basically, I'm fucked.

I force myself to stop walking once we reach the doorway but don't take my eyes off her until she's in her office, and I hear the subtle click of the door closing.

I smile to myself. She's just as affected as I am. Now I just need to decide what I'm going to do about it. Do I continue to fight this pull? Can I fight it working with her every day? How will this affect our working relationship?

*I'm so fucked.*

# SEVENTEEN
## *Berklee*

THIS WEEK HAS flown by. I completed more interviews and I'm happy to report that Club Titan is now fully staffed. We now have four full-time security—one of whom is also trained behind the bar—six servers with one also trained behind the bar, and six regular bartenders. Club Titan is open Wednesday through Sunday for now. Crew mentioned possibly not being open on Sundays, so we're going to see how the numbers are before we decide for sure.

I found from my online search that the local supply store gives free next-day delivery. Crew grumbled that he could've taken me, but he handed over his American Express and said to get whatever I wanted. I don't know if I could've handled another trip in his truck, although thoughts of being pushed up next to him are not unwelcome. Only this time it's just the two of us, so there would be no reason for that. A girl can dream. After Monday, all I've done is fantasize about my new boss. This week has been full of innocent touches and heated looks, a brushing of my hand here, hand on the small of my back there. It's driving me crazy. They're innocent, but every damn time my heart races so loud I'm sure he can hear it.

I hear the door buzzer sound; it should be the company here to install the booths and tables. Crew insisted that the buzzer be installed when he realized I would be here some days on my own. I was given strict instructions that I am not to open the door unless I'm one hundred percent certain it's a delivery for the club. Even then I'm supposed to keep my phone in my hands at all times. He even went as far as buying me pepper spray, which he insists I carry. I argued with him, but in the end I gave him what he wanted. This time, Zane was actually on his side, taking this head of security title more seriously than I've ever seen him. He even had panic buttons installed throughout the club—the bar, each of our offices, even the restroom. I just smile and nod and let them run wild with their ideas. It's not my money.

Grabbing my phone and the damn pepper spray that Crew conveniently placed on a Club Titan lanyard, I throw it around my neck and make my way downstairs. Through the high-tech security system, I can look at the screen and see who's outside. We have screens upstairs in a small closet that Zane dubbed the security closet, as well as the security room downstairs. I opted to use that one today since I'm expecting the delivery. Clearly the guy wearing the company logo on his shirt is who he said he is, but Zane and Crew both insisted I never take that at face value. "Can I see your ID please?" I ask as nicely as possible through the speaker. I feel like an idiot, but I'd rather not deal with Crew when/if he ever found out I didn't ask.

The guy holds up his badge and the name matches the one Crew gave me. "Be right there," I say into the speaker before rushing toward the door.

"Hi. Right this way." I open the door and let him in.

"Thanks, we have a team of four today. Should be in and out of your hair in a couple of hours."

"Sounds good. I'm Berklee. Let me know if you need anything."

With that, I leave them to it. We got in a shipment late yesterday of paper towels, soap, towels for the bar, straws, plastic cups, and a whole host of other items. I didn't get time to put it away yesterday, so this is as good a time as any. I'll be close in case the delivery guys need anything, and I'll knock this off my to-do list—win-win.

I run upstairs and grab the labeler and utility knife from my desk, then make my way to the supply closet and just start slicing open boxes. I'm quickly lost in my own little world, my phone sitting on the bottom shelf playing my eclectic taste of all genres of music.

Down to the last box, I reach the dish towels for the bar. I slice open the box and grab the first pack, standing on tiptoes to slide it on the top shelf. It's a reach but doable.

Grabbing the next pack, I repeat the process, but this time it's different. I feel him as soon as he steps behind me, his hands on my hips, his body close to mine. Too close for a boss to be next to an employee, but you'll never hear a complaint from me. I've lived for these small touches this week.

"What are you doing, Berklee?" he asks next to my ear.

I close my eyes and relish the feel of his body aligned with mine. "Unpacking," I finally say.

He steps even closer, eliminating the space between our bodies. "You need to be careful." Slowly he runs his hand up my arm that is still in the air and takes the pack of towels, setting it on the top shelf. Then he wraps me in his arms and buries his face in my neck. "Fuck, Berklee. I keep fighting this and I don't know if I can do it anymore."

"Don't." It's barely a whisper, but judging from his intake of breath, I know he heard me.

"You work for me."

"We're adults," I counter. We are, and I've thought about this a lot this week. The way his simple touches make me feel. I know I'll regret it if I never know what it feels like to be with him. I can always call Carrie and beg for my job at Coffee House.

I feel his lips against my neck. "So fucking sweet," he murmurs.

I tilt my head to the side, giving him free rein. This is further than he's ever taken things, and my inside voice is begging him not to stop. I don't want to fight this chemistry we have.

"Crew! Where are you, man?" Zane yells.

He squeezes me tight and then let's go, stepping back. I immediately miss his warmth. "Leave the top shelf for me," he says before walking out to find Zane.

Leaning forward, I rest my head on a shelf. I can't believe I just offered myself up to him like that.

After my breathing is under control, I finish unpacking the towels and placing them on the top shelf, even though he told me not to. I then break down all the boxes and grab the labeler. I'm a fan of organization, and it'll be easier to pinpoint what supplies need to be ordered in the future if their location is clearly labeled.

Once finished, I carry the boxes out back to the dumpster. I hear the guys talking about booth placement and I'm able to slip past them and up to my office.

Opening my laptop, I read through the new employee manual one more time before I print it to present to Crew.

"Berklee!" I hear him shout about a half hour later, followed by his heavy footsteps up the stairs. He stops when he reaches my office. Standing in the doorway, he raises his hands over his head and grabs the frame. "I thought I told you I would get the towels."

"I was perfectly capable, so I finished the job I started," I say, locking my gaze with his. It's a challenge because the way he's standing, his shirt has risen and I can see the V. You know the one. Yeah, keeping my eyes on his is difficult, but I hold steady.

"Do you have to challenge me?" he asks, exasperated.

I shrug. "I didn't see it as challenging you. I finished the job I started. The job I was capable of doing."

He steps into my office and shuts the door. The twist of the lock echoes throughout the room. "You do challenge me," he counters as his long legs carry him to where I'm still sitting at my desk.

I sit statue still and keep my mouth shut.

"Every fucking day, it's a challenge to be around you, to see you. To be close to you and not be able to touch you." He reaches out and cups my cheek with his calloused hands. "I fight with myself on a daily basis to stay away from you, yet every day I stumble. I find myself walking too close to you, holding your hand longer than necessary when handing you paperwork." He drops to his knees so we are eye level. "It's fucking wrong, Berklee. The way I want you, it's wrong. I'm your boss." He clamps his jaw shut.

I point to my laptop, not taking my eyes off him. "There's no rule against it," I say. He studies me but doesn't say anything, so I keep going. "In the handbook, there isn't a policy." His dark eyes smolder with heat as his thumb traces back and forth across my cheek. "What if we didn't tell anyone?" I suggest. I'm desperate for him. This is like nothing I've ever felt, and I want him.

"Berklee." My name is a strained whisper from his lips as he leans in closer.

"You can trust me. I won't gossip about us or what we do behind closed doors." The more I talk, the more an idea forms. It's perfect. We can have a benefits-only relationship other than boss and employee. Something has to give with all of this sexual tension between us. I want to concentrate on my new job, and him, the club. We have the same goals in mind, so we'll work together, making it convenient and discreet. I tell him this and he says nothing, just studies me.

Deciding to go all-in with my plan, I place my hands on his face and pull him toward me. He comes without complaint and I lock my gaze on his. "You can trust me. I can't fight this anymore either. It's the best for both of us. We don't have the stress of a relationship, and there's the convenience of being at the same place most of the time. I know you feel it," I whisper.

His eyes soften just a fraction and I know I'm wearing him down. "I'm a big girl, Crew. We do this until one of us wants out or meets someone. We don't sleep with anyone else while we're together." Placing my hand on his cheek, his beard is rough against the palm of my hand. Leaning into him, I kiss the corner of his mouth. "Say yes," I whisper. I have no idea where this seductress is coming from, but I burn for him. I've never wanted anyone or anything like I do Crew Ledger.

I open my mouth to keep trying to convince him when he leans in and whispers "Fuck it" before smashing his mouth against mine.

# EIGHTEEN
## Crew

**M**Y FIRST TASTE of her is intoxicating. Addicting. I don't go easy on her—I can't. I claim her mouth, pushing my tongue past her lips, and she opens for me with a small moan from the back of her throat. With my hand on the back of her neck, I pull her as close as I can, bruising her lips with mine. I want to fucking devour her, mark her so that when other guys see her they'll know she's been claimed.

I was ready to turn her down, this arrangement that she's proposed sounded like trouble with a capital T. My mind was racing with how it would work, how we would manage keeping it a secret working together. Then she kissed me effectively changing my answer. No way can I turn her down after just a simple taste of her lips. I need more.

Needing air, I pull my lips from hers and trail kisses down her neck. "Crew," she moans, and my rock-hard cock stiffens even more. I don't stop kissing her skin, making my way to her collarbone and then journeying further until I reach the button of her shirt. Her chest is rising and falling, her hands knotted in my hair.

Lifting my eyes, I gauge her reaction. Her blue irises are liquid pools of desire staring back at me. Loosening her grip on my hair, she gently runs her fingers through it. That's all the confirmation I need as I proceed to slowly unbutton her shirt. I make sure to lavish her with my tongue with the release of each one. When I reach the swell of her breasts, I just about lose my shit and take her hard on the desk. Instead, I pull down the cups and find pert pink nipples just begging for my mouth. Ever so gently I flick one with my tongue, and her grip on my hair tightens. I suck her, gently nipping with my teeth while rolling the other between my fingers.

"Crew," she moans. "Don't . . ."

I switch it up, placing my mouth on her other nipple, needing to taste every fucking inch of her. Her taste is intoxicating and I want more. I want her naked so I can taste every delectable inch of her. Just as I go for another button, there's a loud knock at the door.

"Berklee, you in there?" Zane asks.

"Fuck!" she hisses.

Letting her nipple fall from my mouth, I carefully pull her bra back up and cover her. She immediately begins to button her shirt. Once she's done, she tries to stand, but my hand on her thigh prevents her from doing so. "Tell him you'll be right there."

"Just a minute," she calls out, her voice a little shaky.

I cup her face. "So, we're doing this? No one else, Berklee, not while we're together. Regardless that this is not a relationship. I won't share you."

"We're on the same page," she says.

Leaning in, I kiss her, soft and slow. A promise of what's yet to come. I want to lavish her body and I plan to. Very very soon.

I stand to my full height, adjust my cock and head toward the door. I flip the lock and pull it open. Zane is leaning against the wall.

"Hey, I was looking for you. The guys with the booths are done. You need to see them before they go?" he asks.

"No, but I'll check it out before they leave." I head for the stairs and fight like hell not to turn back and look at her. I have no doubt Zane knows what was going on; he is my best friend, after all. I don't give a fuck. I want her, and after tasting her, this is happening. Nothing he says can change my mind.

The booths and tables are set up and a thrill shoots through me. The club is finally coming together. We're ready to bring staff in and start training. Opening weekend is just a few short weeks away.

After I sign the invoice and send the delivery guys on their way, I turn to head up the stairs. I tell myself it's to go to my office, but it's really to see her. Zane is up there with her and they're friends. I don't want him giving her a hard time about what he walked in on. I won't let him change her mind.

Just as my foot hits the first step, I hear, "Yoohoo, Crew." My parents. I've been expecting them to stop by all week, and just my luck it would be the day that my mind is all wrapped up in Berklee. Then again, that's pretty much been how things have been since the day I first laid eyes on her.

Turning, I head toward the front of the club to greet them. "Hey," I say, leaning in to kiss Mom's cheek before shaking Dad's hand. "Took you long enough." I laugh.

"Well, you know how things go. You get busy," Mom excuses.

"We had to wait for this to come in." Dad hands me a gift bag.

I take it from him. "You know you didn't have to do this," I tell them.

"Pfft, you don't even know what it is. And we do it because we love you," Mom fires back.

Dad just shakes his head and smiles.

I motion to one of the new tables. "Have a seat." I remain standing, remove the gift's tissue paper and pull out a frame. "This is great. Where did you get this?"

"The Internet. You know, you can get anything online," Mom says.

I bite back my laughter as I take the gift in my hands. It's a framed mirror that says "Club Titan" in fancy script. At the bottom, it has my name and the established date of this year. I'm not gonna lie; I'm a little choked up right now. "Thank you." I force the words over the lump in my throat.

"I thought you could hang it in your office," Mom says.

"Yeah, I think I will."

"So let's see it." Mom stands and Dad follows suit.

I nod. Cleaning up the tissue paper, I place it and the frame back in the bag and lead them upstairs. "This is our lounge area, and the first door is Zane's office."

"Oh, is he in? I've not seen him in far too long." Mom peeks into Zane's office. "Come over here and give me a hug, you," she tells him.

I breathe a sigh of relief that he's not with Berklee.

Mom and Dad are in Zane's office catching up, and since they see him as a second son, I know I have some time. I walk down to her door and peek in. She's sitting at her desk, fingers flying over the keys of her laptop. Her lips are still red and a little swollen. My heart beats a little harder in my chest knowing I did that. "You good?" I ask her.

She stops and looks up, her eyes softening when they land on me. "Yeah, just making a few changes to the employee manual before you review it."

I fight the urge to step inside. If I do I'll want to kiss her, and my parents are just down the hall with Zane. I have to keep myself in employee/boss mode.

"Is this your office?" Mom says from behind me.

I turn to face her. She and Dad are standing behind me, and Zane's behind them grinning like a fool. "No." My voice is gruffer that it should be, so I clear my throat before saying, "This is Berklee's office. She's our club administrator or manager, however you want to look at it."

"Well, is she here? Introduce us," Mom says.

For a second I wonder if Zane put her up to it, but then I remember this is my mom we're talking about. Looking over my shoulder, Berklee smiles, and that has an oddly calming effect on me. Stepping aside, I motion for them to enter her office. "Mom, Dad, this is Berklee. Berklee, these are my parents, Dan and Sarah Ledger."

"It's a pleasure to meet you." Berklee stands and walks to my parents, shaking their hands.

"You too, dear. If you need help keeping these two in line, you just give me a call," Mom tells her. Dad throws his head back in laughter.

Berklee grins. "I might just take you up on that. Although, Crew is my boss."

Mom waves her hand in the air. "Behind every man is a good woman."

"That there is," Dad says, placing his arm around Mom's shoulders and pulling her to him.

I chance a look at Berklee and see she's watching them with a soft smile.

"So, how long has it been?" Zane whispers so only I can hear him.

Berklee and my parents are now looking at the view of the club below. "What are you talking about?" I ask him, my voice low.

"Since you've introduced your girl to your parents?" he asks.

"She's not mine," I growl.

"Really? Then why are you all growly and shit?" Zane counters.

*Fuck me.* "Drop it."

He chuckles under his breath. "I'm not blind, man. You've been a mess since the day you walked in and saw her here."

"I said to fucking drop it."

"Where's your office?" Mom asks, ending our private conversation.

"This way," I say, calmer than what I feel inside. I shoulder past Zane, who has a shit-eating grin on his face, and lead my parents down the hall and into my office. Mom gives me suggestions for where to hang my gift and I happen to agree with her. We sit and talk, Mom catching me up on what's been going on in their lives. Dad's just listening to her yammer on. A knock at the door interrupts us.

"Sorry to intrude, but I'm going to order some lunch. Do you all want anything?" Berklee asks.

"Oh no, dear, we need to get going. Thank you." Mom stands and walks to where Berklee is standing, then wraps her in a hug. "I'm so glad you're here to take care of them."

Berklee doesn't seem bothered. She just hugs her back.

"Son, I'm proud of you," Dad says, standing. "You've done well."

I round the desk and give him a hug, Mom waiting for hers when we pull away. "Drive safe," I tell them. "I'll walk you out."

Dad waves me off. "No need, we can manage."

Another quick goodbye to Berklee and they're out the door. I quirk my finger and motion for Berklee to come closer. She stops just a few inches away from me, her blue eyes sparkling.

We're both quiet, staring into each other's eyes as we listen to Mom and Dad say goodbye to Zane. "I'll walk down with you," I hear him say loudly, I'm sure for our benefit.

As their voices grow softer, I reach out and place my hands on her hips, bringing her closer, her body aligned with mine.

"One taste and I'm addicted," I say before leaning in and kissing her.

"Crew," she murmurs against my lips.

"Hmm?" I say, continuing to kiss her.

"Food." She laughs.

Pulling back, I rest my forehead against hers. "Right. Let's get you fed," I say once my breathing returns to normal. I can't remember a time I was breathless after a kiss.

"Incoming!" Zane yells.

Berklee takes three big steps away from me and I want to scold her for it. Instead, I bite my tongue.

Once Zane steps in the room, Berklee holds up the menu that's clutched in her hands. "You want something?"

"Hell yes! I'm starving." Zane takes the menu from her. "I want a mushroom hoagie."

"Crew?" her sweet voice asks.

"What are you getting?"

She bites her bottom lip and takes the menu back from Zane. "I was just thinking about pizza," she says, not looking up.

"That's fine with me. I'll eat anything, so get whatever you want on it. Use your company card."

She nods and walks out the door, not once looking at me. I know this because I watch her go. I don't pull my eyes from the door until I can no longer see her.

Zane bursts out laughing and I scowl at him. I have to have her. This crazy attraction—addiction—I have is not going to simmer until I do.

## NINETEEN

TODAY HAS BEEN . . . thrilling and overwhelming, to say the least. After lunch it was all business, as Crew's phone rang off the hook. No more chances for stolen kisses, but that's okay. I need to start this with slow doses of him, pace myself so I don't let him consume me. I need to keep all emotions detached and just . . . feel.

Looking at the time, I save the file I'm working on and shut down my laptop. Grabbing my phone, I text Maggie.

**Me:** *Heading home now.*

**Maggie:** *K. Eat at the game?*

**Me:** *Perfect.*

I finish closing up and step out into the hall. Crew is still on the phone, something about workers' comp from what I can tell. I decide not to bother him and make my way to Zane's office.

"Hey, I'm heading out. Maggie and I are going to the game tonight."

"Another home game?" he asks.

"Yeah, we like to make it to as many as we can." I point over my shoulder. "Will you tell Crew? He's still on the phone and I don't want to interrupt him."

"He won't mind." Zane grins.

I roll my eyes. "Night, Zane. Have a great weekend."

"Later, Berk!"

He called me out earlier today—well, if you consider teasing me calling me out. He gave me a hard time, then proceeded to tell me that his best friend is a great guy.

"How was your day, dear?" Maggie asks when I walk through the door. I can't help but laugh at her.

"Great." I grin.

"Wait. I know that grin. Tell me everything," she says, clapping in excitement.

"Let me get ready to go."

"Ten minutes," she calls after me. "Oh, and I grabbed us each one of Barry's Garrison High hoodies!"

"Thank you," I reply, stripping out of my skirt. I put on a pair of worn jeans and my Garrison Football T-shirt, pull my hair up into a loose ponytail and grab my tennis shoes. "Ready," I say, plopping down on the couch to put my shoes on.

"Spill," Maggie demands, tossing the sweatshirt at me.

"The sexual tension is off the charts, Mags. We decided we can't fight it anymore."

"And?"

"And I might have suggested we have a . . . benefits-only arrangement. We're going to be spending a lot of time together, so it's convenient."

"Berklee!" Maggie scolds.

"Think about it. It could work. He's hot as hell, and I've never felt this kind of attraction before. I swear, Mags, it's electric. I feel like I've been shocked every damn time he touches me."

"That's risky and you know it, Berklee."

"How is it risky? We agreed that we won't sleep with other people during our . . . arrangement. One of us wants out, we tell the other and go on with life."

"Come on, you know it's not going to be that easy."

"Sure it is. It's mutually beneficial for both of us."

"This isn't you," Maggie counters.

"I agree this is out of character for me, but Maggie, it's just . . . I want him. Plain and simple. I'm willing to risk the fact that my heart could be shattered when he decides he's done with me. I'm willing to take the pain to experience what it's like to be with him."

"Who are you and what have you done with my best friend?"

"It's me, I'm just taking a risk. I don't have the words to describe it. I just know that if I don't let myself experience him, I will regret it."

"Who knows, maybe it won't end."

"Come on, Maggie. Even I'm realistic about this deal. Crew is vibrant and sexy and can have anyone he wants. I'm a means to an end with him. He's been so focused on the club that he's been depriving himself. I'm the cure. I'm close and convenient, and he can trust that I'll keep my mouth shut—well, except for with you. Once things settle down with the club, I see him walking away, and I'm okay with that. I'm not naive enough to say that it's not going to hurt like hell, because I know realistically that I won't be able to keep my emotions out of it. That's not how I'm built. But I'm going in with my eyes wide open, expecting it, but willing to soak up anything and everything he's willing to give until then."

"Well, *if* that happens, I'll be here for you. I won't tell you to be careful, since it sounds like you've got your mind made up and are prepared for the worst. Just remember that you are smart and beautiful and he would be fucking crazy to not want you to be his. I've got your back."

"Thanks, now can we go? We're going to be late." I stand and pull the Garrison hoodie over my head. It's too big, but it's comfortable.

"Okay, so now that the serious is out of the way," Maggie says once we're in her car and headed toward the school, "I need details."

"I don't have many, not really. I mean, he kissed me. Well, we kissed. I kissed him back, obviously."

"And?"

"Electric."

"Damn, I'm jealous."

"You should be." I laugh. "He's like nothing I've ever experienced. Now, enough about me. How was your day?"

We spend the rest of the short drive discussing her class today. She was a sub for the elementary school, and apparently one of the boys in the first-grade class she was covering asked her to marry him.

"I swear the little guy was so damn confident. I had to say yes."

Maggie laughs.

"Aww, what a cutie."

"He really is. I told his mom about it when she picked him up. She just grinned and said he was a charmer like his father."

"She's going to have her hands full."

"That she is." We pull into the lot. "Let's hit up concessions first. I'm dying for a walking taco."

"Sounds good to me." We grab food before finding our seats and settling in for a night of football under the lights.

# TWENTY
## *Crew*

MY ENTIRE AFTERNOON has been spent on the fucking phone. I hate talking on the phone, hence my pissy mood. Looking at the clock, I see it's now after five. I climb to my feet and head toward Berklee's office, thinking maybe she'll want to get together later. The thought alone replaces the scowl with a grin.

When I reach her office door, the light is off and she's nowhere to be found.

"Fuck," I mumble under my breath. I stalk toward Zane's office and stop in the doorway. "Where's Berklee?"

He grins. "She's gone. She and Maggie were going to Barry's game."

Damn it. "Home game?" I ask, already trying to come up with a plan to still see her tonight.

"Yeah. The two of them try to never miss a home game." He's still grinning.

"You going?"

He shrugs. "I've been to a few. Why?"

I don't give myself time to think about the words that are flying out of my mouth. "We're going."

"What? Mr. Workaholic is taking a night off?"

"Yep."

Zane throws his head back in laughter. "Fuck, Crew. She's got you twisted."

"You ready?" I ask, ignoring him.

"Yeah. Let me just shut down." I stand there impatiently as he takes his sweet fucking time shutting down his computer.

Finally, after what feels like hours, he stands and meets me at the door. "Who's driving?"

"I will." I don't say anything else, just turn and head downstairs. I switch off the lights while Zane sets the alarm.

"I hope you know what you're doing," he says once we're in my truck.

"What are you talking about?" I know exactly what he's referring to.

"Berklee."

"I got it covered."

"She's one of the good ones, Crew. She's not a plaything."

I can feel the anger start to build. "I got it," I say again.

"She's like family," he keeps going.

"You want her?" I ask, my voice low and the anger now evident.

He laughs. The fucker actually laughs.

"No. Like I said, she's like family. She lives with my cousins, and she's been best friends with Maggie for as long as I can remember. Barry too, really."

"They've never been anything?" I find myself asking. It shows my hand, but I don't give a fuck. I've been wondering since I found out the three of them live together.

"Not that I know of."

I nod and get lost in my thoughts. Thoughts of her living with another man, regardless of their relationship. I'm not a fan of the idea, but then I don't really have much of a say-so with our current agreement. I need to hear from her lips that there's nothing romantic with the two of them. After that all I can do is trust that she's telling me the truth.

The lot at the high school is packed. Looks like half the town is here. It's been years since I've been to a football game.

"My parents are here. Mom says there are seats by them."

"Berklee?" I ask.

He smirks. "She's sitting right next to my mom."

I nod, grab my keys and climb out of the truck. "Did you tell them that I was coming with you?"

"And ruin the surprise? Hell no. I can't wait to see how this plays out."

I've not given myself the chance to consider what Berklee might think of me being here. I'm just a guy tagging along to a football game with his friend. Nothing more. Except that's an utter fucking lie, and she and I both know it. She'll be able to see right through me, and I couldn't give two shits. No way can I go all weekend without being with her. She's unleashed the beast and I need to feel her.

We reach the bleachers and I step to the side, letting Zane lead the way to his family, to Berklee. I push my hands into my pockets as we climb the bleachers. I have to in order to keep from reaching out for her. She's my addiction. One taste and I'm all in.

"Hey, hey!" Zane says, stopping at the end of a row almost all the way to the top.

Instantly my eyes lock with hers. She's smiling and her eyes are sparkling. That's a good sign. I can only hope that means that she's coming home with me tonight. We haven't talked about where we would be doing this, but tonight I want her in my bed.

Everyone stands to move down the row, allowing us to sit with them. I'm shocked when Berklee stands and moves to the end. Maggie follows and everyone moves down yet again. She leaves room for me to sit beside Berklee with her on my other side. I don't hesitate to take what's being offered, sliding in between the girls and placing my hand on Berklee's knee.

"Hey, beautiful," I whisper in her ear. It's completely out of character for me, but it's the first thing I could think to say.

"Hi." She smiles over at me. "I didn't know you were going to be here."

"Neither did I," I tell her. Understanding crosses her face. Leaning in, I whisper, "Come home with me."

"We just got here."

"After the game, after whatever it is you had planned for tonight, come home with me."

"Is that part of the plan?" she asks.

"It is if we say so. We can do what we want. It's just logistics, although the thought of you in my bed has me hard as a rock," I whisper just for her.

She wiggles in her seat. "Okay." No hesitation, no counter offer, just complete agreement.

"Crew, how have you been?" Maggie asks.

I have to force myself to take my eyes off Berklee to turn and address her. "Good, and you?"

"Good. Hearing great things about the club, congrats."

"Thank you. Berklee and Zane are a big part of that." I'm not above giving credit where credit is due.

"Surprised to see you here tonight. Zane usually comes alone."

She's baiting me, looking out for her best friend. I'm glad Berklee has someone in her corner. "Never had incentive before."

"And now you do?" she asks, watching me closely for my reaction.

Surprising even myself, I reach over, lace my hand with Berklee's and raise them slightly in the air. "Yep."

Maggie looks past me and at her best friend. I turn to look at Berklee and her eyes are shining bright. I want to kiss her, feel those soft lips against mine, but I refrain. That's not part of the deal, public displays. I drop her hand, reminding myself that she's already agreed to come home with me. I don't need to schmooze her. Only that's not how it feels. Not with Berklee.

The game starts and conversation halts as we watch Garrison dominate the field in the first half.

"Bathroom break. Berklee, you need to go?" Maggie asks, leaning over me.

"Yeah, I better." She stands and places her hands on my shoulders as she steps around me. My eyes are glued to her as she walks away. That's when I see the name "Davis" sprawled across her back.

*What the fuck? Why is she wearing his sweatshirt?*

"Why are you scowling at her ass? It's a fine one, if you ask me," Zane asks.

"She wearing his fucking name," I blurt out.

Zane looks back to the girls, but they've since disappeared into the crowd. "What are you yapping about?" he asks.

"Berklee. She has on his sweatshirt. His last name's on her back."

Zane laughs. "Chill the fuck out, man. It's just a sweatshirt."

"I thought you said they weren't involved?"

"They're not that I know of. They live together, so I'm sure she just borrowed it."

I don't reply, just sit and stew. I hate the thought of him claiming her in any way. Or worse, that she lets him. Not able to take it, I stand. "I'm going to grab a drink." I'm a dick and don't offer to get anyone else anything. Normally I would, but I can't think about anything but getting to Berklee and asking her about the sweatshirt. I don't take the time to stop and think about how crazy I sound. It doesn't matter though, not when it comes to Berklee. We have an agreement, and I intend to make sure that she sticks to it. No way am I letting her change her mind before I've been inside her.

Taking the bleachers two at a time, I head toward the restrooms. The girls are just walking out when I reach them. I hold my hand out for Berklee and she takes it without hesitation. "We'll be right back," I tell Maggie.

She grins. "I'm just going to grab a drink. Berklee, you want anything?"

"No, thank you." Her eyes never leave mine.

With her fingers laced through mine, I lead her behind the building that houses the restrooms. It's not an ideal location, but it's as private as we're going to get considering our surroundings.

I guide her to where her back is against the building, cup her face in my hands and kiss her. She doesn't fight it and kisses me back. Before I get carried away, I pull my lips from hers. "What's this about?" I ask, tugging at the hem of the sweatshirt she's wearing. The one with another man's name on the back.

"What?"

"The sweatshirt."

"Oh, it's Barry's. Maggie and I always steal them. They're big and comfy," she explains.

"It's got his name on the back," I growl.

"Are you jealous?" she asks, shocked.

"No. But we made a deal. Just us until this is done."

"The deal that's not even twelve hours old, that one? I haven't violated the terms. Barry is my roommate. He's my best friend's older brother, and he's a good friend of mine. I don't see the problem with that."

Truthfully, there shouldn't be, but I can't stand her wearing his name. "I don't like his name on you," I tell her. Honesty is always the best policy, even if it shows your hand before you're ready.

Raising her hands, she places them on my cheeks. With a gentle tug she brings my face down to hers. "I don't want him. It's you I made the deal with. It's you," she says, softer this time.

My forehead rests against hers. "Can we leave now?" I ask. I'm deadly serious, but she laughs.

"No, we need to finish the game. Then we go to dinner at the place across the street."

"All that before I get you in my bed?"

"Yeah." Her hands drop from my face and she wraps me in a hug. A fucking hug. When was the last time a woman hugged me just to be hugging me, other than my mother? Berklee isn't trying to seduce me; she's just . . . being Berklee.

"Whatever you want, beautiful," I give in. Not that it's a struggle. In this moment I would give her anything she asked for.

"Okay, now we need to go back out there. And about PDA, what's your take?"

I hold her a little tighter. "My take is that I can't keep my damn hands off you."

"People are going to ask questions. My family, Zane's family."

"Yeah, I know. I'll try to control it." Leaning down, I place a quick kiss on her lips before releasing her. I let her walk in front of me and try like hell to ignore his name on her back. It's irrational, but I don't give a fuck.

Maggie is waiting for us. "Ready?" she asks.

"You ladies go ahead. I'll be right behind you." I watch them go until I can no longer see them, then turn for the concession stand. I order a bottle of water and the Garrison apparel catches my eye. "Give me an extra-large sweatshirt too." The girl behind the counter bags it up for me and hands me my water. "Keep the change," I say with a goofy-ass grin.

I make my way back to the bleachers and take my seat next to Berklee. I hand her the bag and she raises her brows in confusion. I just shrug and focus my attention back on the game. I'm sitting close enough that I can feel her shoulders shaking with laughter.

"You didn't," she whispers in my ear.

Turning, I face her. "I fucking did," I say, proud of my idea. If she wants a bigger hoodie, she can wear mine. I tell her so and she smirks.

"Technically, it's not yours. You've never worn it."

Her blue eyes are sparking with happiness, and seeing her enjoying this makes me take it one step further. I shrug off my jacket and reach into the bag, pulling out the hoodie. I pull it on and place my jacket over it.

"Cold?" Zane bites down on his lip. I'm sure it's to keep from laughing his ass off.

"Yep."

Berklee takes the now empty bag and shoves it into her purse. Leaning in to my shoulder, her lips are again next to my ear. It's loud from the cheering fans, so at least it doesn't look as intimate as it feels. "Now I want it. It's going to smell like you."

*Fuck me.*

# TWENTY ONE
## *Berklee*

I'M FIGHTING HARD to keep the goofy grin off my face. Crew, no matter how he wants to spin it, is jealous of *Barry* of all people. He's got this way about him—he's bossy and a little protective, and it's thrilling. I always said I would never be that girl, the type who lets a guy tell her what to do. This though, Crew and all his sexiness, is so different. Regardless of what our arrangement is, he's got his eyes set on me and I love every minute of it.

"He won't stop staring at you," Maggie whispers in my ear. We're getting pizza after the game. Crew and Zane are sitting across from Maggie and me. Barry is at the end of the table between us. Crew and I just so happen to be sitting on the end.

"Yeah," I agree with her. Every time Barry talks to me, Crew's eyes narrow. Like I said, it's thrilling. I need to see how far he's willing to take this.

Maggie giggles from beside me. She got the condensed version on the short drive over here, but it doesn't take a genius to figure it out.

"Barry." I touch his arm to get his attention. "You all did a great job!" I say excitedly. Maggie nudges my leg, and I can only assume that means Crew is not impressed. From the corner of my eye, I chance a look. He is laser focused where my hand rests on Barry's arm.

Crew clears his throat. When I look up at him, he's staring hard. Maggie giggles and I move my hand back to my lap. Visibly he relaxes, resting back into his chair. A few players come over and share a fist bump with Coach Davis, and we all settle into easy conversation. Barry

117

manages to get Crew and Zane talking about the NFL and the current season. I'm thankful for the distraction.

An hour later, bellies full, it's time to head home. Standing from the table, I turn to Maggie. "I'm going." I motion my head toward Crew.

"What about Barry?" she asks.

"What about him?" Crew growls from behind us, and I jump.

"Not like that." Maggie rolls her eyes. "He doesn't know about . . . " She points between us. "Are you keeping it a secret?"

I say "Yes" at the same time Crew says "No. Not from him." He turns, his eyes boring into mine. If he's expecting me to argue, he's not going to get it. I honestly don't care who knows. Sure, it's going to be hard to explain to my parents, but I can play it off as we're casually dating and leave it at that. They're pretty good about letting me make my own decisions. It's not like I'm a wild child; as long as they know this is good with me and what I want, they'll leave it alone. So yeah, I don't care who knows. I thought he wanted to keep it under wraps.

"I guess not," I tell Maggie.

"She won't be back tonight. I'll take good care of her," Crew smirks.

"I bet you will." Maggie winks at him. "I'll wait for you by the door," he whispers in my ear. Crew quickly says goodbye to everyone and walks away.

"We're heading out," Maggie says, knowing I want to slip away before the rest of our gang can see that I'm leaving with Crew. We say quick goodbyes and meet Crew by the door.

"Where are you parked?" he asks Maggie.

"Beside you." She points to her Honda.

"Perfect." He makes sure that she's inside and on her way before we pull out of the lot. "Come here." He pats the bench seat beside him.

I take off my belt and slide over. "Buckle up," he reminds me. I slide the lap belt into place and rest my hands on my thighs. I'm suddenly nervous. I want this, but it's actually happening and now I'm freaking out inside.

Crew grabs one of my hands and brings it to his lips, then places my hand on his leg. He slides his over my thigh and gives me a gentle squeeze. We ride the rest of the way to his place in silence, the radio playing softly in the background.

When we reach his house, I'm shocked. "You live here? By yourself?"

He chuckles. "Yeah, I bought it about a year ago."

"It's gorgeous."

"Come on, I'll show you around."

I take his offered hand and slide out of the truck, our fingers laced together as he leads me inside. When Crew hits the lights, I notice the house is just as amazing on the inside.

"I'll give you the tour," he says, taking off his jacket. "I just have to do this one thing first." He takes off his hoodie. "Arms up," he instructs. I do as I'm told and he pulls Barry's hoodie over my head. He drops it to the floor and replaces it with his. "Better." He kisses my temple.

"This way," he says, grabbing my hand. I follow behind him as he takes me room to room. After the tour of the basement, we end up in the living room. "Thirsty?" he asks.

"No."

"Want to watch TV?"

"No."

"Cards?" he tries again as he steps closer, his eyes locked on mine.

"No."

"What do you want, Berklee?"

"You. Just you." It's the only answer I can come up with. Fortunately, it's also the most honest. In more ways than one.

Crew steps in to me, his hands resting on my hips. "Where do you want me?" he asks huskily. He must see the confusion on my face. "You've had the tour now. Where do you want me?"

"I-I don't care." I just need his hands and his mouth on me.

"Let me help you out. By the end of the night you'll end up in my bed. Right now I need to be inside you, so tell me where you want me and leave the rest up to me."

I look around the living room and honestly, I don't want to wait. "Here," I say, my voice a soft whimper as his lips trace the column of my neck. His beard is rough against my skin.

"As you wish." Stepping back, he drops to his knees. "Kick off your shoes."

I don't ask questions, not that I could if I wanted to; I'm too turned on at the sight of him kneeling before me. Crew unbuttons my jeans and slides them down over my hips, placing a few tender kisses on my thighs. Once my jeans are pooled around my ankles, I kick them off. "Now this," he says, running his finger under the side string of my thong. "This is in the way." The next thing I know he's ripped it from my body, throwing it over his shoulder. That's a first for me, and let me tell you, it's hot as hell.

Crew stands to his full height, tugs off his T-shirt and kicks off his shoes. I don't take my eyes off him, afraid to miss the show as he unbuttons his jeans and lets them and his boxer briefs fall to his ankles before kicking them to the side. I follow every move he makes as he bends down, grabs his jeans and reaches into the front pocket. He removes a strip of condoms and I watch as he rolls one down his length.

Leaning down, he kisses me. "I need to be inside of you, I want you to wrap your legs around me." He kisses me again, hard, his tongue sliding past my lips. "Eyes on mine," he says as he places his hands on my ass and lifts me effortlessly. I do as instructed, and the first contact of skin against skin has me wrapping my arms around his neck, trying to get closer.

"My shirt," I whine. I want to feel all of him against all of me.

"No," he growls. "I want you in *my* shirt." He kisses me hard, and a thrill races through me that he cares that much. One that I immediately tamp down. I know I'm going to get my heartbroken, but I need to steer clear of that kind of thinking or it's just going to be worse in the end.

"Me," Crew says, pulling his lips from my neck. "I'm the one with you, the one those sexy-as-hell legs are wrapped around. It's my cock," he says, grinding against me, "that's about to be inside of you."

"Just you," I pant.

"Say it," he growls.

"Crew," I moan as he slides inside me.

He walks us to the wall, my back pressing against it. I let my head fall back and I close my eyes, just relishing the feel of him inside me.

"You good, beautiful?" he asks.

Forcing my eyes open, I find his. "Yeah."

That's all the ammunition he needs. Crew pulls back and thrusts hard and doesn't stop. I squeeze my legs tight, grip his shoulders and hold on for the ride, leaning my head forward and burying it in his neck to keep from banging it on the wall. He's relentless and I love it. I've never experienced this type of need and it's all-consuming. I never want it to end.

"Berklee," he growls. "Touch yourself. I can't stop, babe."

It's not something I've ever done in the presence of anyone else, but the way he demands it of me has me wrapping one arm around his neck to hold on and sliding the other between us. I get my hand where I need it to be at the same time he picks up the pace, something I didn't think was possible. "Right there," I manage to pant.

"You with me, Berklee?"

"Ye-yes!" I scream as my orgasm crashes over me.

"Fuck yes," he growls into my neck as he stills, losing himself inside of me.

I hold on tight, both hands once again gripping his shoulders. My face is buried in his neck and his in mine. We're both breathing heavy, and I'm sweating like crazy in this fucking sweatshirt. "I want to feel you," I say, my lips next to his ear.

He swivels his hips.

I chuckle. "All of you, Crew. I want this off." Pulling back, I tug at the sweatshirt.

"Hold on to me. Don't let go." He tightens his grip on my ass and we pull away from the wall. I cling to him as we climb the stairs.

"I can walk," I say, feeling bad that he's carrying me.

"Not when I can carry you."

I don't fight him. Instead I hug him tight and hang on just like he told me to. I don't open my eyes until I feel him set me on the cold counter.

"Your eyes. They're fucking hypnotic." He leans in and kisses me.

I kiss him back, keeping my legs around his waist, holding him close to me. He releases a growl before pulling away.

"Off," I say, tugging at the sweatshirt once more. This time he listens, lifting it over my head and tossing it on the floor. My T-shirt and bra are quick to follow.

Reaching up, he gently removes the band from my hair, my curls falling around my shoulders.

"You are a fucking vision, Berklee." He pulls off the condom and tosses it in the trash. Pulling open the vanity drawer, he takes out another.

"Boy Scout," I tease him.

"Not really." He chuckles. "I grabbed a stash when we were on the tour. It was actually the purpose of the tour." He winks.

"Planner." I laugh.

His eyes grow dark as he trains his focus on my chest, rubbing the pads of his thumbs over my tight nipples. "So responsive," he whispers. I grip the counter, preparing myself for the assault of his mouth.

Crew doesn't waste any time lavishing my breasts. His hands and mouth are everywhere, and all I can do is feel.

"Shower," he says, pulling away. I watch as he starts the water and waits for the temperature to heat up. Coming back to the counter, he hands me a condom. "Hold on to this, beautiful." He places my legs around his waist, lifting me off the counter and carrying me into the hot stream.

He sits me on the bench before reaching up to grab a detachable showerhead. The stream above is still falling on him as he wets my hair, then washes it and every inch of my body. "Tease," I breathe as his lips find their way to my neck.

"No, babe, just enjoying you. All of you. I've had you fast because I couldn't stop it. This is me savoring every inch of your creamy skin, tasting every inch before I slide deep inside you again."

I don't comment, just hang on for the ride. I memorize the way his tongue feels as it traces my inner thigh. His calloused hands against my breast. His breath against my cheek when he whispers, "Ready, beautiful?"

Crew takes a seat next to me and slides me on his lap, facing away from him. "Condom," he says, his voice gruff with desire.

I forgot he'd handed it to me. Opening my hand, I present it to him. He tears it open with his teeth, scoots down low on the seat, and pulls me up his chest. His big hand grips his cock, which is now between our spread legs. I watch him as he rolls it on, just from feeling alone. It's the hottest moment of my life. I can't help but reach out and help him finish sliding it on. He scoots back up to a sitting position, his rock-hard cock rubbing against my aching center. I don't wait for instructions, just grip him and guide him inside.

"Fuuuck," he hisses.

I wiggle on his lap until he's fully seated inside me. I'm so full and so fucking turned on, rocking my hips as the water beats down on us. Crew grips my waist and together we catch a rhythm. Leaning over, I brace my hands on his knees and take what I need. He's so deep, I can't stop.

"Fuck, that's hot," Crew mumbles from behind me. "That's it, beautiful. Take what you need."

"So good," I moan as I feel my walls tighten. My nails dig into his thighs as the most powerful orgasm of my life rips through me. I scream his name and jerk against him. I'm sure it's not a pretty sight, but I've lost all control as I experience what can only be described as euphoria crashing down around me.

Crew leans forward and wraps his arms around me, his lips finding my neck. "Hottest fucking moment of my life, hands-down."

I slump against him, feeling myself tighten around him as aftershocks roll through my system. He runs his hands up and down my arms, kissing my bare shoulder.

"How do you want to finish?" I ask him.

"Finish?" he asks, confused.

"I was selfish," I mumble.

Crew laughs. "Babe, I came so hard I thought my head would explode. Your pussy was going crazy squeezing my cock. I didn't have a choice in the matter." He kisses my shoulder again. "You're spent. Let's get you cleaned up and into bed."

"I don't have to stay," I tell him.

"You're staying. I want you in my bed. Even if it's just to sleep, that's where you're going to be. Can you stand up?" he asks. I do on shaky legs. He moves out from under me quickly and places me back on the bench. "Let me take care of this, and then I'll get you." He steps out of the shower and is back in no time. Once again, he takes his time in cleaning us both thoroughly before turning off the water.

# TWENTY TWO
## Crew

AFTER I GET us both dried off, I carry Berklee to my bed. As soon as her head hits the pillow, her eyes close and I know she's out. Staring down at her, hair spread out on my pillow, her naked body against my black sheets, she fucking takes my breath away. Literally. She blew my mind tonight. I thought once I felt her, I'd be able to distance myself a little. I should've known better. This is Berklee, after all; it's been different with her from the beginning.

Dropping the towel from around my waist, I hit the light and climb into bed, pulling the covers over us. Lying in the darkness with nothing but the sound of her gentle breathing, I feel unsettled, though I can't put my finger on it. Berklee mumbles my name. My heart picks up its pace. To hear her call for me in her sleep, that's . . . something. Something more.

I don't have women sleep over. Never saw the point, and I certainly never wanted the awkward morning after. So when Berklee seeks me out, throwing her arm and then her leg over me before burrowing into my chest, I go with it and hold her close. Her breathing evens out once again and I relax into the mattress, enjoying the feel of her in my arms.

As I lie here running my fingers through her wet curls, I realize that I no longer feel unsettled. It's her. She has that calming effect on me. It freaks me the fuck out, but no way am I running from it. Maybe things will look different in the light of day. That's my last thought as I drift off to sleep.

The ringing of my phone wakes me up sometime later. Reaching over to the nightstand, I come up empty. Replaying the night before, it all comes crashing back to me.

Berklee.

Rolling over, I reach for her and once again come up empty. My cell stops ringing just to start again. Climbing out of bed, I peek in the bathroom—no Berklee. Making my way downstairs, I stop in the doorway of the living room and I know she's gone. Her clothes that were scattered with mine are missing. Even her thong that I tore from her sexy little body. "Fuck!" I scream into the quiet house. My phone starts to ring again and suddenly I'm worried it's her. *How did she get home? What if something happened?* I'm tripping over my own feet to get to my jeans lying on the floor. Pulling my phone out of my pocket, I don't even look at the screen before answering. "Hello," I pant into the phone.

"Did I interrupt something?" Zane laughs.

"No," I growl.

More laughter. "What are you getting into today?"

"Nothing," I grumble. I wanted to be getting into Berklee, make her breakfast and maybe lounge in bed all day, but she ran.

"Getting a group together to take the Jeep out. You interested?"

"What time?" I glance at the clock on the wall—it's a little after eight. I wonder what time she snuck out.

"Around noon. Just going to take it out at Mom and Dad's place."

"Yeah, count me in. Meet you there?"

"Yep. See ya." He hangs up.

I immediately pull up Berklee's name and hit Send. It rings and rings and rings before finally going to voice mail. "Berklee, it's Crew. You left. Why? Call me."

I toss my phone on the couch and head to the kitchen to make some coffee. I pop a couple of pieces of toast in the toaster and stare at the pot. By the time I've had my toast and first cup of coffee, fifteen minutes have gone by.

Refilling my cup, I move to the living room, grab my phone and call her again. Again, I get her voice mail. "Berklee, if you don't want to talk to me, fine, but at least let me know that you're okay."

Grabbing the remote, I turn on the TV and scroll through the stations mindlessly. Before I know it another twenty minutes have passed. Again, I call her. "Fucking voice mail," I grumble. "Berklee, pick up the fucking phone. Just tell me you got home safely."

Hitting End, I slam my phone down on the couch. *Fuck, this shit. She won't answer, I'll go to her.* I assume she's just ignoring me, but what if she's not? What if something did happen to her? That thought alone has me running upstairs to get dressed. I'm out the door and on the road five minutes later.

On the drive over, I call her again. This time it goes straight to voice mail. "Berklee, fuck!" I end the call and toss my phone in the cup holder. I make the fifteen-minute drive in half the time. Throwing the truck in Park, I grab my keys and run to the door. I pound on it, not giving a single fuck if I wake the entire neighborhood. "Berklee!" I shout. Time seems to stand still as I wait for her to open the damn door. When it finally flies open, there's a pissed-off Barry staring back at me.

"What the hell, Crew?" he asks. I can tell he just woke up.

I push past him. "Where's her room?" I ask, walking toward the hallway.

"Who? What the fuck is going on?" he says, following me.

"Berklee!"

"What did you do to her?" he asks, anger lacing his voice.

I turn to face him. "Not a fucking thing she didn't want. Then I woke up and she was gone. She won't answer her phone."

"Maybe she doesn't want to talk to you," he offers, his voice calmer.

"I don't give a fuck," I call over my shoulder. I need to see if she's all right and find out why she left.

"Second door on the right," Barry yells.

I stop in front of the door and try the handle. It's unlocked. The bed is empty but the shower is on. I run my fingers through my hair. She's here. I take a minute to let that sink in. I'd assumed she was avoiding me, but damn, the thought of something happening to her shook me to the core.

I debate on what I should do. Join her in the shower? Surprise her when she comes out? The water turns off, making my decision for me. I kick off my shoes and make myself comfortable on her bed.

"Glad to see you're okay," I say when she emerges. She screams until realization sets in that it's me.

"Crew, what are you doing here?"

"Well, when I went to bed last night, I had this hot little redhead tucked into my side, her body wrapped around mine. When I woke up, she was gone. Then when I tried to call her, she wouldn't answer her fucking phone," I growl.

"I was busy," she says defiantly.

"Yeah? Well, I was worried something had happened to you on the way home. I had no idea what time you left, and you didn't have a car." I'm barely hanging on by a thread between my anger, the relief that she's okay, and looking at her in nothing but a towel wrapped around that tight little body of hers.

"I'm fine." She sighs.

"I can see that." I stand and in two steps am in front of her. "Why did you leave?" I ask, my tone softer now.

Looking down at her feet, she moves them back and forth across the plush carpeting. "I wasn't sure you really wanted me to stay," she says, never making eye contact.

Placing my fingers under her chin, I lift so her eyes meet mine. "I told you that's where you'd be."

"Yeah, and then I was exhausted and fell asleep. I know this is a benefits-only arrangement, and that's new to me. I wasn't sure that included spending the night."

"Did I ask you to leave?"

"No, but—"

"No. No buts. I wanted you there." I step forward, my body aligned with hers. "I wasn't done with you," I say, leaning down and running my lips over her neck.

"We need parameters."

"Why?"

"Are we hiding this? I mean, Maggie and Barry know, and Zane knows. I thought the point was to keep it on the down low? It's not a relationship, after all."

"I don't give a fuck who knows. We're adults."

"We are, but that opens it up to questions. Questions that are uncomfortable to answer."

"This was your idea," I remind her.

"I know that," she snaps. "I just think we need to set some rules. No public displays and no sleepovers."

"Berklee."

"Crew, if I were anyone else, would I have even been allowed at your place last night? Allowed to be in your bed?"

"Fuck no," I growl.

"See, that's my point. We're crossing lines. We have to keep them straight and defined."

Shit. I let her words sink in and I know she's right, but I don't want to. I crave her. "So no PDA, no sleepovers. What else?"

"I think we need to spread out our time."

*What the fuck?* "Why?"

She's quiet for a few minutes before those baby blues seek me out. "I have to keep my feelings out of this, Crew. If you keep insisting that I spend more . . . intimate time with you, time with you at your place and in your bed, my heart's going to get involved and it's going to be shattered when you're done with this"—she waves her hands in the air—"arrangement."

"So . . . what? You're done? We've barely gotten started." I need more of her. One night wasn't enough. No way can she walk away. Not yet.

"Gah! You're not even listening to me. No, we're not done. I just need to space our time out a little. You're a great guy, Crew, and if I let you hold me all night, the lines are going to blur, and that's not what either of us signed up for."

I don't like it, but she's right. I close my eyes and think about how it felt to fall asleep holding her close. Lines were definitely beginning to blur. "Okay, so tell me what's next." I place my hands on her hips and pull her close. "I've not had my fill of you, beautiful."

I watch as she takes a deep breath and slowly exhales. "We've had fun this weekend, but Maggie and I have plans tonight, so I'll see you at the club on Monday."

"What kind of plans?"

"Crew, casual, remember? You don't have to worry about me holding up my end of the bargain. No one else while we're together."

I nod. "Fine. Be safe. Call me if you need anything."

129

"We will. I'll see you on Monday," she says, trying to leave my embrace.

"We're not in public," I tell her.

Those big blue eyes stare up at me in confusion as I lean down and capture her lips with mine. I take my time tasting her, holding her close. "I'll see you on Monday." I give her one more chaste kiss before turning and walking away.

"Later," Barry calls from the couch as I pass him.

I wave over my shoulder and stalk out to my truck. Grabbing my phone from the cup holder, I send Zane a message.

> **Me:** Supplies?
>
> **Zane:** Ice for the Yeti.
>
> **Me:** Food?
>
> **Zane:** I picked it up last night. Good to go.
>
> **Me:** Be there in 20.

I throw the phone back in the cup holder and pull out onto the road. A day hanging out with the guys is just what I need to get my head straight.

# TWENTY THREE
## Berklee

W HEN I HEAR the front door slam, I drop back onto the bed and
groan. That conversation went better than I expected. I know I
shouldn't have just taken off like that, but when I woke up this morning,
his arms were locked around me and my heart leapt into my throat. I
went into this with eyes wide open, but that feeling of completeness
waking up in his arms, that's bad news. That's more than a broken heart;
that's soul-deep pain that I'm not sure I could come back from.

When I called Maggie at six this morning, she didn't hesitate when I
asked her to leave her warm bed to come pick up me. To my surprise,
she didn't badger me for details either. I think that comes from our
lifelong friendship. She knows me well enough to know I need to sort
shit out in my head first.

When we finally got home, she told me that Zane and the guys were
taking the Jeeps out and he'd asked if we wanted to go. She had already
told him that we would be there. It was the exact distraction that I
needed.

"Incoming," Maggie yells through my door before she peeks in.
"Hey, you okay?"

Throwing my hands over my eyes, I groan. "Yeah."

"Let's try this again," she says, lying down next to me. "You okay?"

"No. Yes. Hell, I don't really know."

"What happened?"

"It's stupid," I admit.

"I want to hear it anyway."

"We went back to his place, and things got . . . heated." Maggie giggles and I elbow her. "Anyway, he carried me to his bed and I fell asleep. I woke up to him holding me and I freaked."

"Too much?"

"Yes and no. I mean, yes because I could feel myself falling, but no because it was . . . comforting to wake up wrapped in him. I knew I had to put some distance between us. I can't let myself fall into the 'couple' thing I need to just focus on the sex part of this agreement. That's what it's supposed to be."

"The heart wants what the heart wants."

"So, who all is going today?" I ask, changing the subject.

"You and I are with Barry in his Jeep. Matt's going to be with us."

"Hmmm, you going to make your move?" She's been crushing on Matt for a couple of years now.

"Doubtful." She sits up. "Anyway, Zane is coming and a few others. I didn't catch it all, just that it's going to be a big group."

"It's been forever since we've tagged along."

"I know, that's what Barry said too. Thankfully, I had agreed before I knew Matt was coming. Barry doesn't have that to tease me about relentlessly."

"Good call. What time are we leaving?"

"Around eleven thirty. We have to stop and get some ice for the cooler, drinks and food, that kind of thing."

Glancing at the clock, I see it's almost ten. "I need to get in gear." Maggie gives me a big hug, then leaves me to get ready.

I decide on a pair of old ripped jeans and one of Barry's hoodies that I stole from him freshman year. Mentally I know Crew won't see it, but inside it's my way of defying what he wants. I'm not his. We have an arrangement, nothing more. Wearing the sweatshirt is just a testament of that.

Forgoing makeup, I pile my curls in a knot on top of my head, grab my old mud boots, socks and my sunglasses, and I'm good to go.

"Great minds think alike." Maggie laughs as I walk into the kitchen. She's dressed the exact same way, old hoodie and all.

"I swear the two of you share a brain. I remember those." He points between the two of us and we laugh. "You girls ready to go?"

"Yep," we say at the same time.

Barry just smiles and shakes his head. "I've got the Jeep loaded. I threw the chairs in the back, and we'll stop to get the food. You got what you need?"

"Yep," we say again.

"Let's roll." Barry grabs his travel mug of coffee and heads outside. Maggie and I get our phones and follow.

"Let's divide and conquer," Maggie suggests once we reach the store. "Barry, you grab the ice and drinks, and we'll take care of the food."

"Anything special you want?" I ask him.

"Nah, I'll eat anything. Just grab enough for Matt too. You know how we all share once we get there."

"We got this," Maggie says, hopping out of the truck. I slide across the seat and follow after her.

By the time Maggie and I reach the checkout, our cart is full. We both just shrug; we know how these guys eat. Back at the truck, Barry is leaning against the bed on his phone.

"All right, man, be there in ten." He grabs the bags and places them in the bed of the truck. "That was Matt. His truck won't start. He thinks it's the battery. I told him I would swing by and pick him up."

"You have a standard cab," Maggie reminds him.

"One of you is just going to have to take one for the team and sit on his lap. It's not a far drive, and it's back roads to Aunt Jenny's and Uncle Jeff's."

Maggie sighs loudly. "I mean, it's going to be a hardship." She raises her hand trying to look put out. "I guess I'll take one for the team."

I can't keep the laughter in.

"That's big of you, Mags." Barry rolls his eyes.

"Hey, I'm all about being a team player." She winks.

The ride to Matt's is short, just long enough for Maggie and me to sing along with Bon Jovi's "Living on a Prayer." The windows are down, and Matt's laughing when we pull up. He throws a bag into the back of the truck and opens the door.

"This day just got a whole hell of a lot better." He grins when he sees Mags and me.

"Let me out so you can scoot in," I tell him. My face is serious.

"Wait, what?" he asks, and Barry roars with laughter.

"She's fucking with you. Mags is on your lap for the ride."

"I have two knees," Matt says to me with a flirty grin.

"Don't let Ledger hear you say that."

"No! Really?" Matt asks.

"No, really what?" I look from one to the other, trying to figure out what I missed.

"Apparently," Barry says.

"Well damn," Matt retorts.

"What?" I say, louder than I should.

"You and Crew?"

I feel my face heat. "No, not me and Crew. We work together."

"Uh-huh." Barry laughs. "Is that why he stormed into our condo this morning looking for you?"

"A concerned employer," Maggie adds, trying to be helpful. It's no use; they see right through it.

"Why the big deal, anyway?" I ask.

"Just shocked is all. He's not one known to stake his claim," Matt tells me.

"He has no claim." I cross my arms over my chest.

"Right," the three of them say in unison. I don't bother correcting them. She who protests too much and all that.

Reaching over, I turn up the radio and Maggie gets the hint. We sing along, urging Barry and Matt to join us. When we reach Zane's parents' house, there are already a few trucks there, and excitement races through me.

Maggie starts singing "The Time of My Life" from *Dirty Dancing*. I chime in and we get all dramatic about it. The guys are laughing and join us for the chorus. Matt hops out of the truck, more stealth than I would have thought possible with Maggie on his lap, then grabs her hips and lifts her in the air.

134

"We can't let them show us up." Barry laughs, hopping out of the truck. I scoot over and he grabs me, holding me in the air.

I'm laughing so hard he has to put me down. I fall into him and he hugs me.

"Berklee."

I would know that voice anywhere. I step out of his embrace on wobbly legs.

Barry makes sure I'm steady on my feet before releasing me. Then he walks around Crew and starts unloading the Jeep.

"Hey, I didn't know you would be here."

"Obviously," he sneers.

"What the hell is that supposed to mean?"

"Your little show." He jerks toward Barry.

"We were just goofing around." I tug at the hem on my sweatshirt, a nervous habit. It's a mistake this time. I see the minute it registers with him that it's not mine, or the one he bought me.

"Turn around, Berklee." His voice is low and barely controlled.

I close my eyes, knowing he's going to lose his shit. Slowly I turn in a complete circle, stopping to face him once again.

"His," he scoffs.

"Mine now. I've had it since high school. It's just a piece of clothing, Crew."

"His fucking name is on your back, Berklee."

"Yes, he's family. Learn to deal with it. If this is a deal breaker for our arrangement, then so be it." I hold my head high.

"Damn it, Berklee." His fists clench at his sides as he steps closer. "I want to tear it from your body and devour you. We agreed that it would only be me."

I soften a little at his words, taking a small step closer as well. "It is you, Crew. You have to trust me. This?" I pull the sweatshirt away from my body. "It's a piece of clothing. It's not him."

"I don't like it," he grumbles.

"Okay, but that doesn't change anything."

"Hey, man." Matt steps beside us and holds his hand out to Crew.

"It's been a while."

The guys shake hands, and then Matt turns to me. Innocently, he lays his hand on my shoulder. "We're getting ready to head out."

I see the fire in Crew's eyes. "Thanks, give us just a second." He nods and walks away. "I see that look in your eyes, and you need to calm the hell down. I'm not with anyone but you. We're with friends today. Let's enjoy it."

"You're riding with us," he says, reaching out for my hand.

I see it coming so I step back. "No, I'm not. I'm riding with Barry, Maggie, and Matt. You go ride with Zane. We'll see each other at the breaks."

"Berklee." This time his voice is more pleading and less anger.

"Crew." I place my hands on his chest. "Boundaries, remember?"

"Fuck boundaries."

"Go." I motion to Zane's Jeep. "I'll see you soon." I remove my hands and run off toward Barry's truck.

"You good?" Maggie asks.

"Yeah, just saying hi." I smile at her.

"Uh-huh," the three of them say at once.

Looking over, I see Crew watching me, so I wave at him and smile. I see him relax a fraction, blow out a deep breath, and then head toward Zane and his Jeep.

# TWENTY FOUR
## Crew

STALKING TOWARD ZANE'S Jeep, I glare at him. That fucker knew she would be here. Would've been nice to be given a little warning. When I reach him, he's checking the air in the tires.

"What the fuck, Zane?"

He looks up at me, confused. "You knew she was coming and you didn't tell me."

He grins. "You're welcome. I thought you would want the chance to spend the day with your girl."

*Tell her that.* "Yeah, well, she has other plans. Apparently, it's with Barry and Matt," I grumble.

Zane's smile falters. "I thought you two were . . . "

"We are," I say, frustrated, running my hands through my hair. I don't want to explain it to him because I don't like it. I agreed to it, but I fucking hate it. One night with her and I want to change the rules. "It's fucking complicated."

Zane stands and dusts off his hands. "So un-complicate it."

"Easier said than done," I say, heading to my side of the Jeep.

"Stay with them," I tell Zane once he's in the driver's seat. We start the train, Barry's Jeep leading the pack, Zane and I right behind them. I don't take my eyes off her.

"You might as well go ahead and wipe that scowl off your face. You think that's going to give you brownie points with her?"

I ignore him.

"Look, she's made her choice, for today at least. Berklee is not the kind of girl who's going to bend to what you want. You have to give and take with girls like her."

"Girls like her?" I ask.

"Yeah, the good ones. The one's you want to take home and introduce to your mother. Those girls."

"She's already met my mother."

Zane rolls his eyes. "No shit, Sherlock. What I mean is that she's better than the casual hookup. Honestly, that's so out of character for her. I was shocked when she told me."

"What did she tell you?"

"Just that you two had come to a mutually beneficial agreement and that she knew what she was doing."

"That makes one of us," I mumble.

"What's that?" He glances over at me, then back to the trail.

"Nothing." I force myself to tear my eyes from Berklee and try to enjoy the day.

We ride for a couple hours before stopping at the makeshift campsite at the back of the property. "Let's start a fire. I'm sure the girls will want to get warmed up after being in the wind."

Zane and I unpack the firewood from the back of his Jeep and start the fire. I hear female laughter and turn to see all five of the girls who are with us today gathered around, holding their hands out to get warm. I catch Berklee's eye and she smiles brightly, her cheeks red from the wind. I want to go to her, to hold her against me and warm her up.

"So, who are you all here with?" one of the girls asks.

"My brother Barry and his friend, Matt," Maggie answers.

"Damn! They're both so hot."

"Who are you here with?" Berklee asks her.

"My brothers, Scott and Craig. We whined until they let us tag along."

The girls all laugh. "So, you're with Barry and you're with Matt?" another girl asks.

That's my sign to walk away. I know the answer is just going to piss me off. She'll say she's not with anyone, but that's a lie. She's with me. Or she should be.

I join the guys over by the grills. I've met Craig and Scott before, so we shake hands before I go to Barry and Matt. "Hey, man." We bump fists. "She's stubborn," Barry tells me. "Always has been. Both of them stubborn as hell and loyal to a fault."

"Women," I mumble, taking a swig of my Gatorade.

"Your sister's looking good," Matt says with a grin.

"Man, I don't want to hear that shit." Barry shakes his head.

"Just telling it like it is." He looks over at me like he's going to say something else, probably about Berklee, and I stop him with a glare. He holds his water up in salute and takes a drink.

*Good choice, asshole.* Fighting today would really piss Berklee off.

I finish my Gatorade and decide to grab a chair and sit by the fire. I walk to the opposite side the girls are on and push my chair far enough back that I won't be able to hear what they're saying. My temper is barely hanging on by a thread as it is.

I pull out my phone and scroll through my e-mails, letting myself get completely distracted.

"Why are you over here by yourself?" Looking up, I see Maggie taking a seat on the stump next to my chair.

"It's better that I do." I go back to scrolling through my phone.

"Can I ask you a question?"

I lock my phone and slide it back in my pocket. "Shoot."

"This morning, were you just pissed off that she left, or were you worried about her?"

"Both. At first, I was just upset that she left. I didn't like waking up without her. Then when she didn't answer, I was worried. I knew she didn't have a car."

Maggie just gives me a soft smile. "Nice day," she comments.

"Yeah, warm for this time of year."

"Berklee tells me the club is really coming together. Opening night is, what, a couple of weeks away?"

"Yeah, she's been great. We start training staff this week."

"She's excited about it."

"Yeah, me too. It's been a long time coming. Glad to see it all fall into place."

"Things have a funny way of working out." Maggie taps my knee, then stands and walks away.

"Time to eat," Scott yells.

I wait until the crowd dies down to make my way to the grill.

"Smells good," Berklee says from behind me.

"Which one do you want, beautiful?" I ask her.

"Burger, please." She grins, her blue eyes sparkling.

I grab a burger with the tongs and place it on the bun on her plate. "Where are you sitting?" she asks.

"Other side of the fire."

"Want some company?"

"Only if it's you."

She chuckles. "Yeah, thought we could eat together. I don't like us not getting along."

"You good?" I tilt my head toward her plate.

"Yeah, just need a drink."

"Water?" I know that's what she wants.

"Yes, please and thank you."

I grab two bottles from the cooler and we walk to where I was sitting. "You take the chair. I'll take the stump." I could walk to the Jeep and grab another chair, but I'm not leaving her. Not while I have her attention.

"We can—"

"It's fine, Berklee. Sit, eat." She does and we're quiet at first. "You look like you're having a good time."

"Yeah, we haven't done this in forever."

"I can't believe that you and I haven't run into each other before. It's a small world."

"Yeah, I spent a lot of time in college working at Coffee House. I really only worked and went to school. I went out occasionally, but I was focused on school."

"Not much of a partier?"

She laughs softly. "Not really. I mean, I like to go out, but give me comfy clothes and a good movie—or, even better, a book—and I'm good to go. What about you?"

"I was always good for a beer after work on Friday or Saturday nights, but nothing routine. When I decided to build the club, I put everything on the back burner. I focused all of my time on the club and making it happen."

She drops her napkin on her plate. "I'm stuffed."

Standing, I grab her trash and mine and throw it in the fire.

"I inherited some money," I tell her when I take my seat back on the stump. "My dad's mom. I didn't even know she was still alive. My dad apparently grew up wealthy. His parents insisted he marry for business and he wanted to marry for love. He met my mother and they gave him an ultimatum—her or them. He chose her."

Looking over at Berklee, her eyes shimmer with tears. "Wow," she breathes.

"Yeah, apparently Dad didn't hesitate, just packed up and moved in with Mom and her parents. It's been a little over a year ago that I learned all this. I got a certified letter telling me I had an inheritance. That's when my parents spilled the details."

"Were you upset with them?"

"No. I mean, I was shocked, but not mad. You've met them but to see them, he worships her, and I know he made the right decision."

"That's romantic." She smiles softly.

"So, I guess I said all that to show that I don't trust people, really. I tried to keep it hush, but somehow the vultures found out about my newfound wealth and I had women coming out of the woodwork, throwing themselves at me. Luckily, I was smart and turned them all down. For the most part, it doesn't happen, but sometimes there will be one who still tries."

"That's awful."

"Yeah, so I swore off women until I could get the club up and running. I bought my house, tried to buy one for my parents, invested half, and then the rest I'm starting the club with. The only thing left after that is her house. I have it listed with a relator now. I've had a few bites, but nothing. I'm eager to sell, you know? I mean, I'm grateful, but that house holds no memories for me. It's not even where she lived. It was their vacation home from what Dad tells me. It's the only property she held on to when she moved into the assisted living home."

"They wouldn't let you? You offered to buy them a new house and they wouldn't let you?" she says to clarify.

"Nope. I didn't want to take the money either, not at first. My parents were the ones who convinced me to. I quit my construction job, and that brings us to now. That brings me to you."

She stares at the fire. "Me?"

"Yeah, you. From the minute I laid eyes on you, I wanted you, no matter how hard I fought it. When I walked in and learned that Zane had hired you, I knew I was in trouble." I nudged her knee with mine.

"We can—" She stops when I shake my head.

"No. Not turning back, not changing my mind, not letting you go. I told you this morning that I need more of you. Last night wasn't enough for me."

She's quiet, and if I wasn't watching her I might have missed her whisper, "Me either."

"Hey, man, you mind helping me put the fire out? We're going to start packing up and heading back," Zane asks.

I nod and Berklee stands. "I'll see you back at the house?" she asks.

I fight the urge to reach out and grab her. "Yeah, see ya," I say instead, then watch her head back over to Maggie and the rest of the girls.

Zane and I put the fire out while everyone else packs up the grills, coolers, and the rest of the trash. On the way back, I think about how the day started as shit, but just an hour of sitting and talking with her turned it all around.

# TWENTY-FIVE
## *Berklee*

MONDAY ROLLED AROUND too quickly. I think it's partly due to the fact that I'm nervous to see Crew, my boss, my . . . friend with benefits. After we got back to Zane's on Saturday night, we all went our own way. I waved to him and we left it at that.

"Morning," I yell, walking up the steps to the club. Zane's office light is off, but I can see a glow coming from Crew's.

He steps out just as I reach my door. "Morning, beautiful." He walks over to me, stops when we're toe-to-toe, then leans down and kisses me. "Too fucking long, Berklee. It's been too fucking long since I've tasted you."

I don't say anything, since he's technically not breaking the rules—we're at work, not at either one of our houses, and we're alone. He's got the bases covered, and his cocky grin tells me he knows it.

"I have a delivery coming today," he says, kissing my neck.

"Oh yeah?" I manage to ask.

"Yeah, a couch." His lips find their way to my ear. "If it has to be here, we need a soft place to land."

*Holy hell.* "Good call," I murmur, breathless from his assault.

"I thought so," he says, standing to his full height. "Should be here any minute. I also added a few things to the lounge." He points across the room.

Turning to look, I see a mini fridge and a Keurig. "You did that for me?" I state it as a question, but I know he did.

"Yes, and because I don't want to waste time on coffee runs. Zane will be downstairs in the security room most of the time. This"—he sweeps his hands out—"is all us." He smirks.

"Looks like you've put a lot of thought into this."

"You have no fucking idea." He leans down and kisses me again just as the buzzer sounds on the door. "There's our couch." He swats my ass and takes off downstairs to let them in.

I boot up my laptop and pull up the schedule. The staff will be here at nine for server training. I've hired a serving specialist—yes, they have them, apparently. We'll see how good she is. After talking with Crew, I decided everyone would be trained in all areas. They may not be working that position, but if everyone has a good understanding of what the other does, this place will run that much better. It's also good if we're in a pinch for coverage; at least having the basics is better than going in blind.

"Last door on the right," I hear Crew's deep voice instruct. "Staff's starting to arrive," he says, peeking his head in my office.

"Thanks." I grab the stack of notebooks and box of pens for everyone to take notes and head downstairs. I included myself in all the training sessions as well, figuring if we get desperate I can fill in. I didn't tell Crew that part. I'll let that be a surprise. One I'm sure he will not be impressed with.

Turns out the server specialist is just that, giving great instruction and examples of how to handle difficult customers. She's worth every penny.

"That's all for today," Macie, the instructor, says. "I'm here all week, so think of any questions you might have and we can address them with the group throughout the week."

"Thank you so much. I'll see you in the morning at eight?" I ask her.

"Yep, see you in the morning." She's chipper and focuses on the "kill them with kindness" method. Club Titan is going to have a serving team that's on point.

I see everyone out, then make my way upstairs, dropping my notebook on my desk and flopping down in my chair. Crew left a few hours ago, something about an issue with the outside signage. I was hoping he would be back before now, but it looks like it's going to be a late one for him. After checking a few e-mails, I shut down my computer, pack up and head out.

I've been home for a couple of hours when his text comes in.

**Crew:** *I missed you.*

I try not to let that go to my head or my heart. *He "missed me," not "misses me." Focus, Berklee.*

**Me:** *Yeah, I was exhausted. Headed home around 5:30.*

**Crew:** *Sleep well, beautiful.*

**Me:** *You too.*

As I lie here awake, I think about him. I'm half tempted to spend some time with B.O.B., but it's a poor substitute for Crew Ledger. I fall asleep thinking of the man himself.

The next morning, I wake up late, having tossed and turned most of the night, my dreams of Crew waking me from a deep sleep. It took forever to finally fall back asleep, hence the oversleeping.

**Me:** *I overslept. I'll be there before training starts.*

**Crew:** *Be safe.*

I toss my phone in my purse, grab my heels and rush out the door. When I make it to the club, Macie is there already, as well as the rest of the staff. "Sorry, I'm late. Please go ahead and start." I run up the steps in my heels; it's a miracle that I don't fall and break my neck. I toss my purse and keys on my desk, grab my phone and notebook, then hightail it back downstairs. I managed to wave at Zane on my way past his office, but I didn't make it to Crew. I'm sure he'll look down and see that I've made it.

Macie has started the training, and even though I haven't missed much, I feel like my entire day is going to be out of sync. I hate it when I oversleep.

I'm engrossed in what Macie is saying about being seen but not heard, making eye contact, and if the customer doesn't engage, leave them be. Most who come to a club don't want to be bothered; they're here to socialize. It's a good point that I wouldn't have thought of. I'm in the middle of making notes when I feel a hand on my shoulder, and suddenly a steaming cup of coffee and a granola bar are placed in front of me. I don't need to turn around to know who it is; I would recognize that hand, those tattoos, anywhere.

"Thought you could use this," he whispers in my ear.

I turn to look over my shoulder and mouth. "Thank you." He nods and heads back upstairs.

I take a drink and sigh. This is what I needed. Opening the granola bar, I take a huge bite as my eyes travel up to the window of our offices. He can see me, but I can't see him. That doesn't matter; I can feel his gaze on me.

Grabbing my phone, I send him a text.

**Me:** *Creeper.*

**Crew:** *You're hard to look away from.*

**Me:** *Charmer.*

**Crew:** *Beautiful.*

I don't reply, just set my phone back on the table beside me and try like hell not to look up. You would think it would be creepy being watched like that, but it's not. Not when it's Crew. Not when I know the look is heated and promises more of the best sex I've ever had in my life.

# TWENTY SIX
## Crew

ALL FUCKING WEEK it's been one thing after the other. All I've managed are a few stolen kisses with Berklee.

Today is Friday and it's looking to be more of the same. The signage company screwed up the outdoor signs, both on the street and the building itself. I've been there three times this week making sure it's exactly what I asked for. How hard can it be? They have the image.

Today, it's not the club—it's Berklee. I overheard her telling Zane earlier that she and Maggie are going to the game tonight. It's just in the next town over, but that means that my chances of getting her to work late, to get her alone, are slim to none.

"What are you scowling at?" Berklee asks from behind me.

My eyes find hers. "It's been a week today since I've been inside you."

She coughs, placing her hand over her chest. "Yeah, it's been a crazy week," she agrees once she has herself under control.

"Skip the game," I say walking toward her.

"I promised Maggie I would go. I can't cancel on her last minute."

"So, I have to wait until Monday?" I ask, stepping closer.

"Looks that way. Can you handle that?"

"A week ago I would've said yes. Today the answer is fuck no." I step closer and take her hand in mine, guiding her away from the door. Once she's standing in my office, I shut the door and lock it.

"Crew?" she questions.

"I can't wait another second. It's cruel and unusual punishment to

147

keep me from this," I say, my hand going between her legs.

"We're not alone," she reminds me while pulling her shirt over her head and tossing it to the side.

"Then you better be quiet." I crush my lips to hers and kiss her like she's mine. Like I own her. I slide my tongue past her lips and she opens for me, her hands in my hair. It's happened before, other women gripping my hair, but with Berklee it sends jolts of awareness through my body. She's not putting on a show. She wants me closer; she wants me to devour her.

"I can be quiet," she pants as I move my lips to her neck.

I smile against her skin. "Legs around my waist, beautiful." I lift her off her feet and she complies. Her arms wrap around my shoulders, her face buried in my neck. My chest swells with something . . . something more. All for her. I carry her to the couch and sit down. "Lie with me." I stretch out on the couch and she quickly gets situated. She's facing away from me—not exactly what I had in mind. I wanted to watch her when she came all over my hand, but at this point I'll take anything and everything she's willing to give me.

Putting my arm around her, I pull her in close. I can never seem to have her close enough. Quickly, I move her curls to the side and my lips find her neck once more. I easily slip my hand under the waistband of her leggings, sliding beneath the silky fabric of her thong. Berklee arches her hips when I reach my destination.

"Crew," she gasps when I apply pressure. Her fingers wrap around my arm, her nails digging into the skin.

"You missed me, beautiful," I say, my lips next to her ear. She moans. "Tell me," I demand. I want to hear her say it. I need to know that she's not as cavalier about all this as she seems. That she wants me with the same intensity that I want her.

"I did," she says, her voice soft and breathless.

"You did what?" I push my erection into her ass.

"I missed you," she whispers.

My chest expands with the breath I didn't realize I was holding. Remembering that we're not alone at the club, I know I need to make this quick. I speed up my efforts, my tongue on her neck mimicking my fingers in her heat.

Her nails dig deeper into my arm. "Don't stop," she begs.

"Fuck," I growl. "You're so fucking wet. So hot." I bite down on her earlobe and feel her orgasm. Her walls are squeezing my fingers as my thumb works her faster. I don't stop until she relaxes into me. "I need to feel you, Berklee. I need my cock buried deep."

She gives me an answering nod before she rolls over and I move under her, allowing her to straddle me. "Like this?" she asks, her blue eyes hazy with desire.

"Any way you want me, babe. I just need to be inside you." Reaching into my pocket, I hand her the condom that I've been carrying around in that very spot all damn week, just waiting for the chance to feel her from the inside.

Standing, she slips out of her pants and thong as I unbutton my jeans and slide them and my boxer briefs down my hips. I kick them off, not giving a fuck where they land. My attention is on Berklee, her auburn curls hanging over her shoulders as she tears the wrapper open with her teeth and leans forward to slowly—painfully slow—slide it over my hard cock. Without a word, she takes her place on my lap, straddling my hips.

She grips my cock and licks her lips. Those blue eyes captivate me, stealing my attention. I don't even blink as she raises her hips and guides me inside her. She closes her eyes and releases a soft moan from the back of her throat. I don't risk looking away or closing my eyes. Fuck that. I don't want to miss a single fucking second of her riding me.

"So full," she murmurs, eyes still closed as she begins a slow yet steady rhythm, rocking her hips against me.

Resting my hands on her thighs, I just watch her, letting her take what she wants, what she needs from me. It's a first for me, to not take control, but this is an experience I'm not willing to miss. It's sure to be a memory that will forever be ingrained in my mind.

I can't take my eyes off her as I memorize every detail. The way her curls cover the tops of her breasts, but not quite enough to hide those pert pink nipples that are begging for my mouth. The feel of her heat wrapped around me, her thighs as they squeeze me tight.

Slowly her eyes open and she stares down at me. I cup her cheek and she leans in to my touch, my heart skipping a beat in my chest. "So fucking beautiful," I say, caressing her cheek with my thumb. Turning her head, she sucks my thumb into her mouth and I raise my hips, needing to be closer. Sitting up, I wrap my arms around her. She grasps my shoulders and begins her assault on me, rocking her hips, bouncing, moaning. I'm so fucking close just by watching her, not to mention the way her walls are squeezing my cock.

"I'm close," I pant. It's taking all my effort not to blow. Sliding one hand between us, I rub her clit. She throws her head back and moans. I should worry about someone hearing us, but I don't give a fuck; I want them to know she's mine. And she is. I'll do whatever I have to do to prove it to her.

"Now," she says, biting down on my shoulder.

That one word has me releasing inside of her. I hold on to her as we both come down from the high. I don't want to let go.

"We should get back to work." She pulls away from me and before I can stop her, she's standing and grabbing the tissues from my desk. She pulls out a handful and tosses the box to me. "Shit," she says, looking at her watch. "I'm going to be late." She rushes through getting her clothes back in on

I take care of the condom, grab my clothes and barely have my jeans pulled up when she's heading to the door. "Berklee." She stops, turning to face me. I try to read her expression but I can't. "Come here," I say, pulling my pants over my hips but not bothering to button them.

"Crew, I'm going to be—"

"Come here," I say again.

She sighs but does as I ask. "I'm going to—"

Leaning down, I kiss her, slow and deep. A kiss made of promises of what's yet to come between the two of us. "Be safe tonight, beautiful. Call me if you need anything."

On tiptoes, she kisses my cheek. "Bye, Crew."

"Berklee," I call out just as she reaches the door. "Text me when you make it home tonight."

Her eyes soften and she nods her agreement. Then she's gone, taking a piece of me with her.

# TWENTY SEVEN
## Berklee

"CALL IT A day," Crew says.

This week has been packed full of bartender training. The staff has put in some long days, and all of their hard word has paid off: All of Club Titan's signature drinks can now be made to perfection by every single staff member, along with a few other fan favorites. At least that's what the trainer tells us.

"Great job this week. I'll be back on Monday and we'll review and learn a few more. You all are a great class," Susan, the bartending trainer, says.

Crew and I say goodbye to the staff. Zane left earlier today, something about helping his dad. "It's just you and me," Crew says as soon as the door closes.

"It is," I agree. "However, I have to meet Maggie. I'm already running late."

Crew pulls me into his arms and holds me close. "We're not late. I told Barry to tell Maggie that we would meet her there."

*Wait, what?* "What?" I ask, pulling back from him.

He winks. "It's been another long-as-fuck week where I didn't get my Berklee time. I know I can't *be* with you, but I'll be *with* you, and that's the next best thing." He taps the end of my nose with his finger.

"I'm going to my place after," I say, trying to sound more certain than I feel.

"I know." He sighs. "I'll take you any way I can get you." He pulls me close so we're just a breath apart. "Now, let me kiss these lips." He runs the pad of his thumb across them and leans in, pressing his lips to mine.

All rational thought leaves as I surrender my lips to him. I moan and dig my hands into his hair, pulling him tighter, closer. I want more of him.

When he slows the kiss, I whine. Not my finest moment, but you would too, trust me.

"Fuck, Berklee. We gotta go, babe. One more minute and we won't be leaving."

I giggle. Yes, fucking giggle like a schoolgirl. It's a heady feeling knowing that this man wants me. That I can make him lose all sense of control.

"Come on, boss man. Let's go watch us some football."

"I'm driving. Leave your car here, and I'll get it back to you tomorrow."

"Crew, I can—"

"Not happening, beautiful. This is my Berklee time and I'm soaking up as much of it as I can. I drive, you ride."

Sometimes he makes me forget that this is just an arrangement. The things he says, the way he treats me, they make it hard to remember that we have an expiration date. One that's sure to come as soon as I fall over the cliff and hand him my heart on a silver platter.

Pushing his words to the back of my mind, I smile up at him. "I have to change."

"We'll run by your place."

"Crew—" He stops me with his lips.

"Let me drive you, Berklee. It's not a play to get you in my bed again. It's just me wanting to be around you. Nothing more, nothing less." He kisses my nose and steps away. "We need to get moving."

"How about I drive home and we can leave there together. That way you don't have to bring my car over tomorrow."

"Did you ever think that I wanted to bring your car to you tomorrow? Did you ever think that maybe that was a damn fine excuse to get to see you outside of our work schedule?"

Shit. No, but now that he's said it, I can see the appeal. And that's an issue. No, him following me tonight is the better option for sure. "That's not what we agreed on."

He exhales loudly. "Come on, beautiful, I'll follow you home." He laces his fingers through mine and leads me out of the club.

On the drive to my place I replay our conversation over and over in my mind. I know I shouldn't but it's hard not to. He's sending me mixed signals, and I need to keep my head on straight.

"I'll just be a few minutes," I say over my shoulder as he starts to climb out of his truck.

"I'll come with you," Crew says, ignoring my hint that he should stay behind.

Running up the steps, I unlock the door and race down the hall to my room. I slip out of my skirt and heels, then grab jeans, my Garrison High T-shirt and a hoodie. This time, I wear the one Crew bought a few weeks ago. I smile knowing it'll make him happy. I don't bother with my hair or makeup; it's just a football game. Finding a pair of boots in the bottom of the closet, I make my way back to the living room. I expect to find Crew hanging out on the couch, but he's standing in front of the two built-in bookcases on either side of the TV. In his hands is a picture of Barry and me for his senior prom. "He hated being all dressed up, but his mom insisted that they never miss a rite of passage," I comment, stopping to stand beside him.

"Were you his date?" he asks with a tick in is jaw.

I laugh. "Hardly. I'm wearing jeans. Did you miss that little aspect of the picture?" Crew shrugs and places the photo back on the shelf. I point to the one right beside it, identical except it's Maggie held tight against him in a bear hug instead of me. "Same day."

"Hmm" is his reply. Finally he turns to face me. A slow sexy smile pulls at his lips when he sees my hoodie. He reaches out for me but he's too slow; I saw it coming and jumped back.

"We need to go. We're going to miss kickoff the way it is."

He grumbles but doesn't argue as he places his hand on the small of my back and leads me to the truck. Instead of the passenger door, he brings me to the driver's side and opens it up. "Hop in," he says with a light pat to my ass. I jump, not expecting it. "Don't go far," he says, climbing in behind me. He slides behind the wheel, places his hand on my thigh and pulls me toward him. "Too far away."

"This isn't a good idea. What if someone sees us? We discussed this."

Reaching over me, he slides the seat belt around my waist and makes sure it's secure. Looking up, I find him staring at me. He's so close I can see the small specks of gold in his brown eyes. "What we agreed on is that we would spend time together intimately. This week I've not had any time with you. None. Zero, Zilch. That's not okay with me. You have plans, and now those plans are mine." He kisses the corner of my mouth. "And fuck them. I don't care who sees."

With that, he starts the truck and pulls out of the driveway.

# TWENTY EIGHT
## Crew

I KEEP MY hand on her thigh. Not once do I lift it for any reason. I may not be able to fuck her tonight, but you can bet your ass I'm going to touch her.

I meant what I said. I don't give a fuck who sees. If they have an issue they can look the other way. I'm going to drive myself crazy trying to keep my hands off her. It's not worth the effort or my sanity.

Climbing out of the truck, I hold my hand out for her. She takes it without hesitation and slides out. I place my hand on the small of her back and lead her to the gate. She reaches for her purse, "I got this, babe," I whisper next to her ear before digging my wallet out and finding a twenty.

"This isn't a date," she says softly.

"You don't pay with me. Ever." I kiss her temple and we head to the bleachers. "Same section?" I ask, bending so she can hear me over the crowd.

"Yeah." She nods.

We reach the end of the section and Berklee heads up the steps. I fight like hell to not come off as a creeper and stare at her ass; her family is here, after all.

"Hey, baby girl," her dad says.

He was at the last game, but I was a mere acquaintance then. At that time I'd not been inside her. Felt what it was like for her to be wrapped around me and let go. That changes things. So, tonight, I offer him my hand. "Good to see you, sir," I say.

"You too, son. You two just get off work?" he asks.

"Yeah, we had bartending training all week," Berklee explains.

"Oh, how did it go?" her mom asks.

"Sit, babe," I say, pointing to the bleachers. She grins at me and sits next to her dad. I take the very end right beside her. Berklee is in full conversation with her parents, so I try to focus on the game until my phone vibrates. Pulling it out of my pocket, I see Zane's name.

> **Zane:** Didn't know you were coming.
>
> **Me:** Yeah.
>
> **Zane:** Pussy whipped.

My finger hovers over the screen. I can't help but chuckle because he's right. Although it's more Berklee-whipped, if you want to be one hundred percent accurate. It's everything about her that draws me in: those curls, her lips, that tight ass, her personality. I could go on and on.

> **Me:** Don't knock it until you try it.
>
> **Zane:** Is that you giving me permission to try Berklee?

*Fucker!* I clench my phone on my hands. I know he's giving me shit, but just the thought has me seeing red. Leaning forward, I look down to where he's sitting next to his parents. He's laughing uncontrollably.

> **Zane:** You're face. Priceless!
>
> **Me:** Fuck you!

I shove my phone back in my pocket and take a deep breath. Berklee must sense my anger, her small hand landing on my knee. She's turned and looking right at me. "You good?" she whispers.

I want to kiss the hell out of her. Not a good plan with her parents sitting right next to us. I settle for a nod and slide my fingers between hers. She situates the Garrison blanket that she brought and spreads it where it's not obvious that her hand is clasped with mine.

I don't let it bother me that she wants to hide it. This was the deal. This is what I signed up for.

Only problem is I no longer like the terms.

Before I know it, it's halftime and Berklee is standing. "Mags, I need to use the restroom. Walk with me?"

"I can go," I say, tapping lightly on the back of her thigh.

She peers down at me. "It's fine. You need anything?"

*You.* "No, I'm good. You need money?" I have this need to take care of her.

Her eyes soften. "No, but thank you." She turns and asks the rest of our row if anyone needs anything. They all decline. I stand to let her pass by me, running my hand down her arm as she passes. I feel her shiver. Damn, she's so fucking responsive.

I remain standing, stretching out my legs. "How are things at the club?" her dad asks.

Turning to the side, I answer, "Good. Opening night is next weekend. Things are really coming together."

"Berklee keeps telling us to come by, but we don't want to bother her while she's at work," her mom chimes in.

"You're more than welcome anytime. Berklee knows her schedule."

I turn back and survey the crowd, seeking her out. When I spot her I can't help but grin. She's a knockout, especially with the gentle sway of her hips when she walks. *Fuck me, I want inside her again.* My cock twitches at the thought.

"You're fond of my girl," her dad states.

*Well fuck me. Nothing like having to talk with dear old dad while thinking about sliding balls-deep into his little girl.*

"I am."

"She know?" he asks.

Does she? She knows I want to fuck her and kiss her and touch her every minute of every damn day. And I think she knows that I value her as my right hand at Club Titan? But does she know that I long to have her in my arms at night? That she's both my first and last thought each and every day? Doubtful. "No."

He nods. "She's my little girl."

I know what he's trying to say. "She's safe with me," I tell him. And she is. I'll make damn sure of that.

"She is, but is her heart?" he manages to whisper just as Berklee and Maggie reach us.

"This is sooo good," she moans as she takes another big bite of her walking taco. "You don't know what you're missing."

"That good?" I manage to push the words past my lips. Her moan and those lips wrapping around the fork have me thinking about them around my cock.

"Mmmm," she answers.

I can't take my eyes off her. At least not until I hear a throat clearing, which snaps my attention back to her dad. He's watching me intently, waiting for an answer to his question. *"Is her heart safe?"* Without hesitation I give him a stern nod. He does the same, turning back to face the game.

*What the hell just happened?*

Berklee blissfully finishes her walking taco and then covers back up with her blanket. Not able to resist, I slide my hand underneath and rest it on her leg. She bumps her leg against mine and a small smile tips my lips.

*Loving my Berklee time.*

This is how we watch the remainder of the game: legs pressed together, my hand on her thigh, her hand on top of mine. She cheers in all the right places, even jumps out of her seat every now and then, but she always snuggles back in next to me. I can't tell you if we won or lost, but judging by the smile on her face right now as she throws her arms around my neck, I'd say Garrison took home another win.

"You kids coming to eat?" Berklee's dad asks us.

I defer to her, knowing she'll want to go.

"Of course. We'll see you all over there," she replies.

"Garrison!" Maggie cheers, wrapping her arms around Berklee.

"Come on, crazy. Let's go eat." Zane laughs at her.

"Hey!" Maggie swats his arm. "You're cut from the same cloth, my dear cousin."

"True that." He grins. "Come on, I'm starving." He rubs his belly, as if that will prove his point.

Berklee laughs. "We're right behind you." She turns to me, blanket in her arms, purse on her shoulder. "Ready?" she asks, her eyes smiling bright.

"Yeah." Reaching out, I take the blanket from her and link her fingers through mine. Zane smirks and Maggie is grinning so big I'm afraid her face might split. Berklee, she's all calm, cool and collected as she allows me to lead her down the bleachers.

I don't look back for Maggie and Zane. I don't stop at all, just keep a tight hold on Berklee in the crowd as we push through to my truck. Once we're there, I press her against the side and claim her mouth with mine. There was no other option; I had to kiss her, taste her, have her in my arms. Even if it's just for a minute.

It's dark out and due to my speed walking, we've beaten the majority of the crowd. That's my guess as to why she opens for me, her tongue seeking mine. A wolf whistle along with a loud "Get it" has me chuckling and pulling my lips from hers. I can imagine her face is flushed, and I'm almost glad it's dark out and that I can't see it. Not sure I would be able to step back if I could.

I pull open the driver's door and Berklee slides in across the seat, stopping in the middle. *Good girl.* Taking my spot behind the wheel, hand on her thigh, I drive us across the street to the pizza place. We could have walked, should have walked, but no fucking way am I going to pass up having her with me like this. Just us.

We take our seats at the table, same as a few weeks ago. The spot at the end is reserved for the star of tonight's festivities, Barry. I know the minute he walks in because the room erupts in cheers, and Maggie and Berklee are jumping out of their chairs to rush him and give him a hug. It's an odd group hug thing and the three of them laugh like it's the funniest thing to happen in their lives. Me, not so much. I'm watching his arm as it snakes around my girl, the kiss he places on the top of her head. Yeah, he mimics the action with his sister, but my Berklee, she's not his sister.

I don't know what the fuck my issue is. What I do know is that she's unexpected and refreshing and mine.

Dinner goes smoothly and we're now saying our goodbyes.

"You just want to ride with us?" Maggie asks Berklee.

*Fuck me.* "I actually have a few things to talk to you about before Monday," I tell Berklee.

"Okay. We'll be right behind you," she tells Maggie and Barry, who are both watching us closely.

"I'm out, peeps," Zane says, laying a hand on my shoulder.

"Be safe," Maggie and Berklee respond at the same time.

"Always." He waves and heads toward the door.

"Ready, Mags?" Barry asks. "I need a shower," he complains.

Berklee laughs. "I didn't want to say anything."

"Listen, you." He reaches out and tickles her side. She yelps with laughter.

"I mean, she just said what we were all thinking," Maggie chimes in. Barry goes after her next.

As soon as he drops his hand from Berklee, I put my arm around her and pull her in to me, so close that there's no way anyone would not think we're together. It's to show the fucker that she's mine, and also to keep from strangling him for touching her. Berklee, still wearing a huge grin, looks up at me. Her eyes are sparkling. I'm expecting her to rip me a new one for pretty much claiming her, but she doesn't. To my amazement she wraps her arm around my waist and rests her head on my chest.

Bending down, I place a kiss on top of her head. "Ready?"

When she looks up again, those blue eyes captivate me. "Yeah." She turns back to her friends. "We're heading home. See you all there."

I nod as a way of saying goodbye, not willing to let go of her. I keep her close all the way to the truck. She knows the drill by now, so when I open the door, she slides into the middle of the seat and waits for me to take my spot behind the wheel. I start the truck and get the heater going, then turn to her, cupping her face in my hands.

"W-what did you need to tell me?" she asks, her voice a whisper.

"This." I lean in and kiss her slowly, trying to show her that things have changed for me. That I want all of her, every minute of every day. I caress her cheeks with the pads of my thumbs while my lips softly take hers. She grips my wrists but doesn't try to pull me away from her. No, it's like she's holding on for the ride.

My tongue traces her lips. "Crew." It's almost like a plea—for what, I'm not sure. Loud voices and laughter from the car next to us have me reluctantly pulling away from her. I rest my forehead against hers.

"I guess we should go," she whispers against my skin.

"Yeah, beautiful. Let's get you home." With a quick kiss to her lips, one final taste, I turn around and adjust my cock in my jeans. Berklee surprises me when her hand rests on my thigh, her head on my shoulder. She came to me. Finally, I feel like I'm getting somewhere with her. As soon as I get on the road, my hand is on her thigh too. I can't not touch her when she's near. It's almost like it calms me to touch her, to know she's right here.

I pull into her drive and cut the lights, but don't move to turn off the truck or pull away from her. Instead, I put my arm around her and she snuggles closer, burrowing into my chest. I'll sit here all fucking night if she'll let me.

"I guess I need to go inside," she finally says.

"Nah, we're good right here."

She chuckles softly. "All night?"

"All fucking weekend if we stay right like this." I kiss the top of her head.

This causes her to pull away and look up at me. "What are we doing, Crew?"

Reaching out, I tuck a stray curl behind her ear. "Falling," I whisper. The word just falls from my lips without thought.

"That wasn't the plan."

"Plans change, beautiful."

She starts to speak, but Barry and Maggie pull into the drive, so she sits up and pulls away. "I'll see you Monday," she says, sliding toward her door. Before I can stop her, Barry is there opening it for her. I grip the steering wheel, my knuckles turning white. I don't want to fucking leave her, and it makes it worse to know he's here with her and I'm not. "Night," she says with a small wave before closing the door.

*Fuck this.* I hop out of the truck. "Berklee!" She stops and turns. "You forgot something," I say, not quite as loud, and it works. She heads toward me while Barry and Maggie head inside.

"What did I forget?" she asks, looking down at my hands.

"This." One hand on her hip, the other on the back of her neck, I pull her in to me and kiss her. I put all the desperation I feel into the kiss, my grip on her hip tight. I hold her to me, my hand under those beautiful curls, caressing the soft skin of her neck. I steal her breath as it mingles with mine.

Her hands on my chest, pushing back, has me slowing the kiss but not letting her go.

"Wow," she murmurs.

"Sweet dreams, beautiful." I kiss her one more time, just a simple taste of her lips before I reluctantly let her go.

"Night." She looks up at me wearing a dazed smile.

Leaning in, I give her yet one more kiss. "Night." I release my hold on her and watch until she's in the house before getting back in my truck and driving away without her.

# TWENTY NINE
## *Berklee*

IT'S SATURDAY NIGHT and I'm home alone. By choice, mind you. Maggie's on a date with a new guy she met through one of her sub jobs. He's a teacher too, so that sounds promising. Barry is . . . I don't really know, but he's not here.

I need the time to think about Crew and what's happening. He's says that he's falling, but what does that mean? Is his heart falling, or is he falling more in lust with this agreement we've made? My heart votes for door number one, but I won't let it.

I've just settled on the couch with a big bowl of popcorn and my Kindle when my phone alerts me to a message. My heart skips a beat when I see his name on the screen.

> **Crew:** *What are you doing?*

I decide to show him, snapping a picture and sending it to him.

> **Crew:** *Wild Saturday night.*

> **Me:** *Ha! Not hardly. A night in is exactly what I needed.*

> **Crew:** *Me too. Next week being opening week and all.*

> **Me:** *We're ready.*

> **Crew:** *I agree.*

I don't really know what else to say. He reached out to me, so I set my phone on the arm of the couch, grab a handful of popcorn and wait. I've barely stuffed my mouth full when my phone pings again.

**Crew:** *Can I see you?*

*Be still my heart.* If I've learned anything about Crew Ledger, it's that he rarely asks permission for anything.

**Me:** *When?*

**Crew:** *Now. I'm a few minutes from your place.*

*Shit!* I look down at my boy shorts and tank top. My hair is in a knot on top of my head and I have zero makeup on.

**Me:** *You okay?*

I need to ask because maybe there's something wrong. Maybe he needs a friend or there's an issue with the club. It can't be what I think it is.

**Crew:** *No. I miss you.*

**Me:** *Yes.*

My fingers typed those three letters and hit Send before I could think about what I was doing. Staring down at the screen, I realize he's on his way. I hop off the couch and barely avoid spilling my huge bowl of popcorn, my Kindle not as lucky as it clanks to the floor. I grab it and the popcorn and get them safely on the table when there's a knock at the door. Standing tall, I take a deep breath and head that way.

Opening the door, he's standing there, hands over his head, holding onto the frame. Neither of us says as word as he takes me in, my eyes on him while his travel over every inch of me. I watch his throat as he swallows hard before his eyes rake back up my body. "You're fucking breathtaking," he croaks out.

"You want to come in?"

He drops his hands and reaches for me as he steps through the door. "We alone?"

"Yeah," I manage to answer as his hands roam over my body.

He leans down and buries his face in my neck causing me to giggle from the tickle of his beard. "Here or your room?"

"My room." I turn out of his hold, trying not to freak out that he's here, that he came to me. I just need to remind myself why he's here. He needs release and we agreed no one else. No matter how badly I wish it were more.

I hear the click of the lock on the front door but don't look back. Stepping into the room, the door closes behind me, followed by the unmistakable sound of him locking it.

I don't have time to turn around before he's behind me, wrapping his arms around my waist, my back to his front. I tilt my head to the side, giving him access to my neck, and he takes full advantage as his lips drop gentle wet kisses along the length. I want him. I'm risking my soul letting him in here like this, but let's be honest—I'm already too far gone. He's just one of those people you can't help but give yourself to.

"I need you," he says between kisses to my neck. "I need to be buried deep inside you." He nips at my neck. "Now."

"Okay," I murmur.

I feel a rush of his hot breath as he exhales, one hand on my hip as the other slides under my tank. He takes his time, caressing every inch of me as he works his way up to my breast. He rolls my already hard nipples between his fingers and I can't stop the moan that escapes. "So fucking responsive to my touch," he says, moving to the other breast and repeating the process. Sliding his other hand under my shirt, he captures both breasts and kneads them. "Arms up." His voice is husky. Even though they feel like Jell-O as I'm consumed by his touch, I do as I'm told and lift them over my head.

"Son of a bitch," Crew hisses, palming my ass that is still covered in boy shorts.

His hands leave my body, but only seconds pass before I feel his bare chest pressed against my back.

"Skin to skin," he says, running his tongue over my shoulder. "Nothing better," he declares as his hands once again find my now bare breasts.

He pinches both nipples, causing me to lean back against him, surrendering to him. He can have his wicked way with me and will get zero complaints on my end.

One hand still working over my hard nipples, the other travels down my belly. It doesn't faze him when he reaches the hem of my boy shorts, his large hand sliding underneath the waistband, never missing a beat as he seeks out my heat. "Fuck, babe, you're soaked."

"For you," my inner hussy goads.

"Fuck yes, for me. Only me," he says before pushing one long thick finger inside. "Need these gone." He moves the hand that was occupied with my breast to grip my boy shorts, tugging on them. The next thing I know I'm in his arms and being placed on the bed. Crew grabs my shorts with both hands and pulls them down my legs. Standing to his full height once more, he unbuttons his jeans and within seconds we're both naked.

Reaching out, I grip his hard cock. He groans, closing his eyes and tilting his head back. Sitting up, I scoot to the edge of the bed and take him in my mouth. No warning, just my mouth wrapped around the most sensitive part of him.

"Fuck" falls from his lips and his hand finds its way to my hair. "Need to see this, memorize it," he says, holding my hair back from my face in his tight grip. "My cock in your mouth, best fucking thing I've ever seen. Just like that."

His praise fuels my desire to bring him to his knees. I use my hand in tandem with my mouth, holding on tight to the back of his thigh with the other. I make a humming sound and he pushes me away.

"Can't," he pants. "I refuse to come down your throat. Not this time. I need to be inside you, now." Reaching down for his jeans, he searches through the pockets until he pulls out a couple condoms, throwing them on the bed.

The look in his eyes, the one that tells me that he's barely controlling himself from taking me fast and hard, has me sliding back on the bed and resting my head on the pillow. "I want you," I say, letting my legs fall open. He stands stock-still, staring at me. Only he's not looking at what I'm offering him—he's looking at me. In a way it's even more intimate, the way his eyes bore into mine.

Not breaking eye contact, he climbs on the bed, resting on his knees as his fingers trace through my desire for him. "Only me," he says again.

"Just you," I confirm, closing my eyes, enjoying what he's doing to me.

"I don't think you get what I'm saying, baby. Open your eyes."

I do and find him still watching me. "You're mine. No arrangement, no bullshit about how you work for me, none of it. You're mine."

I blink a few times, trying to clear my head of the lust he's stirring inside me so I can decipher what he just said.

He slides not one but two fingers inside, and I fight to not roll my eyes to the back of my head. "This is mine, this pussy." He leans over me. "These lips," he says, kissing me softly, then running his lips down my neck and to my chest. "Your heart." He kisses me right over where my heart is beating furiously. "It's all mine."

"Crew." His name is a whisper on my lips.

"Tell me you get me. I need the words, Berklee."

I sift through what he said. I'm his. . . . My heart. . . . Did I imagine that part?

"You heard me right, beautiful," he says, reading my mind. "Every fucking word." He pats his chest, over his heart. "Right here, all you, all the time. I need to hear you say it." He leans down and kisses my lips softly. "Tell me you get me."

"I-I get you."

"Say it. Say you're mine."

"I'm yours."

"Mine." He removes his hand and replaces it with his cock. Resting his weight on his elbows on either side of my head, he holds my stare. "Wrap your legs around me," he orders, kissing the corner of my mouth.

I do as he says, digging my heels into his back.

"Good girl." He rolls his hips, causing me to squeeze my legs even tighter. He does it again, over and over again until I'm on the edge of orgasmic bliss. Arms around his neck, I pull him down to me and hold on. He keeps a steady rhythm, moving his hips as he thrusts inside me. "I feel you, babe. Your pussy squeezing me tight. You ready to go?"

I don't have words; all I can do is feel.

"That's it, beautiful. Fuck, you're squeezing me so tight."

With one more thrust and roll of his hips, I lose control and cry out his name. "Crew!"

"Right." Thrust. "There." Thrust. "With you." He stills as he finds his release.

Slumping forward, careful not to crush me, he kisses me on the forehead. We lie like this, both breathing heavy, neither of us willing to break the connection. Finally, he slides out of me. "I need to take care of this. Be right back." He kisses my chest right over my heart and then climbs out of bed.

I instantly miss his heat but am thankful for a minute to try and wrap my head around what just happened. Condom! I didn't even think about protection. When did he put it on? He had me so blindsided with want for him that the thought didn't even cross my mind.

Crew comes back from the bathroom with a wet cloth. "Open for me," he says, tapping my knee. Without thought, I do so. "So damn sexy," he croons while taking his time, wiping away the evidence of what just happened. Doesn't matter; I still feel it. Feel him. Everywhere.

Tossing the washcloth to the side, Crew climbs in beside me and pulls the covers over us. His arm snakes out and pulls my back to his front as he buries his face in my neck. "Sleep, babe. I'm going to need you again and you'll need it." He kisses my shoulder.

"I—"

"I'm staying. Unless you want us to go to my place, we're spending the night right here. You're going to stay right here." His voice is a husky whisper. "I meant it, Berklee. Every fucking word, I mean it." He adjusts his hold on me, tightening further. "Night, beautiful." With a kiss to my shoulder, he says no more, and I lie awake until his breathing evens out.

I hear Maggie and Barry come home, but I don't dare move to go talk to them. I know they saw his truck, my night of lounging in front of the TV still spread across the living room. They're smart; they can put two and two together.

I'm not ready to answer questions, so instead I let myself have this moment. Where it feels as though I'm being cherished by the hold he has on me and let myself fall asleep in his arms.

It's too late to fight it.

I've already fallen.

# THIRTY
## Crew

I'VE BEEN LYING here wide awake for the last couple of hours. I woke up with Berklee's tight little ass pressed against my hard cock and I had to have her. Her eyes opened instantly at my touch but she welcomed me with open arms, and I took everything she was offering as I made love to her. That's what it was, making love. Hence the reason I'm still wide awake. My girl dozed off, head on my chest, soon after, but I've just laid here running my fingers through her hair, listening to her deep, even breaths as I think about the last twelve hours.

The second time was different. Neither of us were in a hurry, just gentle and slow, taking and feeling with everything in us. It was a life-changing moment for me—the minute I realized that I'd fallen in love with her. I knew I cared for her, that she was under my skin, but it's more than that. It's the way those blue eyes smile up at me, so trusting. The way she treats me, not like a meal ticket but an equal. It's just her, Berklee. It's who she is, and I love her more because of it.

I'm still not certain how things will go when she wakes up. Sometimes in the light of day, everything looks different.

A soft knock on her bedroom door catches my attention. It's gentle and then nothing.

"She in there?" I hear Barry ask.

"It's locked," Maggie tells him.

I hear their footsteps as they walk on past. Berklee stirs in my arms, stretching her limbs.

"Morning, baby." I kiss her temple.

169

Her eyes pop open and she blinks a few times. I see the minute it all comes rushing back to her. Our night together, the reason she's curled up in my arms, in her bed. "Hi. You stayed," she states the obvious.

"I did."

"Last night . . ."

"Was amazing. What are we doing today?" I ask her.

"We?"

"Yes, we. I'm not ready to let you go yet. What are your plans today? I'm supposed to go to my parents' for dinner, but I can cancel." All I have to do is tell them that I'm spending the day with Berklee and they'll get it.

"Oh, you should go. Don't let me keep you." She starts to roll away but I stop her.

"If I go, you go."

"Crew."

"Berklee."

"What is this? What are we doing?"

There it is. I was waiting for it. "We're us," I tell her, tapping her ass with my hand.

"What does that mean?" she says, almost whining.

I chuckle. "We are us, you and me. Crew and Berklee. You're mine."

"Are you mine?" she fires back.

I roll on top of her and kiss her, morning breath be damned. "All yours," I say against her lips. No truer words have ever been spoken. I've given her all of me.

"You're my boss."

"I'm your man," I counter, and she tries like hell to fight her grin. "We'll figure it out as we go. Right now, you need to decide what you want to do today."

"I-I don't really have any plans."

"Good. You can come to my parents' with me."

"I can't just crash dinner at your parents.'"

"Not crashing, attending. Trust me, the more the merrier, especially when the more is you."

"Berklee, your phone's blowing up. Your mom has called three times," Maggie says through the door.

"I'll get it." I climb out of bed, slide into my jeans and open the bedroom door, just enough for my arm to snake out and reach for the phone. I don't want to risk anyone seeing her still lying naked in her bed.

"Why, Berklee, what nice ink you have." Maggie laughs, placing the phone in my hand.

"Thanks," I say, shutting the door and twisting the lock before she can try and weasel her way in.

I toss Berklee the phone and then head to the bathroom. Once I'm done, I find her still on the phone. "Mom, I kind of have plans today."

"Tell her yes. Whatever it is, yes," I whisper in her ear.

"Sure, okay fine. Yeah, I'll be there in an hour."

"I'm going with you," I say, kissing her neck.

"Uh, I might have someone with me." She's trying to keep her voice from giving away the fact that I'm kissing her. "Yeah, uh, Crew. He, uh, might come with me." She's quiet and then says, "It's complicated, Mom. I can't answer that." She listens again. "Okay see you soon." She drops her phone to the mattress and sighs.

"What's complicated?" I ask immediately.

"This." She points her finger back and forth between the two of us. "What was I supposed to say to her?"

"That we're dating." I don't see what's so complicated with that.

"Is that what we're doing? I'm still kind of processing the last twelve hours."

"Yes."

"She invited me over for lunch. It's been a while since I've been there."

"I'll call my parents and move our plans to later today so we can do both."

"Are we really doing this? Are we taking each other home to the parents? Isn't this crazy to you?"

"The only thing crazy in this situation is the fact that my girl is naked and I'm about to push her off to the shower instead of sliding inside her heat." I climb out of bed and pull her with me. "We're doing this, babe.

You and me. We've been skirting around it for weeks and it's happening. Now go get ready. We don't want to be late. I still have to swing by my place to shower and change."

"I could—"

"Nope. Not letting you out of my sight. Not giving you the chance to second-guess this." I pull her naked body close. "We." Kiss. "Are." Kiss. "Doing." Kiss. "This." I smack her ass. "Shower, woman, before I take you back to bed." She actually looks like she's contemplating what the right decision is, and I throw my head back and laugh. "Go." She grins, turns and runs for the shower.

While she's gone, I finish getting dressed and check my e-mail. Next weekend is the grand opening of Club Titan, and no matter how much I want to just get lost in her, I can't. I have other responsibilities.

"You sure about this?" she asks, pulling my attention from my phone.

She's wearing tight pants and a long sweater, her wet curls hanging over her shoulders. "You ready to go?" I ask, ignoring her question.

"I need to dry my hair. You didn't answer me."

"That question doesn't deserve an answer. I'm in this, babe. You and me. Never been more sure about anything."

She looks a little worried but turns back to the bathroom to finish drying her hair.

Fifteen minutes later, she's stepping into the room, soft curls now dry. "Ready," she says, going into her closet and grabbing a pair of boots. Sitting beside me on the bed, she slides them on. They're sexy as fuck, reaching up to her knees. "What are we going to tell them?" She points to her bedroom door.

"Why do we have to tell them anything?"

"You spent the night."

"I did, and it's none of their fucking business what we did in this room, behind that closed door."

"Crew, they're my friends. More like family."

"Then tell them the truth, that we're together."

"Maybe we should keep this just between us for a little while. You know, just until you're sure."

I pull her onto my lap and lift her chin with my finger, forcing her to look at me. "Baby, I'm sure. Nothing and no one can change my mind on this. I want you, and we are happening. I don't want to hide how I feel about you. I don't want to have to control myself when I'm out in public with you. I want to touch you whenever I want, kiss these soft lips when the urge strikes." I place a chaste kiss on her lips to bring the point home. "No hiding."

"Okay," she agrees. She still looks unsure, but I'll prove it to her. I've had more time to accept the fact that we're more, officially, than she has. I need to remember to give her time to catch up.

I grab her hand and bring it to my lips, placing a kiss on her wrist. Her shoulders relax a little.

"Okay." She goes to the door and turns the lock as I follow close behind her. Maggie and Barry are both in the living room. "We're headed out. Be back later," she calls out to them.

"Where you headed?" Barry asks, looking over his shoulder from where he sits on the couch. He's watching us with an expression I can't quite name. I step a little closer to Berklee and place my hand on the small of her back, close enough to get my point across but not too much to freak her out.

"Mom and Dad's for lunch," she gives them the honest answer. *That's my girl.*

"Tell them we said hi," Maggie says from the recliner.

"Will do," Berklee calls out, then leads me out the door.

# THIRTY ONE
## Berklee

CREW IS READY in ten minutes. Men have it so easy. Is it too much to ask that he take his sweet-ass time so I can freak out in private?

He insists on driving and, of course, I'm in the middle of the seat. I would love to say that his caveman ways piss me off, but then I'd be lying. I want everything he's offering.

"Just pull in behind Dad's truck," I tell him when we reach my parents' place. He parks and hops out, offering me his hand to help me down just like he always does.

"I'll be good, promise." He kisses my forehead and links our hands together, leading me to the front porch. Not one ounce of apprehension with this man; he knows what he wants and doesn't let anything stand in his way.

I don't bother knocking, just walk right in. "Mom, Dad, we're here," I call out.

"In the kitchen, sweetie," Mom calls back.

I take a deep breath and head that way, my hand still held tight in Crew's. "Mom, Dad, you remember Crew," I introduce them again like an idiot. Of course they remember him. We just sat when them at the game two days ago.

"Of course we do, dear," Mom says. "Come on in and sit down. It's ready. I just make pulled pork sandwiches and those homemade steak fries you love."

"Crew, good to see you, son." Dad offers him his hand.

*Son?*

"You too, sir. Thanks for having me," he says politely.

"Sit, sit." Mom waves us toward the table.

Dad takes his seat at the end, Mom beside him. Crew and I are across from her, me sitting next to Dad. Just in case. Mom begins telling me everything I've missed, like how her hairdresser is pregnant again. She's only two years older than me and this is her second child. I know this is a hint that she's more than ready for a grandchild. Crew just sits beside me eating his food, none the wiser, thank goodness.

"So, what are you two kids getting into the rest of the day?" Dad asks. He must sense my unease.

"Dinner with my parents this evening. Nothing else that I know of, right, babe?" Crew asks.

He just called me "babe" in front of my parents and let the fact slip that we both are indeed doing the family thing today. Together.

"Do your parents live around here?" Mom asks. I can already see her wheels spinning. If this gets serious, will he want to take me away? It's the jinx of being an only child.

"They do. Just on the other side of town, about fifteen minutes from the club."

Mom beams at this information.

"It just kind of worked out that way today. Crew already had plans with his parents and asked me to join them. He was with me when you called, so we figured why not make a day of it." It's not until the words are out of my mouth that I realize my parents have more than likely put two and two together and realize why Crew was at my house just a little after nine this morning. They know I'm not some virginal angel, but I like to keep that shit locked up tight when the parents are around. No need to air the dirty laundry.

"Have you met his parents?" Dad asks. He's on to me, for sure.

"Yeah, actually. They stopped by the club and I met them."

"Speaking of, why don't you all come by this week? Berklee can show you around," Crew offers.

"Yes. That sounds exciting. We've been meaning to but didn't want to intrude," Mom says.

"No intrusion. You're family," Crew states matter-of-factly.

176

"So, have you all decided on your trip this year for your anniversary?" I ask, changing the subject. Mom and Dad start talking about the Alaskan cruise they're planning for their anniversary next August.

The conversation flows and the next thing I know over three hours have passed. I look over at Crew. "We should probably get going."

"Whenever you're ready," he says, leaning in and placing his arm on the back of my chair.

"Don't let us keep you." Mom stands. "We'll stop by one day this week before the opening. Crew, good luck to you," she says sincerely.

"Thank you, but I've got this one." He taps my shoulder. "I think she's all the luck I need."

He's got them eating out of the palm of his hands. Oh, who am I kidding—he's got me doing it too. This man and his words.

We say our goodbyes and we're back in the truck on the way to his parents' house.

"Did you tell them I was coming with you?"

"No, I thought it would be funny to see the surprise on their faces. I've never brought a girl home before, so they're in for a shock." He pats my knee and lets his hand linger there.

"Crew!" I scold him. "You should've told them. I don't want to just barge in on them. Maybe you should just drop me off at my house on our way."

"Not happening. Trust me, okay? They're fine with it. In fact, they're going to be thrilled. Relax, babe."

*Relax, he says. Pfft, hell of a lot easier said than done.* The rest of the drive is quiet, but not uncomfortably so. I think Crew was letting me get my thoughts together, giving me time to have a mental freak-out. He knows me better than I would've thought.

"Here we are," Crew says, pulling into a long circular drive. He's out of the truck before I can ask him yet again if this is a good idea. "Come on, Berklee." Once my feet are planted on the ground, he leans down and kisses the corner of my mouth, lacing his fingers through mine and leading us to the front door. Much like at my parents,' he doesn't bother knocking. "Where is everyone?" he calls out.

"Living room," a male voice yells back—I assume Dan, his dad.

Crew leads us down the hall and into a room with a large flat-screen

TV, his parents snuggled on the couch together under a blanket.

"Hey, guys." He leads us to the love seat and pulls me down with him.

"Berklee," Sarah, his mom, says with a smile. "We didn't know you were coming." She looks at Crew accusingly.

Crew chuckles. "What? Can't a guy bring his girl to his parents' house to surprise them?"

Dan's face lights up with a knowing grin and Sarah hops off the couch and rushes us, pulling first Crew and then me into a crushing hug. "When did this happen? You've been hiding her from me," she pouts.

Crew's eyes find mine and he smirks. "Not hiding, just seeing how it goes. Wanted to see what was there before we broadcasted it to the world. You know, working together and all that."

"Well come on, you two. I've got a roast and potatoes in the Crock-Pot." Sarah grabs my hand and pulls me from the couch.

"Hey now, where are you taking my girl?" Crew calls after us.

"Girl time," she fires back. I can hear Crew and Dan laughing behind us as we reach the kitchen. "Have a seat. Can I get you something to drink?" she asks me.

"No, thank you."

"So tell me, how are things at the club?"

"Good. We're ready for opening night. It's exciting to see it all come together and be a part of that. Crew's meticulous." I laugh. "I don't think failure is in his vocabulary."

She laughs too. "He's always been that way. Once he decides, that's how it's going to be. Stubborn child, so much like his father."

"Trust me, I know all too well."

"Oh honey, they're all bossy and possessive, but what you need to understand is that you are truly the one in control," she says, lowering her voice.

"You've met your son, right?"

She chuckles. "Oh yes, and like I said, he's just like his father. You're the first girl he's brought home, so I know you're the one to share this wisdom with." She looks around me at the door, making sure the coast is clear, I assume, before she bestows her wisdom up on me. "Let me guess. He's demanding, jealous, pushy. Am I getting close?" She smirks.

"Nail on the head."

"Figured as much. The apple doesn't fall far from the tree. He likes to act as though he's the one in charge, but that's not the case. Trust me, if and when the time comes for you to put your foot down, he will bend to your will. It's almost comical." She laughs under her breath. "Dating his father was the same way. I got fed up one day and took a stand. He started to see things my way."

"Interesting," I tell her. "Although, we're still pretty new, so I don't think I hold that kind of power yet, but it's good to file away for a later date."

Before she can answer, Crew and Dan join us. I watch as Dan rests his hands on his wife's hips. "Can I help with anything?" he asks, kissing her cheek.

I look away, not wanting to be a voyeur, and feel strong hands wrap around my waist. "You good, baby?" Crew asks. He doesn't bother to lower his voice.

Sarah looks over at me and winks. "You have more than you realize."

"That's cryptic," Crew says, humor in his voice.

"Grab some plates," Sarah tells Dan. "Honey, drinks, please," she tells Crew. It's amazing how she commands them and they jump to it.

"Well done." I hold my hand out to her for a high five.

Once everyone has plates and we're all seated, we start to dig in. "Mmm, this is amazing," I tell Sarah.

"Thanks, I'll have to give you the recipe. It's one of Crew's favorites."

"You ready for the opening?" Dan asks.

"Yeah, we've got everything under control."

"Behind every man is a good woman." Dan chuckles.

Crew grabs my hand, places it on the table and laces his fingers through mine. "I couldn't agree more."

"You all go sit where it's more comfortable. We'll get the dishes." Dan stands and starts grabbing plates. Crew kisses my temple and joins him.

"More girl talk," Sarah says as I follow her to the living room.

"Thank you so much for dinner." I started to say, "for having me" but she really didn't get much choice in that part.

"You're welcome here anytime. So, how was your day?"

"Good. We, uh, we had lunch with my parents at their place, and now we're here."

"Crew, my son, went to your parents' for lunch?"

I nod. "He did."

"Oh, Berklee, sweetheart, you have no idea how excited that makes me."

"What's making my wife excited that I don't know about?" Dan asks as he and Crew join us.

"Well, Berklee was just telling me how they had lunch with her parents today."

I chance a look at Crew from where he now sits beside me to gauge his reaction. Is he going to be pissed that I told her?

He smiles at Sarah. "We did, and they're great. I'm sure you'll meet them soon enough."

Dan's the one to speak up this time. "Ah," he says, like he finally gets it. He glances over at me and must see the question in my eyes. "My boy here once declared that meeting the parents was something he would never do. We've tried for years to get him to bring his dates over. He assured us that if and when that happened, we would know he was in it for the long haul."

I can feel the heat coat my cheeks as embarrassment floods me. Crew leans in front of me, blocking me from his parents' view. "Mine." One word. That's all it takes for the embarrassment to fade.

He and Dan talk about the club, Sarah and I chiming in here and there. I mostly just sit back and watch his interaction with his parents. It's an all new side of Crew Ledger, one I'm glad I'm getting to see.

"We better get going." He stands and offers me his hand. *Always the gentleman. My bossy gentleman.* I know now where he gets it.

"If we don't see you before the opening, best of luck. And you"— Sarah walks toward me—"come back any time. We'd love to have you."

"Thank you. Dinner was amazing."

After a round of hugs, we're on our way back to my place.

Crew pulls into the drive and turns to face me. "Come home with me," he says, running his knuckles down my cheek.

"It's been a long day. I need to get some laundry done and get ready for this week."

"I'll buy you more clothes." He leans in to kiss me.

I laugh against his lips. "That's crazy talk. Go home. I'll see you at the club in the morning."

"Please?" He juts out his bottom lip and pretends to pout. Let me tell you something—Crew in full-on pout mode is cute as hell and hard to say no to, but I hold strong.

"Come on, goof, walk me to the door." I push on him until he relents and opens the door.

"Invite me in," he says, placing kisses on my neck.

"No."

His grip tightens on my waist. "Babe, how am I supposed to sleep alone after I finally know what it feels like to hold you all night and wake up with you in my arms?"

"I'll see you in the morning. Kiss me and say good night."

He turns me so that my back is pressed against the door. "I don't like the word 'no' when it comes to you," he says huskily.

"Kiss me," I say again. This time he listens, fusing his mouth to mine. I'm lost in the feel of his lips, the taste of his tongue, when the porch light comes on.

"Fuck," he grumbles.

"I'm sure that's Maggie. She's probably dying to know what's going on with us."

"You gonna tell her you're mine?"

The conversation I had with Sarah filters through my mind. "No, I'm going to tell her you're mine."

"Yours." He kisses me one more time and then backs away.

"Text me when you get home," I say.

"You got it, baby. Get some sleep. I'll see you in the morning.

As soon as I'm inside, Maggie pounces. "Girl! I've been waiting all damn day for you to get home. Spill!" she says, bouncing on the balls of her feet.

"We're . . . together."

"Together, yes, I know this. But he stayed and you spent the day together."

"No, Mags, I mean we're *together*. As in no more hiding together."

"No shit!" she exclaims.

"What's all the racket about?" Barry asks, joining us in the living room, carrying a half-eaten slice of pizza.

"Oh, you know, nothing much. Just Berklee telling me that she and Crew are an official couple." Maggie claps.

"Official, huh?"

"Yeah. It's still new, obviously, but we're going to go with it and see where it takes us."

"I'm so happy for you. He's got it bad." Maggie grins.

"She's right, you know. All I have to do is look at you and he's ready to piss all around you and mark his territory." Barry laughs.

"He's . . . protective. That's not a bad thing."

"Of course it's not. He's good to you?" Maggie asks.

"Like you wouldn't believe," I tell her honestly. Crew would never hurt me. I feel it in my bones.

"That's all that matters."

"I agree. Now if you'll excuse me, I'm exhausted. I need to change and start some laundry." I leave my roommates to talk about me, because that's totally what they're doing. I sort out a load of laundry, start the washer and head back to my room. I have a text waiting from Crew.

> **Crew:** I'm home.
>
> **Me:** Good night.
>
> **Crew:** Night, beautiful.

# THIRTY TWO
## Crew

TONIGHT IS OPENING night and I'm ready. *We're* ready. The staff is on point, security tight, and my girl went dress shopping this week. All week I've tried to get her to stay with me, or me with her, but she continues to shut me down. Tonight, however, she's coming home with me. I need her in my bed. Not to fuck her, but to hold her and wake up with her. She robbed me of that the first night, and I will get it back. Tonight, I'm not taking no for an answer. I've tried to not push her for fear that I'm too much. Mom called me Sunday night and lectured me about letting her get there, so that's what I've been doing, but I've reached my limit.

She's mine, after all.

I park my truck in her drive and stare at her front door. I insisted that she ride with me tonight. She didn't give me much of a fight, but then again, I've been here every day this week to drive in together.

I knock on the door and it swings open. "Hey, Crew," Maggie greets me. "Come on in. Berklee's almost ready."

"Thanks. You going to make it to the club tonight?"

"Definitely. I'm so excited to see it after hearing so much about it."

"You could have stopped by."

"Nah, this is Berklee's thing. It's better that she gets to see our reaction to the final product."

"Sorry," Berklee says, walking into the room, and my mouth drops open. Her hair is in curls down her back, her nails and lips red. She's wearing a short black dress, made of some kind of lace, I think. She

183

looks at Maggie. "I have a slip on underneath but you can still see," she whines.

"You look hot. Tell her, Crew."

Two steps. That's how long it takes me to get to her. My hands settle on her waist and I pull her to me. "You're fucking beautiful, and I'm trying really damn hard not to insist you go change right now. How about a compromise? It's not too revealing, but every guy in the place is going to want to see what's mine, so you don't leave my side tonight. I want you stuck to me like glue."

She giggles. "How is that different than any other day this week?"

Okay, so I might have been up her ass this week. When she was in her office doing paperwork, I brought mine in and sat on the opposite side of her desk. During the final day of bartending training, I tagged along and yeah, so I sat right beside her. When it was Berklee's turn to create the new drink, I went behind the bar with her. It's not something I can control—not that I want to. She's magnetic and beautiful and, finally, all mine.

"It's not." I lean in and gently press my lips to hers.

"Come on, you. I want to be there when the staff starts arriving. You know, pregame pep talk and all that." She pats my chest.

I step to the side and wrap my arm around her waist. No way am I letting go of her. I can't take my eyes off her as she says goodbye to Maggie.

"Crew," she says, waving her hand in front of my face. "You ready?"

I nod, mouth suddenly too dry to speak. I do manage a wave to Maggie as I usher her out the door. We reach my truck and I open the door for her. Her heels are high and dress tight. She's looking at the seat, trying to figure out how to climb inside and not flash the neighborhood.

"Turn around," I say, my hands already on her hips and turning her to face me. "On three." I lean in and kiss her softly. "One." Kiss. "Two." Kiss. "Three." I lift her by the hips and set her on the seat. She scoots to the middle and stops.

Once I'm settled behind the wheel, I place my hand on her bare thigh. "You're gorgeous."

She blushes. I love that I have that effect on her. "Thank you. You clean up pretty nice too."

Not hardly. I have on dark jeans and a black button-down with the sleeves rolled up to my elbows. That's about as dressed up as I'm going to get.

I park behind the building and help Berklee out of the truck. We're hours early, but we need to be here for everything to make sure it goes off without a hitch.

Inside, I keep the lights turned off and lead her upstairs to my office, closing the door behind us. "Come here." I unbutton my shirt, slide it off and toss it over the chair.

She turns to look at me. "No way, mister. I worked hard on this look. I am not letting you mess me all up before we even open the damn doors."

I walk to the couch and sit down. "Come sit with me, then."

She comes toward me and I capture her hips, pulling her onto my lap. "Feel that?" The little minx wiggles her tight ass against my already-hard cock. "How am I supposed to wait when you look like this?"

"What do you want?" she murmurs.

"I want you to crave me the way I crave you."

"I do." She stands and slowly pulls her dress over her head, then straddles my hips. She's wearing a black sheer slip and my cock grows even harder. Leaning down, she kisses me. "You have to go slow. I don't want to wear a freshly fucked look for opening night."

The word "fuck" on her lips? So hot. "Whatever you need."

I have one hand on her ass and the other on her back, not willing to let her get away. On her knees, she braces her hands on my chest and rests her forehead against mine. "I just want you," she whispers.

They say when the moment comes, you'll just know. This is that moment for me. I know without a doubt that she owns me—heart, body, soul. I'm in love with her. I think I've always been there, teetering on the fence since the minute I laid eyes on her, but that simple confession pushes me over the edge. It's on the tip of my tongue to tell her before I make love to her when there's a loud knock on my office door.

"Crew, man, you in there? I saw your truck parked outside," Zane's muffled voice carries through the door.

"Fuck," I growl.

Berklee laughs.

"Shh. Just be quiet and he'll go away."

"I heard that," Zane says, way too damn chipper to be breaking up the action. "Come on, love birds, the DJ is here and the staff is starting to arrive."

"I'm going to strip this sexy little number off you tonight. Then I'm sliding inside you and I'm going to stay there for hours. All week, I've thought of nothing else. Be ready, baby."

Her blue eyes heat with desire. "Always for you," she says before kissing me way too quickly and climbing off my lap.

I help her back into her dress, although there's groping involved so it takes longer than it should. I then pull my shirt back on and reluctantly open the door. Zane is sitting in the lounge area scrolling through his phone.

"That was fast. B, you ever want a—"

"Don't you fucking finish that statement," I warn him.

He throws his head back in laughter. "You're too easy to fuck with. I can't help myself."

Berklee, who is tucked in to my side, is shaking with silent laughter. "You." I stare down at her, trying to appear pissed off, but her laughter dissipates just as quick as it started.

"What?" She bites her bottom lip. "It's funny when you go all caveman."

I smack her ass and she yelps. "I'll show you caveman," I say just for her.

"All right, break it up," Zane scolds us. "We've got work today. Club Titan is ready for business, baby."

His excitement is contagious, and a feeling of absolute completeness washes over me. My vision has come full circle and comes to life tonight. I have the woman I love in my arms, and my best friend along for the ride.

Life is fucking good in the world of Crew Ledger.

# THIRTY THREE
*Berklee*

AS I WALK around talking to the staff, I can't keep the grin off my face. I'm so excited for tonight, for Crew and everyone else. The hype around the club has been crazy this week, and local news stations have come by to interview us. We left that up to Zane; he's our little social butterfly and doesn't mind the attention. My parents stopped by this week with a basket of goodies that are sitting upstairs in the lounge area. Mom called me that night, after they were here, and gave Crew her and Dad's seal of approval. Not that I needed it, but it makes the fact that I've fallen head over heels in love with him a little easier. I can't imagine what it would feel like to not have my parents like the guy I want to spend all my time with.

"Ms. Hanson, we're ready when you are," the lead guy on the production team tells me. I hired his company to document the occasion. I want Crew to be able to look back on this day and remember everything about the moment that his vision came to life.

"Thank you, I'll be right back."

Inside, I find Crew talking to Tank, one of the security guys. "The photographer's here," I tell Crew. "We're ready for the ribbon cutting ceremony. Zane's already outside."

"Let's do this." He grabs my hand and leads the way.

"Mr. Ledger, here are the scissors." Someone on the production team hands him a pair of scissors the size of his arm.

The red ribbon is already strung across the front entrance, and the camera guy is behind the camera giving a thumbs-up. "I'm so proud of you," I say, standing on my tiptoes to whisper in his ear. I kiss his cheek and step back.

His head whips to the side. "Where are you going?"

I can't help but smile at his protective ass. "Just standing off to the side. I'll be here the entire time, I promise."

"Come here." He holds his hand out for me. I know his stubborn streak and he'll hold this up if I don't take it. As soon as I'm within his reach, he snakes his arm out and pulls me close. "You belong right here, beside me, always." He watches me and I know he's waiting for me to argue with him, but when he says things like that, I can't seem to find the fight in me. "Zane," he calls out, his eyes still on me.

"What's up?" he asks, appearing in front of us.

"Going to need you here too." He nods to the ribbon, breaking our connection. "You two helped make this happen, so you deserve to be here as much as I do."

Crew nods at the camera guy and takes a deep breath. Stepping forward, he places the scissors up to the ribbon and cuts through it. The patrons who are already in line to check out the newest club in town cheer. Crew waves to them while handing the scissors back to the production team.

"Thank you," Zane says to the crowd while Crew and I slip back inside. "Doors open in less than an hour," he announces, and the roar of the crowd grows.

He rushes inside to join us, closing the door behind him. "Holy shit, they're stoked!"

"Make sure the security team is on it. I don't want things to get out of hand," Crew tells him.

"We're all over it. We have all hands on deck this weekend."

"Good. Okay, so let's do a walk-through, check in with the staff, and then sit back and watch all of our hard work."

That's exactly what we do, and before I know it the time has come to open the doors. I'm nervous. I want people to love this place, for Crew's vision to become his legacy. After all, that's how all of this came together in the first place.

"Maggie and Barry are here. I told them to park around back. I'm going to go let them in." Zane hurries to the back door.

"You ready for this?" I ask Crew.

He pulls me into his arms and kisses me. It's just a quick chaste kiss, but it heats my body all the same. "I am."

"Berklee," Maggie yells.

I pull out of his arms and brace myself for her hug. Barry steps up next to us and takes his turn as well, lifting me off my feet. "So proud of you."

I feel him right behind me, so I quickly drop back to my feet and pull away from Barry. Crew is there to pull me to his side.

"Berklee, Crew, this is Alan," Maggie introduces us to the guy she's been seeing. She gave up on Matt after only one date with Alan.

"Nice to meet you." Crew holds out his hand. He's much friendlier with me by his side. I follow his lead and offer my hand as well.

"Let's do this," Zane cuts in. "Ready, boss?" he asks Crew.

My man chuckles. "Yeah, I'm ready." Zane rushes off to officially open the doors. "Help yourself to the bar. It's on the house for the three of you tonight. I already told them Barry and Maggie, so Alan I'll make sure I add you to the list."

"Thank you," Maggie says. Barry and Alan give that head nod thing that guys do and then saunter away.

"You," Crew says, wrapping both arms around me. "I want you to stay close to me tonight. One, you look sexy as fuck, and two, I don't know what kind of crowd we're going to draw in. I need to know you're safe."

"Okay," I agree without an argument.

"You're giving me my way an awful lot tonight."

"I trust you." I would trust him with my life.

"I thank God every day for helping me find my way to you."

Crew is hardly ever not his dominate protective self, so this is a rare moment of vulnerability from him that I savor. It's in these moments that my heart cracks wide open and the love I have for him flows. I squeeze him as tightly as I can, letting him know with my touch that I feel the exact same way.

# THIRTY FOUR
## *Crew*

IT'S JUST AFTER ten and we're at capacity. Have been since about an hour after we opened the doors. I've been sitting back at a table with Berklee tucked into my side, Maggie, Alan, Zane, and Barry, both of whom have club patrons on their laps. I never thought I would say this, but I don't miss it. Not one bit. What I miss is my girl and the feel of her in my arms. Sure, she's been at my side all night, but I miss that connection, the way it feels when I'm buried inside her. Nothing like it. Nothing.

"Oh my God! I have not heard this song in years," Maggie screams as Salt-N-Pepa's "Push It" comes blaring through the speakers. "Berklee, we've got to." She stands, reaching for my girl's hand.

We're all laughing at her enthusiasm. That is until they step out on the dance floor and begin to move. My eyes are locked on Berklee, just like every other motherfucker in this club. When she begins thrusting her hips, I jump to my feet.

Zane's hand lands on my arm. "Let her have fun. I told the guys to watch out for her, and I know you did too when you talked to Tank earlier. This is what they do," he tells me.

"He's right, you know. I can't tell you how many times growing up they would have dance parties to this song in our living room. They heard it on a movie one night and never looked back." Barry laughs.

I hate that just as much, that he has that side of her.

I remain standing, watching my girl dance and laugh with her best friend. Her face is flushed, and even from here I can tell those blue eyes are sparking with happiness. I stand vigil with our friends and watch as she shakes that tight ass—turning every dick in the place hard as a rock, I'm sure.

The song changes to Blackstreet's "No Diggity," and no way am I leaving her out there for some sleazy fucker to grind against her. "Alan, I don't know about you, but my girl needs a dance partner," I say before walking away. I hear the scraping of his chair, and then he's beside me as we make our way through the crowd. Berklee sees me coming and a grin spreads across her face.

Arms in the air, hips swinging, she moves toward me. My hands find her hips and I begin to move with her. Berklee leans back, knowing that my strength will hold her up as she wiggles her body down to the floor, arms still in the air while singing along. When she comes back up, she kisses my chin, then turns in my arms. That tight ass of hers rubs against my cock when she bends over and grinds, and any control I was pretending to have has snapped. When I roll my hips into her ass, I know she feels me. She confirms it when she looks over her shoulder at me. Her blue eyes are smoldering with desire.

Catching Alan's eye, I point up to the windows that hide the offices upstairs. I don't want them to worry when we disappear, because we *are* going to disappear. I have to be inside her right now.

When she stands, my lips find her ear. "Need you. Now."

She nods, grabs my hands and shakes her ass as I follow her off the floor. I drop her hand and place mine on her hips, leaving no doubt that this girl is mine. Her arms immediately go back in the air and she sways to the beat, her hips somehow rock as she walks. She leads us upstairs and I'm on her heels, not willing to take my hands off her.

"Let's change it up," the DJ says to the crowd. The next song begins and it's Trey Songz "Na Na" pumping through the club.

Once we clear the top of the steps, Berklee looks over her shoulder at me. I see the same desire I feel staring back at me in those big blue yes. "My office," I say, my voice low and laced with every ounce of need I have for her.

I close the door and click the lock, then start taking care of my buttons as I take small, calculated steps toward her. For every step I move forward she takes one back. I finish with the last button just as I reach her. She rests her hands on my abs, running them up to my shoulders where she tugs my shirt down and then tosses it across the room. When her lips land on my chest, I fucking shiver at the contact. Bracing my hands above us on the window, I watch as she traces her tongue across what feels like every inch of my exposed skin. She slides her hand over my cock that's pressing against the zipper of my jeans, begging to feel her.

"I need you," I tell her.

She peers up at me. "Take me."

I crash my lips against hers, grabbing her ass. I know what she has underneath this dress and I plan to strip it off her later. Right now, I need to be deep, so deep inside her that I won't be able to tell where I end and she begins. Her small hands get to work on unbuttoning my jeans. When I feel her soft grip on my hard cock, I almost lose it. I'm barely hanging on by a thread.

"You're ready," she says as she strokes root to tip, driving me crazy.

"Always with you." I pull away and kick off my jeans and boxer briefs. My lips are on hers within seconds, and I push my tongue past her lips and taste her. I command her mouth, taking from her. Hands on her ass, I lift her.

My girl knows the drill. Arms around my shoulders, she clasps her legs tight around my waist. Reaching between us, I move her thong to the side and align my cock at her entrance.

"Need you," she mumbles as she trails kisses down my neck.

Without warning I push inside her, causing her to tilt her head back against the window. "So fucking tight. So hot." I bury my face in her neck, trying to keep myself from ending this before it even gets started.

"So full," she says as she tilts her hips. "Need more."

Who am I to deny my girl anything? Pulling out, I slide home once more, thrusting hard and fast. She moans and I do it again, over and over with the beat of the music, the packed club beneath us. I fuck her—that's what this is—hard and fast. So fucking good.

"There," she pants. "Don't stop. Please don't."

I can't speak, so I work on keeping my steady rhythm as I bury my cock deep with each thrust. I couldn't stop even if she asked me to. She's tight and hot, and I can feel the walls of her pussy as they squeeze my cock. It's a feeling like nothing I've ever felt before. "Need you there, baby. Touch yourself," I command. I can't let go of her and chance losing this rhythm.

"I'm—" That all she gets to say before I'm crashing my lips to hers as our orgasms wash over us at the same time. We stay there, her back pressed against the window, my cock inside her, my face buried in her neck as we try to catch our breaths. It's not until I slide out of her, setting her on shaky legs, that I understand why it felt so good. Bareback.

"Fuck, Berklee, I'm sorry."

"What?" she asks, confused.

"Condom. I forgot. I never forget and I'm clean—"

She places her tiny hand over my mouth. "I trust you. I'm on the pill, and it's been over a year before you. I'm clean too."

I exhale a sigh of relief. "That's good news. Although it's on the bucket list, I don't think we're ready for little Berklees just yet." I grab some tissues to clean us both up.

She rolls those blue eyes at me while a slow, sexy smile curves her lips. "It was different."

"It was. Between your sexy ass and being bare, I'm surprised I lasted as long as I did." She giggles and the sound soothes me. "We better get back down there."

"Do I have that freshly fucked look?"

I take her in: her curls are mussed, her cheeks are pink and her lips are swollen. "You look completely fuckable."

"Come on, you," she says, tossing the tissues in the trash. "I need to freshen up in the restroom first."

"I can help." I wag my eyebrows at her.

"You got me into this mess." She laughs. "I'll just be a minute."

When we make it back downstairs, we go back to our table of friends, all of them wearing knowing looks. I take my seat and pull Berklee onto my lap. I just had the most intense sex of my life with this girl and I'm not ready to let her go. I need her close.

Before I know it, it's last call. The patrons have already started to thin. The security staff does a good job of clearing the place out, calling cabs for those who appear to be too inebriated to drive. We say goodbye to our friends, including Zane. We don't have to worry about cleaning up, as we have a company that will be here first thing in the morning to take care of that.

"Successful night," Berklee comments.

"Yeah," I say, closing the safe built into the wall of my office. I don't want to deal with the deposit or counting or anything that isn't Berklee.

"I can do that real fast," she tells me.

"Nope. I need you in my bed, all night. This will be here in the morning. You have everything you need?"

"Yeah, all I brought was my phone, and it's in your desk."

After grabbing her phone, we walk through the building, turning out the lights as we go. I make sure the security system is set, and then we're on our way.

The drive is quiet. Berklee rests her head on my shoulder and dozes off on the way there. She's so peaceful. I somehow manage to get her out of the truck and in the house without dropping or waking her.

As soon as she hits the softness of my mattress, her eyes flutter open.

"Will you hold me?" she asks in her sleep-laced voice.

"Forever," I tell her. I know she's sleepy and probably doesn't realize what I just confessed, but that's okay. She's here in my bed and that's good enough for now. After getting both of us stripped of our clothes, I climb in behind her and pull her to me, holding her tight as I drift off to sleep.

# THIRTY FIVE
## *Berklee*

I T'S BEEN A month since the club opened, and today I'm having a staff meeting. Crew's not staying; he has a meeting with his attorney. His grandmother's house in New York has an offer. He seemed relieved and hopeful that it would sell so he can take that off his list of items to worry about.

Zane is also not going to be here, something about a meeting with an outside security company. We've been filled to capacity every night and the guys thought some added security would be helpful, at least until the crowd dies down. We've not had any issues, but Crew is all about safety. Especially with me. He insisted that if I'm downstairs someone be watching me at all times. It's silly yet sweet at the same time. I just let it roll off my shoulders. He's coming from a good place, and really, the guys are all already here. He just tells them all to keep a close eye on me.

I grab my notebook and head downstairs. I don't really have an agenda for today's meeting; I just want to meet with the staff and see if there are any struggles or issues that might need to be addressed. After a month we should know if there are any inconsistencies or processes that need tweaking.

Crew is at the bar where Carly, our bartender/server, is leaning over and showing him the goods. He doesn't take the bait, but it still pisses me off. They all know at this point that we're together. He makes it known to anyone who gets near us.

Biting back my irritation, I walk over to them.

"Beautiful," Crew says in greeting. He snakes his arm around my waist and kisses my neck. I relish the feel of his scruffy beard against my skin. It's a feeling I've grown to love. "I need to get going. I'll see you in a few hours." He kisses me softly, and then he's gone.

Carly watches him leave with a sour look on her face. *Take that, bitch!* I'm her boss, so of course I don't say it, but I want to. She needs to keep her eyes off my man. "All right, guys, let's take a seat," I say, getting everyone to come together.

The staff all have great ideas, and I thank them all for their hard work at the end of the meeting before I set the alarm and head up to my office to finalize the deposit. I finish up, leave Crew a note that it's ready to go when he is, and then lock up.

When I get home, I find Maggie and Barry just hanging out. "Hey," I greet them, plopping down on the couch beside Maggie.

"Long day?" she asks.

"Not really, I'm just exhausted. Maybe I'm coming down with something."

"Too much sexy time." She laughs.

"Is that possible?"

"I agree with Berklee," Barry chimes in. "Never too much when it comes to sexy time."

"TMI, big brother, TMI," Maggie says.

"What?" He laughs. "I have to listen to you girls go on and on, and I can't comment?"

Maggie rolls her eyes playfully and releases a heavy sigh.

"I'm going to change."

I head off to my room, throw on comfy clothes, then lie down on my bed with my Kindle. It seems like forever since I've been able to read a book start to finish, and that's on the agenda for tonight. Me and my book boyfriend, best-laid plans and all that. I'm not even three chapters in when I start to doze off. My ringing cell phone wakes me.

"Hey, babe," I answer.

"Beautiful," Crew says. "The house is sold, finally." He sighs with what I assume is relief. "But I have to fly to New York to finalize everything."

"That's great news. When do you leave?"

"I fly out Friday morning. I tried to change it, but that's what worked for the buyers and honestly, I just want to be done with this."

"Don't worry about the club. Zane and I will keep things running while you're gone."

"Come with me."

"We both know I can't do that. Both of us leaving this soon after opening could be the potential for disaster. Besides, it'll be a quick in-and–out, right?"

"Yeah. I'm going to call Zane and talk security with him for while I'm gone. I couldn't get a flight home until Saturday morning."

"Sounds good." I yawn.

"You okay?" he asks, concerned.

"Oh yeah, just tired."

"Get some rest, babe. I'll be there later. You want to stay there or my place?"

"Honestly, I just want to sleep here. You can just stay home. I'll see you in the morning."

"Berklee."

"Crew, I'm tired. Come on, I'll see you in the morning. I'm home safe and sound and want to curl up in my bed and sleep."

"I'll be there," he says. "See you soon."

Stubborn man. "No. I'm going to stay here and you are going to stay at your place. It's one night, Crew. I'll see you in the morning." I hold strong, mainly just out of stubbornness. Not to mention I'm tired and cranky.

"Fine. I'll be there first thing."

"Thank you. Good night."

"Night, baby," he says, his voice softer.

I give up on my book and burrow into the covers. I think I go to sleep before my head even hits the pillow.

My alarm goes off at seven and I groan. Rolling over, I'm met with an unexpected yet delightful sight—Crew is lying next to me. He's in his boxer briefs, tattooed arm over his eyes. My stubborn man just refuses to stay away. I was so exhausted I didn't even feel him come in.

I scoot closer to rest my head on his chest, listening to his even breathing. His arms softly wrap around me. "Morning," he mumbles.

"Hey, I thought we agreed you would go to your place?"

"Couldn't sleep without you. Came in at five when Barry left for the gym."

I want to be irritated, but how can I when he says things like that? "I'm going to hop in the shower while you get a little more sleep."

When I get out, I feel more human. Crew is still sleeping, so I creep out of the room to make us some breakfast. "Hey, no subbing today?" I ask Maggie when I find her sitting at the kitchen island.

"Nope, and since you're here, I need some bestie time. You've been so busy with that man of yours and the club that I've hardly seen you. Speaking of, is that his truck in the driveway?"

"Yeah, he's sleeping. Said Barry let him in at five this morning. Claims he couldn't sleep without me there."

"Aw, he's so sweet."

"He has his moments, but then again he can be . . . hardcore too." I blush, thinking about opening night at the club.

"Uh-oh, there is most definitely a story there and I am all ears. Spill it, sister."

So I do, giving her the details about that night in his office.

"Holy shit." She fans herself with her iPad. "I'm turned on just hearing the recap."

I laugh at her. "It was hot, and . . . just everything. He kind of freaked a little. We forgot the condom, he took the blame. It was both of us who let it happen. I told him I was on the pill." I chuckle. "He said something like even though it was on his list, he wasn't ready for little Berklees to be running around."

"We've been on the same schedule for years, so you can tell him rest assured that things are good to go. We have proof this week." She laughs. "So he's talking about kids with you? That's pretty serious," she rambles on while I'm still stuck on what she said. I'm due this week. It's not uncommon to be a day or two off from Mags, but for most of our lives, we've been pretty in sync. That happens when you spend so much time together.

*That must be it. We've not seen each other as much and I've been spending more time at Crew's place, so we've fallen out of sync.*

I shrug. "Not sure. I mean, I'm gone for him, Mags. So gone that I know I will never find my way back. If this ends, I'm done for."

"Well, from what you tell me, you don't have anything to worry about, but if that day does come, I'll get you through it. It's what we do."

I hear my bedroom door open and Crew's heavy footfalls as he walks down the hall. He stops to stand behind me where I sit at the kitchen island beside Maggie. "Missed you." He kisses my cheek and rests his chin on top of my head.

"You're interrupting girl time, Ledger," Maggie teases him.

"Don't care," he mumbles.

"Mags, why don't you and I do lunch today?"

"Sure, I'll let you two get going. Noon? Let's go to that sub shop that's just opened beside Coffee House."

"I didn't know it was open yet."

"They opened yesterday. I'll meet you there." She stands, rinses out her coffee cup and heads to her room.

"I need to go home and shower. You coming with me?"

"No, you go. I'm going to head in and get started on paperwork. I have some schedule changes for the staff that came up in the meeting yesterday."

After a kiss that almost has me begging him to stay, we both head out.

When I pull into the club, my phone rings. It's Crew.

"Miss me already?" I ask.

"Always," he says, chuckling. "Listen, Mom called and needs me to pick her up. Her car broke down and Dad isn't answering his phone. He was outside in his wood shop when she left and he doesn't get good service there. I don't know how long I'll be."

"Okay, tell your mom and dad I said hi."

"Will do, beautiful. I'll see you soon."

Time passes quickly as I rework the staff schedule, allowing for some time-off requests. I leave a note for Zane that the security has also been switched up. I'm not worried since I know he's adding more from the outside for now. Glancing at the clock, I see it's time to meet Maggie for lunch.

When I get to the sub shop, she's standing outside on her phone. "Sorry, I'm late. I lost track of time."

"I was just getting ready to call you." She laughs.

"I'm two minutes late."

"I'm starving," she counters.

Maggie pulls open the door and as soon as the smell hits me, I feel like I'm going to be sick. I don't tell her where I'm going, just seek out the sign for the restrooms and head that way. I barely make it before losing my breakfast.

"Berklee," she asks hesitantly from outside the door. "Let me in."

Grabbing a handful of paper towels, I wipe my mouth, wash my hands and open the door.

"Change of plans," she says. "Meet me back at our place. I have a stop to make. You need anything?"

"No. I don't know what came over me. I think I'm coming down with something."

"You okay to drive?"

"Yeah."

"Okay, I'll meet you there."

Barry's car is in the driveway when I get home. "What are you doing here?" we ask at the same time.

"Early dismissal," he states. "You?"

"Not feeling well."

"You need anything?"

"No, thanks. I'm just going to go lie down."

Once in my room, I send Crew a quick text.

> **Me:** Not feeling well. Stomach bug. At home, going to sleep.
>
> **Crew:** Need anything, babe?
>
> **Me:** Just sleep. I'll call you later.

*Crew:* I'll stop by once I'm done here.

*Me:* K.

Actually, I'm not feeling too bad right now. Maybe just lying still is the ticket.

Before I can think any more about it, Maggie is knocking on my door. "Can I come in?" she asks.

"Yeah," I say, not bothering to sit up.

"Listen, B. I have a hunch, but I think you're too close to the situation." She stops and takes a deep breath. "Can you do something for me?"

"Sure, what's up? What are you talking about having a hunch?"

She reaches into the bag that I didn't notice before and pulls out two boxes.

Pregnancy tests.

"No," I say, shaking my head. "I never miss a pill, ever."

"I know that. But these things happen. You've been tired, and today the smell at the sub shop got to you. And I bet you've not started yet this month. Am I right?" she asks, knowing damn good and well she is.

*No use in putting it off.* Slowly I climb to my feet, two boxes in hand, and head to the bathroom. There are two tests in each box, and I use all four. There is safety in numbers, after all.

With the tests lined up on the bathroom sink, I go back to my bed where Maggie sits patiently waiting.

"One said five minutes and one said three. I'll wait five for both." I'm holding strong on the outside, but on the inside I'm flipping out. Crew's words that night about how he's not ready for kids filter through my mind. *He's going to hate me. He'll think I trapped him for his money. Gah! How did I let this happen?* There's still hope that it could be negative, but that's my luck. Fall in love with a guy who isn't ready for kids, get knocked up and lose him. *Strong work, Hanson!*

"Time," Maggie says.

"I can't look. Will you do it for me?"

She nods and disappears into the bathroom. I close my eyes and lie back on the bed. I hear her feet shuffle across the carpet and I slowly open my eyes. There are tears in hers and she's wearing a blinding smile. "Positive, B. You're gonna be a mommy."

I'm frozen in place. I feel the wetness coat my cheeks, but I can't move. *I'm pregnant. Crew and I are having a baby.* My heart cracks open. This is going to be what causes me to lose him. My hand flies to my stomach, and I can't help but laugh through my tears.

"You okay?" Maggie asks.

"Yeah, I was just thinking that, when I lose him over this, at least I will always have the best part of him."

"You won't lose him, B. He's crazy about you."

"You're right, he is. I know that. Hell, the whole world knows that if you've seen us together. What he's not crazy about is the idea of kids. At least not yet."

"That was in the heat of the moment. You have to give him a chance to turn you away. Don't do it for him. Don't take his choice away."

"I won't, I promise. I just need time to . . . process. To mentally prepare myself to be a single parent."

"Knock, knock," Barry says at my door. "You two okay in there? I thought I heard you crying."

Maggie looks at me for approval and I nod. "Come in," she calls out to him.

He joins us, taking a seat on the opposite side of the bed. He looks at Maggie and I know the minute he spots the pregnancy tests she's holding.

"Which one of you?" he asks.

"Me," I whisper.

"Does he know?"

"No. I'm not ready to tell him yet either. I just need a few days to process this. Can you all please keep this between us? Just for a week or so. I just . . . need some time."

"Of course," Maggie assures me.

"He needs to know, Berklee. He deserves to know," Barry says.

"I know that. I won't keep this baby from him, I promise. I just need time. Please, Barry."

He nods. "Okay, but do it sooner than later. If I were in Crew's spot, I would want to know."

"Promise."

My phone alerts me to a text.

**Crew:** *Headed your way.*

**Me:** *K*

"That's him. He's on his way over. I told him I wasn't feeling well. I'm going with that. I just need a few days," I say again.

I don't know if it's for my benefit or theirs.

# THIRTY SIX
## Crew

MY FLIGHT LEAVES in the morning and I've contemplated cancelling more times than I can count. Berklee still isn't feeling well. She looks tired, and I hate leaving her when she might need me. I talked to Zane this morning and reminded him that she's not feeling well and to keep a close eye on her. He assured me that he's got it covered, but I want to be the one here for her.

"Hey," she says from my doorway. "You ready?"

"Yeah," I say, packing up my laptop. "You hungry?"

She grimaces. "Not really. Why don't you just run through a drive-through on the way to your house? I'll grab some crackers or something when we get there. I'm still queasy."

"Babe, maybe I should reschedule the closing and take you to the doctor."

"No, it's just a bug. I'm fine, I promise. Just not hungry. I'll meet you back at your place."

"Okay. Just let me tell Zane we're leaving."

I stop in his office and let him know to lock up, then walk Berklee to her car and make sure she's buckled in before following behind her. I whip my truck into the local burger joint and order a double cheeseburger and fries. I scarf it down before getting home, hating to eat in front of her when she's not able to.

When I get home, I find her curled up in my bed, already asleep. Quietly, I pack my bags by the light on my cell phone, not wanting to wake her up. Once I'm done, I slide in beside her and hold her next to me. Her deep, even breaths lull me to sleep as I hold my world in my arms.

The next morning, I wake and she's still sleeping. I have to leave or I'm going to miss my flight, so I write her a note and leave it on the nightstand under her phone. Giving her a quick kiss goodbye on the forehead, I make myself leave. I keep telling myself that once I get there, sign the papers and get back, it will be over. The sooner we get this over with, the better.

My plane lands twenty minutes ahead of schedule, so instead of checking into the hotel, I drive straight to the attorney's office for the closing. The buyers arrive right behind me and we're able to get down to business. The entire process takes about thirty minutes, with my grandmother's attorney assuring me that the money will be deposited into my account within twenty-four hours. I opted for that versus a check; my grandmother's house was a pretty penny, and I really don't want to be traveling with a check that size.

Checking into the hotel, I order some room service and call my girl.

"Hey, you. I was starting to get worried."

"My flight landed early, so I went straight there. It's done. Can you believe that? Fly all that way for thirty minutes."

She laughs. "It's done. Now you never have to go back."

"Have you ever been?"

"No, but I hear it's an experience." There's humor in her voice.

"You sound like you're feeling better."

"Yeah, today has been a little better so far. Don't worry about me. What are you up to the rest of the day?"

"Christmas is just a few weeks away. Maybe I'll start my shopping."

This she laughs at. Not just her cute chuckle, but a full-on gut-busting laugh. It's infectious and I feel myself relax. "What?" I ask her.

"Sorry, I just can't see you window-shopping in New York City."

"Well, what else am I going to do? I tried to get an earlier flight and still nothing."

"I have a great idea," she says with enthusiasm.

"Yeah?"

"Why don't you try to relax? You've been working yourself like crazy the last year. The club is up and running and doing amazing, and it's in good hands. Take the night to just relax. Hell, even sleep."

"Right. Like I can sleep without you here."

"Try. I'll see you tomorrow."

"Berklee."

"Yeah?"

"See you soon," I say, ending the call. *For weeks I've been trying to find the right time to say I love you and I almost fuck up and tell her on the phone.*

After eating, I decide to venture out, thinking I really should use the time to get her something great for Christmas. Just across the street from the hotel is a Tiffany's. Perfect. I walk inside and head straight for the earrings. Some diamonds for our first Christmas together.

"Welcome! Is there something I can help you with?" an older gentleman asks.

"Looking for a gift for my girlfriend."

"Ah. Well, diamonds are a girl's best friend." He laughs.

"What about those?" I point to a square diamond.

"Excellent choice. Princess-cut solitaire. These are one carat."

"Do you have anything bigger?"

"Sure, step down this way." I follow him to the end of the case. "These are two carats and these are three. You can see the difference."

"Yeah, I think two is what I'm looking for."

"Excellent. Can I help you look at anything else? Engagement rings, maybe?" He winks.

*You know what?* "Why not?" I say, following him to yet another glass case.

"You seem to like the princess cut, so let me show you one of our newest pieces." I watch as he reaches into the case and pulls out the ring. It's Berklee. I can see it on her finger. "This is actually four smaller princess-cut stones in the center diamond at a half carat each, totaling two carats. There is also half a carat of baguette diamonds on each side. And this"—he hands me a diamond band—"is the matching wedding band, totaling one carat of baguette diamonds.

The rings together sparkle, reminding me of her eyes when she's happy. I can see both on her finger. "I'll take them," I find myself saying. "I'm actually from out of town. Can I have them shipped home so I don't have to worry about taking them on the plane with me?"

"Certainly, we can overnight them free of charge. There will need to be someone present to sign for them."

"I'll send them to my work." I rattle off the address while handing over my credit card.

Fifteen minutes later, I'm walking out with a grin. I just bought Berklee an engagement ring, and I have yet to even tell her I'm in love with her. I guess I need to rectify that situation. I'd marry her today if I thought she would say yes, but baby steps and all that. At least when the time comes, I'll be ready.

I hit a few more shops and then decide to call it a day. I call room service again and text Berklee.

**Me:** *Miss you*

**Berklee:** *You too. See you soon.*

Nothing on TV as I mindlessly scroll through the stations. I've already checked my e-mails and responded, so this is what I've resorted to. My phone pings, alerting me to a message. I jump off the bed to retrieve it from the dresser hoping that it's Berklee.

It's a text from Carly, one of the server/bartenders at the club. Opening the message, it takes me a few minutes to figure out what I'm looking at until the second text comes through, that too is a picture. This one is clearer. It's Berklee sitting at a table at the club. Barry's next to her, his arm behind her chair, his lips next to her ear. *The minute I have to leave town, he pounces.* A third message comes in and it's a picture of Berklee kissing Barry on the cheek. From the angle, her mouth is too close to his.

I see red.

I'm pissed and hundreds of miles away. When the fourth text comes in, I grit my teeth before looking at it.

**Carly:** *Thought you'd want to see what your girl is up to.*

I squeeze my eyes closed. *They're friends. Berklee has told me so countless times. She wouldn't do this to me.* I keep repeating that over and over in my head.

Another text alert. This time from Berklee.

**Berklee:** *Miss you. Tonight went fine. I'm heading home now. Zane is going to walk me to my car.*

I read her message over and over again. Do I reply? Do I ask her about the pictures of her and Barry? Fuck! No, she wouldn't do that, not Berklee. If I could only see her, be face-to-face. Then it hits me: FaceTime.

**Me:** *FaceTime when you get home? Drive safe.*

**Berklee:** *I guess. I really will see you soon.*

Would she be willing to FaceTime with me if she was going home with him? That's when I remember that she lives with the fucker. If it weren't for the fact that she would be going there alone, I would have her go to my place.

I pace back and forth in my room, waiting for her to call. When my phone rings, I hit the button so hard I'm surprised I don't crack the screen.

"Hey! Why didn't we think to do this earlier today?" her sweet voice asks.

She's beautiful. Her red hair is up on top of her head and she's wearing one of my T-shirts. Surely she wouldn't be wearing my shirt and then go to him?

"You okay?" she asks.

"Yeah, tired is all. Ready to come home to you." I watch her closely for a sign that she's been with him. Nothing, just my Berklee.

"I'm so ready for you to be home. I know it's only been a day, but it feels like longer."

"You feeling better?" She looks better than she has all week.

"Yeah, a little better every day."

"Good thing or I was going to force you to go to the doctor."

"I um, I went today, actually. Just, you know, for reassurance, I guess. All checks out fine."

"Glad to hear it. So tonight everything went smooth?" Again I watch her reaction and get nothing out of the ordinary. Not even a flinch.

"Yes. Maggie, Alan and Barry, and this girl Amy, who Barry's been on a couple of dates with stopped by. I sat with them for a while. Thought it would give the security guys a break if I stayed in one spot." She giggles and I let the familiar sound wash over me. My eyes are closed when she whispers, "I miss you, Crew."

Slowly I open them and stare at her image on the screen. She's lying in bed, head on the pillow, phone propped up. "I miss you too, baby." She yawns and I suddenly feel bad for keeping her up when I know she's not been feeling well. "Get some sleep. I'll be home in the morning. My flight lands at ten."

"Yeah. Night, babe," she whispers, already half asleep.

"Night," I say. I see her hand snake out, and then she's gone.

Lying there in bed, I try to keep my shit under control. I know I'm a possessive, jealous asshole when it comes to her, but she's my fucking heart. I'd rather be that guy and protect her, keep her with me, than the alternative of losing her. What if the pictures are of the two of them sneaking around? Can I forgive her? Can I live without her? My phone vibrates with another message.

Carly.

I contemplate opening it, but do I want to see any more? Eventually I give in; it's like a bad accident that I just can't look away from. The message is yet another picture, this time of Berklee in the bar, I think by the door. Barry has her pulled in to his chest, holding her, his chin resting on her head. *Motherfucker!* I throw my phone across the room, not giving two shits if it's in shambles. It can match my heart.

She just fucking broke me. The love of my life just ripped my heart out.

Hours later, I turn off the TV and try to get some sleep. It's pointless though, as I toss and turn most of the night. Why did Carly send those pictures? Berklee has never given me any reason not to trust her. But the pictures speak for themselves. Will she admit it? Will she tell me the truth when I confront her? The images will not get out of my head. Eventually I do fall asleep from pure exhaustion, only to be woken up a few short hours later to catch my flight.

Once my plane lands, I pull out my phone that survived being thrown against the wall and text Berklee.

**Me:** *You home?*

**Berklee:** *No, on my way to your place. I was going to try to surprise you.*

**Me:** *You did.*

**Berklee:** *Haha. See you soon.*

I shove my phone back in my pocket and head to the parking lot. I need to see her, hold her in my arms and know this is all in my head. I'll be able to tell if she's hiding something then, when she's in my arms.

I hope it's all just a ploy on Carly's part. She's one of those women who will go to any lengths to get what she wants, and she's got it in her head that she wants me. I've seen the way she watches me.

I don't give a fuck what she wants. She'll never be Berklee.

When I pull in the drive, she's already there. I left a key for her on the nightstand yesterday when I left, hoping this would be the outcome, just not with my mind plagued with questions.

"Honey, I'm home," I call out for her.

"Hey," she says, coming into the kitchen. "I missed you." She walks straight into my arms and holds on to me like she's never going to see me again.

*Please, please let it not be what it looks like.*

"I can see that. I missed you too," I say, lifting her and setting her on the kitchen counter. I cup her face in my hands and kiss her. I give her all of me. She's reluctant at first, but then she kisses me like she always does, responds like she always does.

*She wouldn't be kissing me like I'm the air she breathes if she was with him, right?*

"Hey, can we come back here tonight? I kind of have something that I need to talk to you about," she says, pulling away from my lips.

"Sure. Or we can talk now, if you want?" *Is she going to confess? Was the kiss all just an act? I don't think I can wait until later tonight.*

"No, tonight is good. Unless you have something going on?"

She's wringing her hands together in her lap. She's nervous and I feel the familiar ache, the one that crushed my chest last night when I first saw the pictures. It's true.

"No, but we have time now. We can talk now," I say, not letting her get out of it. Why wait a few hours? It's just like pulling off a Band-Aid; let's get it over with. Not knowing, or knowing and her not knowing that I know, is killing me.

Her phone on the counter vibrates. Looking down, I see the screen and the message it displays. She reaches for it, but it's too late. I read what it said.

**Barry:** *Did you tell him yet?*

**Barry:** *He deserves to know.*

All at once my vision blurs and my heart is pounding in my chest. It's true. I have her up on this fucking pedestal in my mind and all this time, right under my nose. No wonder she was fine with me leaving, acting as if it was no big deal.

I take a step back from her. "So it's true, then. That's what you want to talk about I assume?" I point down at her phone, seething mad.

"Crew, listen. I don't know how you found out but I was going to tell you, I promise."

"Right, later. You needed to 'talk.' Were you going to let me make love to you first? One more night together?" I bark out. "I can't believe this."

"Please, just listen to what I have to say."

"Listen? You expect me to listen after that?" I point to her phone again. "I thought I knew you. I thought I could trust you."

"You can," she sobs. "Please let me explain."

I laugh. "Really, Berklee? No explanation needed. I need you to leave."

"What?" she sobs.

"Leave! I don't want you here. You lied to me. How can I forgive that?"

"I didn't," she sobs. "Can we please just talk about this?"

"No. I'm done. I want you out of my life." Fuck, she's in every facet of my life. She fucking works for me. "I'll be sure you get a good severance package." Closing my eyes, I take a deep breath to prepare for what I say next. "Goodbye, Berklee." It pains me to say it as much as it pains me that she cheated on me. Lied to me.

I turn and walk out of the house. Away from the only woman I'm positive I will ever love. Away from the future I had planned for us.

My world just tilted on its axis, and I have no idea if it will ever be right again.

# THIRTY SEVEN
## Berklee

HE LEFT ME. Just walked out and left me. No discussion. Nothing. Just walked out on me, on us.

I rub my still-flat belly. I had myself convinced that he would be upset but we could work through it. That he loved me like I love him.

I was wrong.

After I get myself somewhat under control, I lock his house, although I'm not sure why I care after the way he treated me. I take my time driving home, tears running unchecked down my face. I try to calm down as I know it's not good for the baby.

My baby. Just mine.

He doesn't want us.

Barry and Maggie are both out today and I'm grateful. I just want to be alone. Turning off my phone, I curl up in bed and cry myself to sleep.

That's how Maggie finds me hours later. I have no idea what time it is, but it's now dark outside.

"Hey, you feeling okay? I was at the Club and Zane said you took the night off, said Crew told him you wouldn't be in. Also said Crew was in a pissy mood. I take it you told him?"

"No." I fight another round of tears threatening to fall. "I didn't get a chance to. He knew. I don't know how he knew, but he did. He saw a message on my phone from Barry asking if I had told him yet and he flew off the handle. He was so angry, Mags."

She climbs into bed with me. "I'm sorry, B. Maybe he just needs time to process it."

"He knew, Mags. He didn't act surprised. He just blew up. I told him I needed to talk to him tonight and he kept pushing to talk then. That's when Barry's text came through and he knew. How did he find out?"

"I don't know, sweetie. I can tell you that neither Barry nor I told him."

"Did I hear my name?" Barry asks from my door. "Hey, what happened? Is everything okay?"

"No, everything is not okay. He doesn't love me. He doesn't want me or this baby."

"What?" He steps back like I slapped him. "How is that possible? I've seen the way he looks at you. Hell, he pisses around you any time another male even gets close."

"Apparently pregnant me is not what he wants," I sob.

"He said that?" Barry growls.

"Leave it," I tell him. "It doesn't matter. I don't want him to be with me out of pity. I don't need him to raise this baby. I'll always have the best part of him." My words end with a sob.

"Come here." Barry joins Mags and me on the bed and wraps me in a hug. "I'm so sorry, B. I thought he would act differently. He's not a man. No man would turn away a woman and his unborn child."

"He loves you," Maggie adds. "I've seen it. He's scared and confused, maybe angry that you waited to tell him, but he loves you. I know he does."

"Tell him that." I laugh humorlessly. "He obviously didn't get the memo."

"What can we do?" Maggie asks.

"Nothing, just thank you for being here. I need to find a job and a place to live, I guess."

"What? Why?"

"He f-fired me too. Said th-that I would get a g-good severance." I close my eyes, take a deep breath and slowly release it, willing myself to calm down for the baby. "You two didn't sign up to live with a single mom. I can't do that to you."

"The hell you can't!" they say at the same time.

"I'm tired. I just want to sleep."

"Have you eaten?" Maggie asks.

"No, I'm not hungry." She gives me a stern look. "I'll get something later, I promise. I just want to sleep for a little while."

"Okay. I'll be here all night, so just yell if you need anything," she says, squeezing my hand.

"I have to run out, but I'll be back soon. No talk about leaving. We got you." Barry kisses my forehead and leaves the room.

"B, I'm here for you, no matter what you need. Just say the word."

"Thanks, Mags. I just need some sleep."

"Okay," she relents. She leaves my room, turning off the light and closing the door. Leaving me to my tears and the pain, and the fact that my worst fear came true.

He doesn't want me.

# THIRTY EIGHT
## Crew

WHEN ZANE ASKED me where my girl was, it took every ounce of self-control I have not to punch him. He caught on to my mood really quick when I told him she wouldn't be in and that I didn't want to be bothered. I stomped upstairs to my office, and this is where I've been ever since. The club opens in an hour, but tonight I'm sitting this one out. I'll be right here, drinking away the pain, or at least numbing it. I don't want to see any of the staff, especially Carly. I'm not ready to answer questions. I'm not ready to deal with what it means to be here without her.

"Hey, man, you coming down?" Zane asks from my door.

"Fuck off," I say, not bothering to even look at him. I can't take my eyes off the two Tiffany's boxes that were delivered today. Express shipping. Two little blue boxes that were for her. She fucking played me for a fool.

"What did Tiffany ever do to you?" Zane asks.

"What?" I turn to look at him. "Who the fuck is Tiffany?"

He laughs and points at the two small boxes.

"Don't you have work to do?"

"I do, and so do you. We have a club to run."

"That's what I pay you for. Whatever it is, handle it. I don't want to see anyone." I look up at him. "Including you."

"That's how you're going to play this?"

"No games. That's not my gig. But Berklee?" I pick up the picture of

219

her from my desk and hold it up for him to see. "She plays games. She's damn good at it too."

"What the hell are you talking about?"

"Nothing. Go handle whatever comes up and leave me be. I need tonight."

"Ledger!" a loud, very pissed-off voice yells as heavy footfalls stomp up the steps. I don't give a fuck who it is; they can turn around and go right back to where they came from.

Zane turns to face the door just as Barry appears. I stand immediately and clench my fists. "What the fuck are you doing here?" I seethe, taking a step toward him.

"You motherfucker! I can't believe you left her. You make her fall in love with your sorry ass and then leave her when she needs you the most."

"Fuck you! I can't believe you have the nerve to show up here after what you did."

"Me? *You left her!*" he roars. "She's a fucking mess because she believed you would be there, and look at what you did."

I take another step toward him. "Look what *I* did? It was you. I saw the proof. You two deserve each other." My control snaps and I throw a right hook, slamming into his jaw.

Zane steps in front of me, hands on my chest. "No more," he orders. "Would one of you jackasses care to tell me what the fuck is going on here?"

"Gladly. Your boy here, he fucked her over. Knocked her up and now he doesn't want her. Kicked her out with the promise of a severance package."

*Did I hear him right?* "Repeat that," I say, my eyes locked on his.

"Cut the shit, Ledger. Don't stand there and act surprised. You fucking *left her!*" he screams.

"No, I . . ." I stumble backward, thankfully meeting the side of my desk. "She was . . . There were pictures . . . You texted her." I run my hands down my face to try and erase this fucking nightmare.

Pregnant.

"What are you rambling on about?"

"The fucking pictures!" I yell at them. "Carly, she sent me pictures of you and Berklee from last night, and she's been distant, and then the text message asking if she told me, that I deserved to know. I. . . ." *Oh God, please say I didn't just walk away from her and my baby.*

Barry scoffs. "You're telling me you had no idea she was pregnant."

Tears prick my eyes. *"I have something to tell you."* Her words filter through my mind. The sickness, her being tired—it's all clear now.

I fucked up.

"No," I say over the lump in my throat.

"Did you give her a chance to explain?" Zane asks. His voice is soft, as though he's speaking to a wild animal that could attack at any minute.

"No," I say again, barely getting the word to pass my lips. *Fuck, Berklee, she thinks I don't want her or my baby. I have to go to her. I have to fix this.* Turning, I grab my keys and phone and see the two Tiffany boxes. I shove one into each pocket. "Is she home?" I ask Barry.

He stares at me, scowl on his face, arms crossed over his chest.

"Is she home?" I say again.

"Why should I tell you where she is? You left her, kicked her to the curb, remember?"

I stalk toward him and stand toe-to-toe, nose-to-nose. "Because I fucking love her. She's my entire fucking world and I fucked up. I get that. I'll make it up to her."

"What makes you so sure she'll take you back?"

"I'll fight for her. I won't stop until she sees that she's it for me. And"—again with the fucking emotion—"my kid. I'm going to be a father to that baby. They're mine, both of them, and I won't stop until she's back where she belongs."

"And where is that exactly?" he counters.

"Right here." I place my hand over my chest. "She belongs right here, and I'll show her."

He stares at me, and I don't blink. Zane takes a step back, seeing that my fight's not with Barry. It's for my family. Berklee and our baby. I'll fight every damn day to show her what she means to me.

"She's at home. She's exhausted from crying and just wanted to be left alone. Maybe you should—"

"No. I'm going to her. I can't let her go to sleep thinking I don't want her or our baby. I'm going, and I would advise that neither of you try and stop me." With that I shoulder past them. I stop when I reach the door and look over my shoulder. "I want Carly fired. Escorted off the premises. Now," I growl. Turning around, I run down the steps and out of the doors to my truck. I don't speak to the staff. I don't even know if I got the door shut. All I know is that I have to get to her.

I make the fifteen-minute drive in half that, breaking a few laws in the process. When I pull into the drive, I'm out of the truck and knocking on the door within seconds.

A pissed-off Maggie opens the door. "What do you want?"

"I need to see her," I say, trying to be nice. If that doesn't work, I'll force my way in. Nothing is going to keep me from seeing her.

"She's sleeping. What else could you possibly have to say?"

"I'll explain later, but not before I talk to her. I need to explain it to her first. She deserves that."

"I thought you loved her. I told her that you would be there for her."

"I do," I say, defeated. "I'm going to be. It's a huge misunderstanding. I didn't know about the baby. I thought. . . . Look, I just need to see her," I plead.

"Fix it." She gives me a look that tells me there's a silent threat behind her command.

I nod. She steps out of the way and I head straight to Berklee's room. The lights are off. I slowly push the door open, and what I find breaks my heart. She's curled in a ball, eyes swollen, face red and blotchy. She has one hand on her belly and the other grasping a picture frame. It's a photo of the two of us. Quietly I close the door, the last remnants of daylight all that remains. I can still see her though. I kick off my shoes and climb in beside her. She stirs and her eyes pop open.

"I'm so fucking sorry," I say softly.

Tears well in her eyes. "What are you doing here?" Her voice is gruff; I can only assume it's from all the tears.

"I didn't know." I rest my hand over hers on her belly. She flinches but doesn't pull away.

"But you—"

I place a finger over her lips. "I'll explain it to you, but first I need to

222

tell you that I love you. I love both of you with everything inside of me. I want you. Both of you. Every minute of my forever I want you."

A sob escapes her lips and I want to hold her, but I know she won't let me. Not yet. "Last night I got a message. Pictures of you at the club, with Barry. I know now that they were innocent, but what I saw and what my mind told me was going on obviously wasn't."

"He's my brother, Crew. I've told you this countless times. I don't know how else to explain it."

"You never have to again. I get it." I push a loose curl out of her eyes. "When I saw your phone, his message asking if you told me, I flipped my shit. In my mind the pictures were real, and you and Barry were going behind my back. I thought you were going to tell me that you were leaving me for him, and I couldn't bear to hear you say it. I couldn't fathom the thought of hearing those words fall from your lips, so I pushed. I ended it before you could. I walked away."

"I would never."

"I know that. I do. I just let my imagination run away with it, although no reason is good enough for the pain I've caused you. Caused both of us. That's on me. I've never felt this ache deep in here." I place my hand over my heart. "Never known the kind of pain that's caused from walking away from the woman you love. That pain, its intensity increases tenfold when you find out that it was all a misunderstanding. When you find out that you made a baby with that woman." I rest my hand back on her belly. "When you find out that a part of you is living and growing inside her and you have no idea if she'll forgive you."

She's quiet, silent tears still coating her cheeks.

"The minute I laid eyes on you, I knew you were different. I knew, even though I wouldn't admit it at the time, that you would turn my world upside down if I let you. Funny thing is, no matter how hard I fought it, I still fell. I've wanted to tell you for weeks how I feel. That you own me. That I'm madly in love with you," I say, my voice almost a whisper.

"I don't need you. I can take care of this baby on my own. You're off the hook." Her words don't match the want in her eyes. She's giving me an out.

"That's not going to work for me, beautiful. I want our family. I want us. Even if this little peanut"—I rub her belly—"didn't exist, I would still be here, begging your forgiveness. Begging you to give my sorry ass another chance to prove to you what you mean to me."

"You love me?"

"I do, baby. So much."

"You hurt me."

My chest cracks open at her words. "I know that." I swallow back the emotion. "Every day, baby. Every day I will fight to show you how sorry I am. I'll show you how much you mean to me." I shift and get jabbed in the leg. The Tiffany's boxes. "Can you do something for me? Can you close your eyes?"

"Crew, I—"

"Please?" I say, placing my finger over her lips. She nods slightly and closes her eyes. "I'm right here. I'm not going anywhere. I just need to stand for a minute." I push my luck and place a kiss on her forehead, then quickly climb out of bed and pull out the boxes. I tear the ribbon off both until I find the one with the ring in it. I set the earring box on the floor along with the ring box, leaving the wedding band inside.

"Open those baby blues for me." Her eyes pop open and she studies me, trying to figure out what I'm up to. "When I was in New York, I said I was going shopping, remember?"

"Yeah."

"I wanted to get you a gift, one that would let you know that I loved you. Something that you could keep and remember our first Christmas together." Her eyes soften. "I found it, but I also found something else. Something that reminded me of you and the love that I have for you. I bought it too. I wasn't sure when I would give it to you, but I wanted it. I knew that it was perfect, and I couldn't chance not ever finding one like it again."

Reaching for her hand, I manage to slide the ring on her finger. "Berklee Hanson, I love you. You are my heart, the very breath I take, and I cannot live without you. Will you do me the incredible honor of being my wife?"

Her tears flow faster and a tiny sob escapes her lips. She raises her hand and inspects the ring, not saying anything, so I keep talking. "I'm not doing this because of the baby. I had already bought it. I've always known from the day I met you that this is where we would end up. Every part of me infused with every part of you. I want this, what we have. I want our future, our babies, our life. I just want you."

She silently wipes at her tears. Finally, she speaks, and they're the sweetest words I've ever heard. "I love you too." She smiles through her tears.

"Is that a yes?"

She nods. "Yes."

I lean in and kiss her. taking my time, tracing her lips. Pulling back, I rest my forehead against hers. "You're mine, both of you. We're having a baby."

She laughs. "We are."

"Thank you. For giving me a second chance. For making me a husband and a father. Thank you for loving me."

"Crew Ledger, you're impossible not to love."

# EPILOGUE
## *Berklee*

TODAY IS OUR four-year wedding anniversary. It also just so happens to be my due date for baby number two. Did I also mention that it's New Year's Eve? Crew badgered me to set a date, and jokingly Maggie suggested New Year's Eve. Crew loved the idea—new year, new start and all that. I didn't care when it was; I just wanted to be his wife. I wanted to start our lives together, and preferably before the baby came.

Our parents were supportive, and when we told them we wanted a destination wedding, they didn't blink an eye. It was beautiful with our closest friends and family. A day I will always remember.

Not only is our personal life fairy tale worthy, at least in my eyes, Club Titan is also thriving. Crew and I have been talking about expanding, maybe opening another branch but no definite plans have been made.

"Hey, B, where are the extra plates?" Maggie calls from the doorway of the kitchen.

"I'll show you." I scoot to the edge of the couch and push myself up. Before I can take two steps, our daughter, Corrine, comes flying at me, wrapping her little arms around my legs and almost knocking me off balance.

"Momma, Daddy said you're going to get a spanking." Her blue eyes, so much like mine, stare up at me.

"He did, did he?"

"Uh-huh. What did you do?"

"She won't sit down and keep her feet up," Crew says, answering for me. He stalks toward us, lifting Corrine in one arm as he rubs my belly and then snakes the other around my waist. "How's my boy?" He nods to my belly.

"Sleeping. Not much activity today."

"Should we call the doctor?" he asks, concerned.

"No, I'm fine."

"But we should probably go, you know, to get checked out."

"Stop! I'm fine. This is not my first time doing this, you know."

"Baby, I just think that—"

"Crew, leave the woman alone. I swear the nurses down at the hospital are still talking about you from when this little angel was born," Sarah says, taking Corrine from his arms.

"But—"

"Babe, it's fine. Let's just enjoy today. I was three days late with Corrine. Caden will come when he's good and ready. Now, I need to show Maggie where the plates are."

"Sit. I'll show her."

I roll my eyes but do as he says. Pick your battles and all that. Crew has always been protective of me, but when I'm pregnant he's like normal, everyday, non-expectant daddy Crew on steroids.

His mom's right. When I was pregnant with Corrine, every little ache, or pain, or funny look I gave him, he was taking me to the hospital to get checked out.

Crew brings me a plate and sets it on the table beside me. "Thanks, babe, but I have to pee. Again."

He chuckles and helps me from the couch. As soon as I stand, I feel something trickle down my leg. At first I think I peed myself. I stand frozen, embarrassed, that doesn't last long as my mom walks in the room, takes one look at me and says, "Her water just broke."

Crew jumps into action, lifting me in his arms and running me outside to our SUV, yelling over his shoulder for I'm not sure who to keep his little girl safe while he's gone. He grips the wheel and badgers me with questions all the way to the hospital.

"I feel fine. No contractions. Yes, Corrine will be okay. Mom can bring my bag later," I answer him dutifully.

He's a good man, honorable. He loves me and our kids with every ounce of his being. He's nervous and protective and I know this. That's why I humor him.

Pulling up to the emergency department, a contraction hits and I scream out in pain. Crew hops out of the SUV and grabs a wheelchair from just inside the door. As soon as he opens my door another contraction hits.

"Sit, babe. Those are close together."

I don't answer him as I focus on breathing through the pain. He gets me in the wheelchair and takes me inside. The nurses see him and laugh—until another contraction hits me and I scream out in pain. They all jump into action and I'm whisked off to a room, my husband hot on our heels, refusing to leave my side. They give him a gown to help me change. As soon as my pants are off, another one hits.

"Can we get a doctor in here?" Crew yells. "You got this, babe. I wish I could take the pain from you. I love you. Thank you for my son, my daughter. I love you," he says again.

The doctor comes in as another contraction hits. "Let's take a look," he says.

"Wait a minute. Are there not any female doctors on tonight?" Crew asks.

"Crew! Get out of the damn way. This baby is coming, so unless you plan on delivering our son into the world, move your ass!"

That snaps him into action and he moves out of the way, never taking his eyes off the doctor.

"How long have you been having pains?" the doctor asks.

"Just minor aching. I know that's normal."

"How long?" he asks again.

"Since yesterday," I say through gritted teeth.

"What?" Crew turns to face me. "You didn't tell me."

"I just thought it was—" Deep breath. "—common. It wasn't—" Deep breath. "—unbearable. Just a slight dull ache, and it wasn't constant."

"Well, this baby is ready to meet his parents. Dad, hold her legs." He nods to the nurse to do that same. "No time for an epidural, I'm afraid. It's time to push."

# Crew

"ON THE COUNT of three. One, two, three," the doctor says. Berklee bears down and a scream rips from her throat. I feel helpless and I'm ready to lose my shit seeing her in this much pain. When she delivered Corrine, she had pain meds, an epidural and something else. She didn't scream like this, like a monster has taken over my sweet wife.

She reaches out and I offer her my hand. She crushes it as the doctor counts her to another round of pushing.

"You're doing so good, babe."

"Shut up," she growls as she tucks her chin into her chest and pushes. I'm just about to apologize because that's the only thing I can think of when I hear a loud cry and Berklee falls back against the bed.

"It's a boy. Dad, you want to do the honors?"

I nod, tears flowing as I lean down and kiss my wife. "I fucking love you, Berklee Ledger." With shaking hands, I cut the cord that separates my son from his momma. They check him over, and then he's being placed on her chest.

"Look at him. He's a mini you," she croons. "His dark hair and those eyes."

"I thought all babies were born with blue eyes?" I learned that little tidbit when Corrine was born. I was stoked that she had her momma's eyes until they told me they were all born with blue and they could change.

"Not this time," she says softly. "Hi, Caden. I'm your mommy. You look just like your dad, my sweet boy." She looks at me with a watery smile. "You want to hold your son?"

I nod; speaking really isn't an option for me right now. Life is full of defining moments, ones that can bring a man to his knees and tears to his eyes. I've had three. The first was the day Berklee became my wife. The second when she made me a father for the first time and I got to see my daughter brought into the world. Then there's today. I thought the second time around, knowing what to expect, I would keep my cool, not cry. Not going to happen.

All too soon the nurses are taking him away to clean him up. I look down at Berklee. She's more beautiful than I've ever seen her. I said that on our wedding day and the day Corrine was born, and I didn't think anything could ever top that. I was wrong.

"I love you," I say, kissing her softly.

"I love you too." She closes her eyes and leans back against the bed.

"Can I get you anything?" She's given me the world, after all.

Slowly, she opens her eyes. "I just want you."

CONTACT Kaylee Ryan

**Facebook:**
www.facebook.com/pages/Kaylee-Ryan-Author

**Goodreads:**
www.goodreads.com/author/show/7060310.Kaylee_Ryan

**Twitter:**
@author_k_ryan

**Instagram:**
Kaylee_ryan_author

**Website:**
www.kayleeryan.com/

# OTHER WORKS BY
## Kaylee Ryan

### *With You Series*
Anywhere With You
More With You
Everything With You

### *Stand Alone Titles*

Tempting Tatum
Unwrapping Tatum
Levitate
Just Say When
Unexpected Reality


### *Soul Serenade Series*
Emphatic
Assured

### *Southern Heart Series*
Southern Pleasure
Southern Desire

# Acknowledgments

My family. I love you. Thank you for your never ending support and encouragement.

Sommer Stein, Perfect Pear Creative Covers, you never cease to amaze me. Thank you so much for yet another amazing cover. You've brought Crew and Berklee to life.

Sara Eirew, you're a genius behind the camera. Thank you for an amazing picture.

Tami Integrity Formatting, you never let me down. You make my words come together in a pretty little package. Thank you so much for making I Just Want You look fabulous on the inside!

My beta team: Kaylee 2, Jamie, Stacy and Lauren I love you! From day one you all have been there and I cannot tell you how much that means to me. Thank you for reading IJWY over and over again. You ladies are amazing!

Give Me Books, thank you for hosting and organizing the cover reveal and release of I Just Want You. I appreciate all of your hard work getting this book out there.

*To all of the bloggers out there* . . . Thank you so much. Your continued never-ending support of myself, and the entire indie community is greatly appreciated. I know that you don't hear it enough so hear me now. *I appreciate each and every one of you and the support that you have given me.* Thank you to all of you! There are way too many of you to list . . .

To my Kick Ass Crew, you ladies know who you are. I will never be able to tell you how much your support means. You all have truly earned your name. Thank you!

Samatha Harris, our chats crack me up. Thank you for your never ending support.

S. Moose, your beta notes crack me up. Thank you for always being honest.

Brooke Rice, Thanks for the name suggestion with Crew. It fits the character perfectly!

Last but not least, to the readers. I truly love writing and I am honored that I am able to share that with you. Thank you for your messages and tags on social media. I love hearing from each and every one of you. Thank you for your continued support of me, and my dream of writing.

With Love,

*Kaylee Ryan*

CPSIA information can be obtained
at www.ICGtesting.com
Printed in the USA
LVOW10s2144051117

555098LV00025B/1003/P